THE
VOICE
HE
LOVED

THE VOICE HE LOVED

Laurel Schunk

THOMAS NELSON PUBLISHERS
Nashville • Atlanta • London • Vancouver

Dedication

for L. and B.

Copyright © 1995 by Laurel B. Schunk

Published in Nashville, Tennessee, by Thomas Nelson, Inc., and distributed in Canada by Word Communications, Ltd., Richmond, British Columbia, and in the United Kingdom by Word (UK), Ltd., Milton Keynes, England.

**Library of Congress
Cataloging-in-Publication Data**

Schunk, Laurel B.
    The voice he loved / Laurel B. Schunk.
        p.   cm.
    ISBN 0-7852-8082-0 (pb.)
    I. Title.
    PS3569.C55533V65   1995
    813'.54—dc20   94-36603
                                                           CIP

Printed in the United States of America
1 2 3 4 5 6 7 — 99 98 97 96 95

Acknowledgements

Thanks To

Dr. Roger Fredrikson, for encouraging me to write and publish this story

John Schunk, for being my best friend

John Schunk, Diana Schunk Tillison, Heather and Timmy Schunk, for being my best readers

Greg and Pin Pin Schunk and Chris Tillison, for being there when it was time to decompress

Cindy, Kate, Margaret, Mary, and Peg, for reading and critiquing

Bonnie Copp, for technical advice on advertising

Lucile M. Lowder, my mother, for being the queen of our family

other supporters, who know who they are

Though one may be overpowered by another,
two can withstand him.
And a threefold cord is not quickly broken.

—Ecclesiastes 4:12

Prologue

The room wasn't dark enough. The man could still see his hands. The backs of his fingers and hands sprouted a red fuzz he hated. He tried to keep them shaved, but the hair grew back too fast.

Busily his hands plucked matches out of a cardboard holder and curved them around his fingers. When he noticed what he was doing, he snatched his hands back as though burned, then forced himself to pick up the matches, take them to the bathroom and flush them down the toilet.

He returned to the living room. Pictures of a beautiful blonde lined the walls of the room. Small photos in frames or in neat stacks covered the coffee table in front of him. The pictures were of the same person, taken at different ages—from six or seven through her teens.

Glossy magazines filled a bookshelf near the couch. Her face was in these too—pictures of her from eighteen to twenty-five or so.

The man picked up a studio portrait in a silver frame. He didn't know what he felt when he looked at the face in the photos. Anger, love, and hatred warred in him. Paige was so lovely. He wanted to own her, but she kept twisting away from him.

At last he had tracked her down. He couldn't decide whether to call her again. But he wanted to hear her voice, liked listening to the fear in it. Sometimes she sneered at him, though, and he couldn't stand that.

Still, there was a musical quality in her voice that he loved. He wanted to hear it again. He picked up the phone and dialed. It rang and rang. No answer.

He dropped the receiver down in its cradle. "She knows when I call. She's just refusing to answer the phone." He clenched his jaw and stared at his hands again. He hated them. So did she, he knew. He wanted to choke her for it.

Chapter 1

Paul Sherman slammed the ball against the wall and won the game. Success! He whooped and leapt into the air. He rarely beat Jamal James at racquetball. "Oh, man," Jamal groaned, "my arm isn't worth anything today."

Paul grinned and punched the big black man's shoulder. "All I can say is, it's about time I won. Seems like it's been years."

"It's just that I've been up late nights studying, besides working all day," Jamal grumbled. "Some people don't have a professor's life of leisure, you know."

"Do the words 'You're not being a very good sport' mean anything to you?" Paul asked, in a never-fail challenge to Jamal to join in their fifteen-year-old game, one they'd invented in junior high. His brown eyes crinkled with humor. His dark hair, wet with sweat, curled on his forehead.

"*Heaven Can Wait*," Jamal countered, "and there's no 'very.' It's just 'You're not being a good sport.'"

"Are you sure? I'm never wrong on these lines."

"Yeah, I'm sure. You are this time."

Paul shrugged. "Lucky at racquetball, unlucky at movie lines, I guess."

"Very funny." The big man grimaced good-naturedly.

Paul opened the trunk of his car and threw his racquet and bag in, then grabbed a grubby gray sweatshirt. Although it was a mild day, it was December, and he needed more clothes on. There was a nip in the air, noticeable now as the sweat from their game dried on his skin. He then doubled over to squeeze his long, lean body into the driver's seat of his beat-up Civic, while Jamal climbed into the passenger's side.

Paul left the park and drove up Hillside toward the university. It was the end of the fall semester. This evening he would give a final exam to one of his classes. "At this point you always wonder how well you taught Eudora Welty and Flannery O'Connor. I can predict, though, which students will do well and which ones won't."

"I wish I could predict how I'll do on *my* final tonight. Man, I hate taking tests. I'm just too old to be back in school." Jamal, a former police detective, was moonlighting as a private detective now and studying pre-law at the university. "I'll be thirty-five when I finish in seven years."

Paul shot him a sidelong glance. "And how old will you be in seven years if you don't finish?"

"Not funny." Jamal spotted a cream-colored BMW two cars ahead of him in the right lane and pointed it out. "It has to be Paige—her car stands out in Wichita."

Paul craned his neck to catch a glimpse of her. "I can see the car, but I can't see the driver. I'm sure you're right, though." He shook his head. "She really confuses me."

Paul's thoughts took him back. Friends since childhood, he and Paige had planned to get married from high school. Then she'd become strange and distant, and she wouldn't say why. Instead, she'd run away, from Wichita and from him. "It's nothing personal, Paul," she'd said. "Just forget me."

It was hard to forget her when they kept meeting. They had run with the same friends in high school, and now that she was back in Wichita, they attended the same parties.

"Am I fooling myself when I keep believing God chose us for each other?" Paul asked Jamal. That thought sounded dumb sometimes, even melodramatic. "Do you think Paige has lost her faith?" The idea niggled at the back of his mind all the time . . . maybe because Paige refused all his invitations to church gatherings now.

Jamal shrugged. "I don't know, man. Her faith was sure the real thing in high school. But now she seems to be fighting some big monster in her head."

Wildly divergent feelings for Paige whirled in Paul's brain: he loved her, but she kept pushing him away. He liked her company because she was bright and funny, but she exasperated him. She put herself in dangerous situations with a crazy bravado that scared him.

Just the week before, Jamal had called him late one evening. "Paul, you're not going to believe this. I was just driving home from work and saw Paige walking up Central. She'd locked her keys in her car and she was going home to get a spare set. On Central, at nearly midnight! What's with that girl?"

Paul's heart had constricted with Jamal's words. What if the wrong person had stopped to help her? "I don't know. One minute she's afraid of her shadow, the next she's making *more* shadows."

How could he still love her when she rejected him as well as her faith? He didn't know how, but he did.

Ahead of them, Paige's car turned east into the Wesley Medical Center complex. Probably going to sell them some advertising. He frowned, then rubbed his chin. Or maybe she was sick. "I have to quit this roller-coastering. She keeps me unbalanced, and I hate the feeling."

"You're digging the same old holes in your mind. Can't you wait on God's timing?"

Paul dipped his head, then smiled ruefully. "You're right, of course. Thanks, pal, for setting me straight."

Jamal laughed. "Mrs. Reimer would be proud. You learned that lesson well."

"I needed to."

Their high school senior English teacher, Lois Reimer, had insisted they all learn that phrase to counter their group's love of verbal battles. Nine of them—Paul, Jamal, Paige Brookings and her twin brother Carter, Jenny Parker, Susan Barsolo, Jerry Keegan—and more on the edges of the close-knit inner clan, Renee Wentworth and Reilly Hoskins—had stuck together, yet had loved to hear the sound of their own voices, to get into arguments, usually over who said what and when. They also had a regrettable tendency—Carter, in particular— to lash out at teachers who corrected them.

"All of you are blessed with a verbal facility that intimidates other people," Mrs. Reimer had said one day when Carter and Reilly Hoskins, a strange boy who seemed to drag a miasma of gloom around with him, enraged the PE teacher by refusing to climb the ropes in the gym. "You must learn to be gracious, especially when adults correct you. Learn to say, 'Thank you for setting me straight.'"

"I've always been thankful for that lesson," Paul admitted. "Helps develop a teachable spirit. Too many of us act like infallible hardheads all the time." He chuckled. "Remember Carter just wouldn't give in on it? He'd say the words, but with a smirk on his face, so you knew he was still defying the teacher. Reilly didn't really care. He just followed Carter's example." He made a right turn onto Campus Drive. "Poor old Flossie hated the very sight of him, he was so cocky. Since we hung out with him, she didn't like us much either."

Jamal grinned at the memory of Flossie Perkins, the Spanish teacher who—Carter had said—looked like a chicken caught in a wringer washer, her thin, ginger hair flying loose like mangled feathers and her skinny arms flapping in perennial dismay. "Yeah, I remember. We were quite something, weren't we?"

"Thought we were, at least. Think we've improved any in the past ten years?"

Jamal straightened in the car seat. "I should hope so."

They drove the rest of the way in a companionable silence. When they reached the northwest parking lot, Paul let Jamal out by his car. "What are you and Sherry and the kids doing for Christmas?"

"Well, I'm sleepin' in every day, to rest my brain."

"Sure, right, with three kids under six. You're fooling yourself."

"I know. Besides, I've missed the little rug rats. I

THE VOICE HE LOVED

can hardly wait to roughhouse them to the floor and tickle them. They love it when I play Sleeping Tiger."

"Sleeping Tiger?"

"Yeah, I lie on the floor and pretend I'm asleep. When they poke me or punch me, I wake up with a roar and grab 'em and eat 'em up. They love it." He rubbed his hand over his face, fatigue evident in the lines at the corner of his wide mouth. "I feel I've been in a hole the last three months. Sherry's managed so well with a husband in absentia. Hope to make up for that some."

Paul nodded. He didn't envy Jamal—his friend deserved the wonderful family he had—but he longed for a family of his own, especially at Christmastime. "Say hi to them for me."

"Come by Christmas Eve, okay? We read the Christmas story, then let the kids open one present each. Sherry always fixes a shrimp and veggies platter. Just yesterday, she was saying she missed seeing you these days."

Paul hesitated. "You guys feeling sorry for the poor widower, so you're doing your duty by him?"

"Yeah, right." Jamal gave a sardonic grin. "It's not like we actually enjoy your company."

"So all right, you twisted my arm. What time?"

"Supper at six. It'll be an early night—I've got to put together a trike for Joshua—so we're aiming to throw 'em in bed at about 8:30."

Paul smiled warmly at his friend. "Thanks, Jamal. I'll look forward to it. Give Sherry my best."

"See you, man."

Before driving off, Paul prayed briefly. *God, thank you for friends like Jamal. I pray that you may rain your blessings on him, Sherry, and the kids. But why am I so dense about Paige? I can't seem to stop worrying about her. Please give me wisdom. And please help Paige. Be with her as she struggles with whatever it is she's fighting.*

He drove back down Hillside to Douglas, then east to his street and north on home. When he let himself in the back door, Paul whistled for Moses, his old collie. In spite of her name, Moses was a female, a big sable collie with a magnificent white ruff. She woofed in greeting from her spot by the heat register, then pulled herself to her feet and ambled over for her customary pat. The big house seemed so quiet. Paul wasn't a person who needed someone around to keep him amused, but he knew he was missing out on human companionship, the "helpmeet" God wanted for every man.

Once, he and Marianna had lived here as newlyweds. They'd entered into their marriage with such hope. The hope had leapt high, like an overbuilt fire, especially when he thought of children to come. And when he'd learned she was pregnant, he'd been hopeful she would straighten out, take care of herself for the baby's sake. She'd refused.

The marriage had been all wrong from the first. Paul had loved Paige first, and Marianna knew she was second choice. Her temperament, which was difficult to begin with, grew poisoned over time. And in retrospect, he could see that the end of their marriage, resulting from her endless bitterness and alcoholism, then her death, seemed inevitable. He should have known they were headed for trouble before they married. *Dear God,* he prayed, *help me never make such a horrible mistake again. I'd rather stay single for the rest of my life.* He thought of Proverbs—was it 15:17?—"Better is a dinner of herbs where love is, than a fatted calf with hatred."

He shook his head. Why did he have such a hard time with this—wanting to be married, yet not waiting on the Lord for his leading on who and when he should marry? *Help me, God, to know your will,* he prayed, *and help me want only that, not just what I want.* It was funny how even the Christian who'd had so much proof of God's lovingkindness and concern for every part of his life sometimes doubted that God knew best.

Paul snapped the red leather leash on Moses' collar, then went out for their daily walk in the park. "Don't you think it would be nice to have someone else in the house to fill it with noise, and light, and warmth? Oh, don't get me wrong, Moses. You're good company. But you're not quite what I had in mind for the long haul."

Four teenagers passing by gave him a funny look. A little embarrassed, he grinned at them. They probably thought he was off his rocker, talking to himself out in a public place like this. "See what I mean? That's what happens when a man is alone too much," he said to Moses once they were out of earshot. "He talks to himself. But even worse, he sometimes answers back!"

Chapter 2

"Are you sure I'm ready to leave analysis?" Paige Brookings asked her doctor as she paced back and forth across his office. She twisted her hands. Her ivory pumps sank deep into the Aubusson carpet, all cream and rust and navy.

From behind his big rosewood desk, Abe Finney watched her pace. In her ivory suit with a peach silk blouse, Paige exemplified the dressed-for-success young advertising executive. Her complexion—like sun-ripened apricots—glowed in the room's subdued light. Even five years before, when she'd abandoned her modeling career and come back to Wichita, humiliated and frightened, she'd worn peach and ivory. In fact, he couldn't remember ever seeing her in any other colors.

Abe shifted in his chair as the pain in his abdomen intensified. He passed a hand over his face, clammy from the ache that never let him be.

He didn't want her to know he was ill. He was sad to end therapy with her, but it was time. "Paige," he said kindly, willing himself to hold on through this session, "I'm sure."

She turned to face him. Her shoulder-length hair gleamed golden as it swung around the heart-shaped face with the high cheekbones and deep-set blue eyes. "It's been five years," she said. "Aren't you afraid I'm too fragile?"

"No, I'm not," he said. He inspected the pipe he held in large, bony hands. His hands were shaking again. He willed them to stop, but they didn't cooperate. He reached over to a side drawer, opened it, and pulled out a tobacco pouch. *I haven't done a great job for you, Paige,* he thought, *but you're a survivor. You'll overcome it in spite of me.*

As he refilled his pipe, the smell of vanilla and aged tobacco filled the room. He struck a match and held it to the bowl of the pipe.

Abe looked over his horn-rimmed glasses at her, his black eyes sad under bushy gray eyebrows. A thatch of salt-and-pepper hair hung over a long, gentle face. Paige had told him he reminded her of a dog she'd had in childhood, a basset named Beauregard DeBussey. She had loved Beau, but some memory of him frightened her, although she didn't know why.

She'd spent years, with no success, trying to remember cruelties at the hands of people who should have taken better care of her. And he'd lost his nerve for digging into people's hurts and fears. How could he blame her for refusing to examine her own?

"But I'm not sure I can leave Carter," she said. "He's more worrisome than ever." Carter, her twin, was a male version of Paige. Abe knew, however, that Carter lacked his sister's strength of character, always had, always would. Paige was steel in a velvet glove.

"You'd think Carter could stand on his own two feet at twenty-eight, and I'd let him, wouldn't you?" she asked.

"You might be surprised at how well he'd do without you."

"You think so?"

"Yes, I do. He might make different choices for himself than you would, might blow things. But he's a big boy now."

Paige shook her head a little. She didn't believe that. Changing the subject, she went on, "I got a letter the other day from Jenny Parker, about our tenth class reunion." She stopped to look out the large window from Abe's fifth floor office that faced west over the gathering December dusk. "She wants me to help her plan the reunion." She traced a snowflake on the window. "If I do, I'll have to stay through the summer."

"Mm-hm?" he responded noncommittally.

"I just don't think I can stand to stay here that long."

Abe fiddled with his pipe and didn't speak. "Paul wants to start dating again. I think he wants me to marry him."

Abe perked up at this comment. At last—the real topic she wanted to talk about. Like all patients, she had saved the big one until the last five minutes of therapy and introduced it with a casual "Oh, by the way." Now he knew why she was feeling pressed to leave. "It sounds like that frightens you."

She turned away from the view of downtown, where the lights were coming on in the twilight, twinkling on the Epic Center and the Plaza. "Why doesn't he know I'm not the right sort of person for him?"

"What's the right sort?"

"Oh, someone like Jenny, so good and sweet. Someone who isn't damaged, who doesn't come from such a wacky family. Someone without such a distasteful past, without . . ."

She paused, thinking of her abortion at seventeen and of her corseted and coiffed mother marching her into the gynecologist's office. Mother had never asked her how it happened or who was responsible. She'd only lectured Paige on using contraception if she was going to be promiscuous, and on not getting caught again.

"Without what?" he asked softly.

"Without so many wounds, I guess." She looked at her hands in her lap and twisted the large single opal on her right hand.

Abe didn't answer. He started to relight his pipe, but instead he laid it aside. "Paige," he said, "I know you're threatened by the thought of ending analysis, but it really is time. I want you to know I'll be here as a friend. You can call me if you run up against some big snag."

She raised her head and took a big breath, a deep gulp of air, to stop her tears. "But why can't I remember everything?"

He wanted to reach out and pat her, to comfort her. "Paige, that's common. You're not ready to remember yet. It will come, never fear." He shifted in his chair.

"You're scared now, with me saying good-bye," he went on, "and that's why you're trotting out all your old issues, to hook me back into taking care of you. But you can do it yourself."

Therapy itself had worked no miracles. A listening ear, and a strong faith in herself—and maybe Someone else—might. Abe had always rejected religion as a crutch, but now he suspected only a healing of the spirit could heal her mind. "Doesn't Paul want you to return to your faith?"

"Did I leave it?" she asked coldly.

"Didn't you? I'm not a Christian, Paige, but I have come to believe everyone needs God. I've returned to the Jewish roots of my family."

"My family had no faith." Her voice was harsh.

"I know. I'm increasingly sure, though, that only God really heals."

She shook her head vigorously. "I can't accept that."

He sighed, then changed the subject. "I'm ready to retire, and it's time for me to say good-bye—as your therapist, that is," he added hastily when she bridled at that. "I'll still be your friend. I'll even give you my home phone number."

"Boy, you must think I'm doing well. I thought you *never* gave it out."

"Almost never, but I want to stay in touch. I'll give you Dr. Lake's card, too. You can call him if something comes up down the road. I'm not throwing you out. I want you to come back in two weeks, and then a month later after that. Okay, Munchkin?"

She smiled through her tears. "Do I have a choice?"

"You always have a choice."

Abe got up and walked around the desk. He put his hand out to her to help her up.

"Speeding me on my way," she said dourly as she rose from the chair.

He lifted her cape off the coat rack and helped her

on with it. The ivory wool swirled around her. "Is that thing warm enough in this weather?" he asked, pinching the fabric between two fingers.

"Yes, it is. See, you still try to take care of me," she said through a watery smile.

Abe smiled back.

Paige turned and made a small movement toward him as she looked into his eyes for approval. "Can I hug you?" she asked shyly.

"Yes, you can hug me—but only because therapy is over," he said with mock sternness as she walked into his arms. He returned her hug, but he knew his long-standing practice not to touch a patient was right. This hug hurt him because he loved her so much.

She turned away from him and rushed out of the office.

As Abe closed the door behind her, he grimaced in pain. His so-called stomach ulcer was no ulcer. He didn't want to face the long months ahead, the pain, the death to come from the evil thing growing in his belly. And he certainly didn't want Paige, or his other patients, to watch him die.

He thought of the enigma that was Paige. She was beautiful, talented, wealthy. She had a knack for drawing people to her, people who loved her for her courage, her kindness, her vulnerability. Yet she saw none of that . . . all she saw was a brightly packaged but unlovable piece of nothingness.

He returned to his desk and stood gazing out the window. Was the psychiatry he'd practiced for thirty-five years a sham? He thought of Freud and his outdated metaphor of the human psyche as a steam engine. Computers made the steam engine obsolete; Abe's knowledge of the human soul made Freudian psychology obsolete. "I've wasted my life on a false premise. God alone knows whether I've helped or hurt my patients," he said to the night.

Chapter 3

Paige looked back at the closed door. "I ought to be glad I'm through! Why don't I *feel* glad?" Shaking her head, she turned and walked slowly to the elevator.

As the elevator glided noiselessly to the underground level of the building, she couldn't help thinking how much of her life she'd spent riding elevators, passively letting life—and other people—move her around. Taking action helped jar her out of the passivity, but she feared the consequences at times. *What if I do the wrong thing?* she constantly asked herself and tried to guess how Abe might answer her question. Be active—make mistakes. Be passive—avoid living.

When the elevator stopped at the garage level, the smells of exhaust, oil, and dust assailed her nostrils. Old envelopes and plastic bags swirled in eddies of wind that entered through the open rectangles in the concrete walls.

She could come up with all kinds of psychological jargon—unmet dependency needs, transference issues, blah, blah, blah. After five years of psychoanalysis, she felt she had lived through and paid for an education in psychiatry. Not that it had done her much good.

No, that wasn't fair, she thought as she strode through the cavernous parking garage to her cream-colored BMW, heels clicking on the concrete. After all these years with Abe, she was much better off now. At least, she rarely had the nightmare anymore, the nightmare where she killed a man, some faceless stranger she knew but could not name, the menacing specter who threatened her sanity.

Thoughts of the man she thought she'd murdered—but realized she couldn't have—had chased her back to Wichita, a failure running from a growing career in New York. She had left the big city because she was frightened, on the streets, in Central Park, everywhere. Wichita—a quiet midwestern town that was outgrowing itself—was supposed to be safe. Wasn't it? Then last summer that nut had started calling her. She didn't know who he was, and he never actually threatened her, but the calls were unsettling.

Blessedly, the calls had stopped two months ago. She could relax again.

She sighed. She had a promising career here too, but Wichita! Wichita, Kansas—everyone's symbol of boredom and blocked exits.

Paige thought back to their group of friends in high school—her and Carter's pals—and how they had all sworn they would get out of Wichita and never come back. She had been the first to rocket out of here, so her return had all the drama of an aborted space flight.

At first, she couldn't face anyone, not even Carter. Over time, though, Abe had helped her break out of that nuttiness and reach out to some people. Mostly, though, she had avoided the old crowd. The imagined questions in their eyes hurt too much.

As she reached her car and fumbled in her purse for her keys, she heard a scraping noise behind the retaining wall to her left. She realized she'd just heard that same noise a few seconds before, but the first time it hadn't made an impression. Now she was scared. As she hesitated, alert to the nature of the sound, the noise stopped. She waited to see whether it would come again. Her knees began to shake as an echo of her old terror rang through her.

Someone was there in the silence!

Paige fumbled with her keys, scratching the paint on the door around the keyhole. At last she found the right one and inserted it in the lock, opened the door, and flung herself into the car. She reached back to lock it behind her, then sat panting and shaking, the sound of her breathing rasping across her nerves in the dead air.

She jumped. *Behind me in the back seat . . . is there someone in the car behind me?*

Paige shut her eyes tight and prayed, *Oh, God, help me!* She forced herself to look. In the gathering darkness, she could not see the floor. She stretched over the back of the seat to make sure no one was there, telling herself as she did so to slow down, to take deep breaths, not to panic.

She reached up and flicked on the overhead light. No one was there.

Of course no one was there.

She bowed her head and covered her face with her hands. *This is ridiculous!* she thought. *I'm just upset over losing Abe.*

Breathing deeply, she inserted the key in the ignition to start the car. The heavy purr of the engine comforted her, and she reversed out of her space.

As she spun the wheel around, she glanced over toward the wall where she had heard the noise. At the base of the wall was a large canvas carryall, army green, half-open, there in the shadows made by wall and floor.

She shivered. Why was that bag there? She wanted to scream.

The rational half of her brain droned sturdily: *It belongs to some workman with sloppy habits. It has no sinister implications.* At the same time, a shrill, hysterical voice shrieked, *He's found me! He's after me again!*

She forced herself to take another deep breath. She had to think logically. She tried to remember when she had parked her car. There had been a young mother at that spot, lugging an infant and a diaper bag and pushing a stroller with a toddler in it. The poor woman had dropped her purse right there, and Paige had picked it up for her. She recalled feeling a wave of compassion for the tired-looking woman and thinking how glad she was that she didn't have any babies to haul around. And there had been no workmen, of that she was sure.

Tremors shook her. She drove carefully to the exit, fearful she would jump out of her skin if she didn't get out of that garage. She took control of herself enough to greet the parking attendant calmly and pay the charges. He smiled at her in the way most men smiled at her, men who admired her beauty and knew she was out of their range. Sometimes the wall between her and men was comforting, sometimes it was lonely.

She drove out of the garage, then stopped a block down from the doctors' building. She stalled the car in her anxiety. She spent a long moment regaining her composure, started the engine, breathed a long, shuddering sigh, then slowly and calmly selected a tape of baroque classics to put into the tapedeck. *A few minutes of Pachelbel's* Canon *will help me,* she thought, as she fast-forwarded the tape to side one and the three-hundred-year-old musical tranquilizer in D major.

She drove the few blocks to her co-op, concentrating on the music. At last the majestic old Skycrest loomed into view. Safe at last! She pulled into the first porte cochere, and the doorman came out and tried to open her door. It took her a few seconds to remember it was locked.

"I'm sorry, Chester," she apologized, face flushed with embarrassment.

The slight old man gave a hint of a bow. Chester's courtesy never failed to soothe Paige's nerves at the end of her busy days at the ad agency.

"Lockin' your doors is a good idea, Ms. Brookings," he said earnestly. "It's a bad world out there."

As opposed to inside the Skycrest, she thought.

The seventy-year-old Tudor half-timber and brick matron dominated the east side and the College Hill neighborhood it bordered. It looked safe, impregnable as a castle.

Chester rang for the parking attendant to come move her car as he held the door into the lobby of the building open for her. Then he scuttled across the Persian carpet to get her mail and back to the old man-operated lift. With his long, thin legs and slightly hunched posture, Paige thought he looked like a gray beetle of some sort. He handed her the stack of mail, then clanged the gate closed and turned the handle to run the elevator up to the eighth floor.

By now she had gained control of her panic sufficiently to ask, "So how is your little granddaughter doing today?" He had told her that the five-year-old girl was getting over a bad case of chicken pox.

"She's doin' better," Chester answered. "The itchin's cooled down, so she's sleepin' better at night, which means her mom and dad are sleepin' better too!" He grinned and rubbed his chin with one hand. "I remember when her father kept *us* up half the night when *he* had chicken pox."

"That's good news, that she's better, I mean," Paige said softly. Chester loved to talk about his family, and she liked to listen. The glimpses of home life he gave her were her idea of what a real family should be, a far cry from what she had grown up with.

As he stopped the elevator and opened the door for her, she gave a little wave to the old man who tried so hard to please.

Paige unlocked the door and entered her cool, uncluttered apartment. Inside, the dominant color was a tranquil ivory, and the effect was that of a high-dollar art gallery. A few good art pieces seemed to float from their pedestals, and quiet oil paintings, symmetrically placed, graced the walls.

Her cat, an orange tom named Marmalade, stretched long and loose from his place on the highboy and then leapt noiselessly to the couch. He meowed a greeting at her. Seeing him, Paige felt her taut nerves unwind a little.

She sighed and hung her cape in the entry closet. For a moment, she stood with her back against the closed door, head against the smooth wood, tears hot in her eyes. This was home. It was safe, it was lovely, but it was, in spite of the cat, lonely. And now there was no Abe to talk to.

She crossed the room and sat down beside the cat and stroked him gently. Marmalade placed his front paws in her lap and stretched up to rub his head under her chin. The softness of his fur sent a poignant little shiver down her spine. He was the only warm thing in this room. She blinked back tears.

Abe said I could call, she silently told Marmalade. She knew full well, though, that she wouldn't— couldn't—short of a catastrophe.

She padded quietly down the hall, the cat trailing behind her, to the bedroom where she changed out of her clothes and into sweats. Picking up the ivory suit from the bed where she had laid it, she brushed it and hung it up. Then she put the blouse in the hamper to go to the cleaner at the end of the week.

When the bedroom was again as neat as it would be the minute after the cleaning lady left, she picked up the cat and, holding him close, went back through the living room and into the kitchen. It, too, was immaculate, all ice-white and stainless steel. She opened a small, hideously expensive can of gourmet cat food, which she emptied into the cat's dish and placed in the middle of his place mat by the refrigerator. Marmalade purred loudly as he ate, ever so neatly. She poured herself a glass of wine.

Taking the glass into the living room, Paige sat on the couch with one leg tucked beneath her and opened her mail. Most of it was junk, catalogs with screaming ads for Christmas gifts, things that required the best advertising Madison Avenue could come up with, merely because no one really needed them.

There was one lone Christmas card from Paul, a quiet card with a peaceful midnight blue scene pricked out with stars over Bethlehem. She made a face at herself, at Paul, at the card.

She thought back to the cards she had received from him while she was in New York, when his wife Marianna was still alive. They had been sweet, homey cards—open doors to storybook houses, with warm fires blazing on fairytale hearths. They'd made her want to cry.

Then Marianna had died in childbirth, the little boy too, and the cards had changed. Now they were more tailored and remote. She liked them better. She needed to be tailored and remote, didn't she?

Paige let her thoughts stray to Paul. He was sweet, too sweet. Why didn't he just give up on her?

She stood, picked up the neat stack of mail, and carried it to the wastebasket by her desk. She dropped it all in, his card on top, and watched it fall to the bottom with a last lingering look before turning her back.

She returned to the couch where she picked up the remote control and flicked on the TV. She hoped to catch some news. But it was too late.

As she flicked the television back off, the phone rang. She froze, staring at the phone. *I don't want to talk to anyone.*

The phone continued to ring. Surely the answering machine would kick on soon.

It didn't. *I must not have turned it on this morning,* she thought. The phone shrilled on.

She walked over to it and stood looking down. At last she sighed and reached for it. "Hello?" she answered hesitantly.

There was nothing but the sound of breathing on the other end, but no one spoke.

"Hello," she repeated, louder this time.

Still no response. She moved to drop the receiver into its cradle. But as she was pulling it away from her ear, she heard a voice and jerked it back.

"Oh, Paige, Paige, I've been waiting for you," came a husky whisper. "I'll meet up with you yet, you know." The caller chuckled obscenely.

"Who are you?" she yelled into the mouthpiece. "Who are you?" She began to sob softly, trembling. It had been weeks since his last call. She'd hoped he'd given up.

"You know who I am, Paige."

She gripped the phone so hard her hand ached and grasped her abdomen with the other hand, fearing she might break apart with terror. But she stood frozen, like a doe caught in the lights of a car at night, unable to escape her tormentor. Bile rose in her throat, and she shook off her trance-like inertia.

Paige threw the receiver down, away from her. It missed the cradle of the phone, landing on the thick carpeting on the floor. Marmalade had returned to the room, and he jumped and hissed when the phone narrowly missed him.

Retrieving the instrument, she slammed it down on the table. She stared at it where it sat, threatening her, like a coiled snake, ready to strike.

Her head started to pound. She felt her lungs constrict. *I can't breathe!* she wailed to herself.

She stumbled into the bathroom and opened the medicine chest. Where was it? There. The brown plastic vial of Librium was hiding on the top shelf, behind the aspirin. She shook out two green-and-black capsules into her trembling palm, then stared at the two small containers of oblivion. The tremors jostled the capsules out of her hand and into the basin, staining the small pool of water a murky gray.

She straightened and looked at herself in the mirror. "No," she said through clenched teeth. "Not again." She picked up the dissolving pills, dropped them in the commode, and flushed them away. She snapped the white lid back on the bottle and replaced it in the cabinet. It would be there if she really ever needed it, but not this time.

She thought of the weeks of recovery from her addiction to the rotten things. Abe had been there, daily, to treat her. He had been so gentle, so kind. *I need you, Abe,* she cried to herself. *I want that kind, gentle treatment now.*

Sinking down on the hard tile floor, she rested her head on her arms, propped on the edge of the tub. Marmalade entered the room silently and settled in her lap as softly as snow on a pine tree. Tears traced the curve of her face and dropped onto the cat's fur.

Paige lifted her head to stare at the bar of globe-like lights above her and thought of her mother, wondering why she couldn't have had the kind of mother she could turn to for comfort. Instead, Candice Brookings was a woman Paige and Carter had merely called "Mother," a woman who had turned her back on both of them soon after their birth.

How many times had Mother said to the two children, "I gave birth to you, what more do you want?" Paige could see the perfect makeup, the surgically lifted face right now. "You've got my looks and your father's money. Use them to get what you want."

"But I wanted a mommy," Paige whispered to the cat now sleeping in her lap. Shaking off her wistful mood, she spoke coldly, trying to duplicate her mother's tone, "But that wasn't what you got, so quit your bellyaching."

The depression hit her then, a wrecking ball to the brain.

It took her hours to calm herself. She brought the bottle of wine, nearly full, into the living room, and spent the evening filling and refilling her glass. If she was lucky, maybe she could drink herself into a stupor.

The phone rang seven times over the long evening hours, but she didn't answer it. She only stared at it as it rang and rang and rang. At some point during the siege, Paige retrieved Paul's card—a talisman of sanity for her—from the trash and tucked it into the top desk drawer.

A little after midnight, she dragged herself into the bathroom for a long, hot soak in the large tub on claw feet. At about one, the phone rang again, rousing her. She realized she had dozed off and stood quickly, dizzy now from the combined effects of the alcohol and hot water. How stupid! she admonished herself and vowed never to take another bath after a night of drinking.

An ugly little voice in the corner of her mind said, *But why not? It might be a good idea to end all this.*

No! she screamed at the worm in her head. *I will not commit suicide. I'll beat this thing. I'll find this person who's tormenting me and . . . kill him if I have to!*

And you won't have a nervous breakdown over it either, another voice in her head assured her slyly. *You'll be glad to see him lying there dead . . . won't you?*

With a shudder of revulsion, Paige threw away the empty wine bottle, resolving to give up alcohol entirely. She wanted to be free from whatever enchained her—pills, booze, the threatening voice. "Help me, God," she whispered.

But why should he help her? She'd turned her back on him long ago. She wrapped herself in a huge peach bath towel and slept, sitting up in a nest of pillows on her bed, Marmalade curled next to her.

Chapter 4

A melancholy mood settled over Paul after he and Moses returned home from their daily walk. The two-story brick house, built in the twenties when craftsmen didn't stint on woodwork or finish details, rose lovely and graceful from the winding walk and flower beds that bound the house to the earth. Once inside, Paul walked through the human-empty house, looking at the comfortable furnishings, the large windows, high ceilings, and glass-fronted bookcases filled with books, Marianna's collection of Capodimonti flowers and birds, and videos of old movies. He opened one of the cases and picked up a porcelain bird, a cedar waxwing. It took him back to the day two years before, when he'd bought it for her. They'd taken a trip to Italy, in hopes she'd snap out of her depression.

"Oh, please, Paulie, just this one more?" she'd begged, big, round, black eyes upturned to his. She smiled at him then, and he'd melted. She really knew how to work him. He hadn't minded so much. He'd always been willing to do nearly anything to make her happy.

She looked like a china doll—tiny, delicate, with black curls and a pretty face. He'd studied her that day and realized there were no character lines in her smooth skin, nothing to show she'd lived and suffered and learned. There was only a sulky cast around her bow-shaped mouth. He'd reached out and touched her cheek. "Poor Marianna."

She cocked her head sideways and pouted prettily. "I know I have so many," she continued, holding the bird up for his inspection, "but this one is special."

He laughed. "Aren't they all?"

"But this one reminds me of you, darling, so handsome, so dignified." She smiled again, her dimples dancing, her eyes flashing. "And I just know I'll turn fat and ugly as this horrid baby grows in me. So let me surround myself with something pretty."

He'd jerked his hand away from her face when she'd spoken the words "horrid baby." How could she think that about the child she was going to bear? He'd bought her the cedar waxwing and then mourned that she would never be the adult companion he'd hoped to spend his life with.

But that was then. Now he looked up from the bird in his hand and through the door into his bedroom. Seeing himself in the long cheval glass inside, he laughed. He looked so morose, like a long, skinny descendent of Emmett Kelly—a clown with a self-pitying frown on his face. He couldn't—didn't want to—hold on to a bad mood for long. He had too many blessings to waste time on any "woe-is-me's."

He put the bird back in the case, then went into his

bedroom to change out of his racquetball clothes. Better try for a little more dignified image for his students, he decided. He chose a tweedy blue-green sweater and gray slacks, then brushed his hair.

When he walked back into the living room, he went to the stereo and put on a cassette tape—Larnelle Harris, singing "I Choose Joy"—and began whistling along with the music. In the kitchen, he fixed turkey divan for his supper, making enough for two. His folks were in Florida for two weeks, and he'd agreed to feed his grandmother each night while they were away. She did quite well on her own, but Kay Sherman felt better if she knew her mother would be getting a hot meal every night. He'd drop it by on his way to the campus to give his final.

Once the food was cooked, he wrapped it and packed it carefully. He needed to rush—he still hadn't eaten his own supper. The phone rang, and he looked longingly at the food on the stove. He was starving. "I'll never have time to eat if I answer the phone."

Taking his plate with him, he answered it anyway. A breathy voice, sounding a million miles away, said, "Paul?"

"Yes? Who is it?"

"It's Renee."

Renee Wentworth, one of the old high school gang he and Jamal and Paige had run around with. He pictured her wounded face and hunched stance. She always looked like she was apologizing for being alive and breathing the same air as the rest of the world. "Yes, Renee," he said gently. If he spoke too loudly, she'd run like a spooked deer. "What can I do for you?"

"I—I know you're busy, but could you come by my

place? I'm afraid. There's been a car out in front off and on for several nights."

"Have you called the police?"

"Oh, no, I couldn't do that."

"Is it there now?"

There was a long pause. He imagined her tugging a curtain aside to look. "No."

"I've got to go to class—have to give a test. I'll be by later. Should I call first so I won't scare you when I come?"

"No," she whispered, "I'll be watching for you."

He heard a rustle as though she were preparing to hang up. "Wait! Lock all your doors and windows, now."

"Oh, okay."

He shook his head as he hung up. Probably hadn't thought of that easy remedy. For some reason, Renee's manner made him doubt her. Was she so hungry for attention that she'd concoct a story about some stalker?

He decided it didn't matter. Either way, she deserved a friend, someone who cared. *Dear God and Father, I pray for your protection for Renee. I don't know what's wrong with her, but something is. Please wrap your arms around her.* He then pictured Paige, beautiful Paige, looking as hounded as Renee, as pathetic. He laughed at the image. Perfect, super-achiever Paige like loser Renee? Yes, somehow, they were alike. *Please protect Paige too, dear God. I'm afraid for her.*

Paul wolfed down his meal, then dashed out of the house, a picnic basket with his grandmother's supper tucked up in a blue and white checked cloth. "I feel a little like Red Riding Hood," he said to Moses as he

31

left. "I should probably be skipping down a woodland path or something."

After the last student had turned in his paper, Paul dropped by Renee's. She lived in an apartment in back of an old house on South Main. The neighborhood wasn't terrible, but it was a little rough, he thought.

He knocked at the door. No answer. He knocked again, more persistently this time.

At last she came to the door. "Yeah, what is it?"

"Renee, you called me three hours ago and asked me to drop by. Don't you remember?"

"Um, yeah, guess so." She didn't look quite awake.

"You were worried about someone in a car watching you."

She looked out the door. "Guess he's not here now."

"Renee, you can't see the street from here. Where was this car?" He struggled to keep a cap on his impatience.

She sighed, like an overworked teacher dealing with a slow child. "I see him whenever I go to the grocery store or something."

He narrowed his gaze, eyeing her curiously. "Right. Well, he's gone now."

"Right." She began to close the door on him.

"Call again if you're concerned."

She nodded but didn't answer.

Paul turned and walked away, shaking his head as he went. "Odd. I wonder if she's on the same planet with the rest of us." He resolved, though, to check on her again.

Chapter 5

The next morning Paige awoke with a splitting headache. Marmalade was gone, probably waiting in the kitchen by his dish.

When she looked at her image in the bathroom mirror, she saw in the harsh light that the ravages of the night before were written all over her face. There were dark shadows under her eyes and pinched, gray lines around her mouth. She made a face at her reflection. "And a lovely thing you are too. Wonder what all your admirers would think if they could see you now?" Maybe this morning face was the thing that killed marriages, at least all the marriages she knew, beginning with her mother's five and her father's three.

She dressed quickly, yet as meticulously as ever. When she was through with her morning routine and had fed and petted the cat, had drunk her coffee and eaten her dry toast, the apartment looked like an eight-page spread in *Architectural Digest*. She wouldn't leave it any other way. As she pulled the door to behind her, she thought fondly of Abe's attempts to "cure" her compulsiveness and of his laughing capitulation near the end: "I give up, Munchkin. I'll never succeed in helping you relax enough to be sloppy, even just once in a while."

The thought of giving up all her comforting rituals, the precise placement of all her belongings, panicked her nearly as much as the man on the phone. At least she had control when things were done just so. She locked the door with a smug smile.

✤ ✤ ✤

By Wednesday, Paige had received no more calls from her tormentor. There had been no strange noises behind her. She was beginning to doubt her senses again, to believe that perhaps she had imagined the person lurking in the garage, the obscene voice on the phone.

At the office, while she was going over the ad campaign for the Fourth National Bank, Carter called her. She was irritated, even before she recognized his voice. The phone had been ringing all morning and she had just discovered that the campaign was going to go way over estimates on cost. Her boss, Hal Fitzpatrick, and the bank were both going to be irate, and she knew she would be the one to get it in the neck.

"Paige, pet, where the heck have you been?" Carter began. "I've been calling and calling, and I don't get an answer. I don't even get that blasted answering machine of yours!"

"I just discovered last night that it's broken," she lied.

"What's going on? Why are you the invisible woman this week?"

Demanding Carter. She bridled a little at his expectation that she make herself ever available to him. Covering her irritation, however, she replied coolly, "I've been busy, Carter. I do work, you know." She looked around the walls of her office, with the framed awards she'd won for different campaigns. She was proud of her Addies and her two CLIOs. They weren't shabby, at all.

"Has it been work, love . . . or one of your grubby men friends?" he asked snidely.

She didn't answer him.

"Okay, okay, don't get ticked," Carter backed off. He couldn't stand to alienate Paige, his one tie to normality, he called her. Paige, on her part, struggled valiantly not to let him know how abnormal she considered herself, how damaged.

"So don't you want to know why I'm calling?" he asked fawningly, like a puppy.

Paige couldn't help herself—she chuckled. "Yes, Carter, honey, I do."

"Well," he said, a mincing tone in his voice, "I'm planning a big Christmas bash, and of course, I need you to come."

"Of course."

"And not just to bring food, child. I need your presence, P-R-E-S-E-N-C-E, not gifts, you know."

"And what do you need my presence for?" She doodled on the pale gray legal pad in front of her, drawing a likeness of Carter's head, mouth open like a hungry baby bird.

Liz, Hal's secretary, stuck her head in Paige's door. Paige raised one hand in acknowledgment. Liz pointed to her watch and mouthed, "Hal wants to see you in ten minutes."

Paige nodded, then turned her attention to Carter on the other end of the line.

"There are three agents coming from Hollywood," he was saying, "and you never know, some of them may be put off by my pansy friends. You would provide a nice balance."

"Gee, thanks," she said sarcastically. "I'd be so glad to provide a balance for your pansy friends." She x-ed out the face on the legal pad.

"Now, now, don't get miffed. You know I need you."

Paige redrew her brother as a cherubic infant, fat cheeks and an aureole of curls. "And will I be the only non-pansy there—other than perhaps an agent or two?"

"No," he said earnestly, "I've invited a few old friends from school. Paul is coming," he threw out, proffering the information like a delicacy to tempt her.

"Paul!" she exploded. She snapped the pencil in her hand and threw the fragments into the corner of her office. "Carter, you know I'm trying to keep away from him." She knew her voice was too loud, so she made an effort to quiet down. When Liz stuck in her head, with its tumble of black curls and a quizzical look on her face, Paige smiled ruefully and lowered her voice. "Paul thinks he wants to marry me, and I'm trying to discourage him."

"But why?" Carter wheedled. "He's so nice."

"I know he's nice . . . as in boring and staid and dull and dreary." She picked up a new pencil to lengthen the cherub's face, making it lean and bony, like a living death's head, sprouting horns and mustache. She sketched in the small scar above his eyebrow, the one she'd put there when they were six. She'd lost her temper with him—again. He was constantly teasing her and nagging her to trade her toys, Barbie stuff, usually. Even then, he'd liked decorating and playing dress-up.

He'd grabbed her favorite Barbie, so she'd picked up a crystal alarm clock and flung it at him. She shivered involuntarily, recalling the scene as if it were yesterday.

The cut wasn't that big, but like all head wounds, it bled profusely. He screamed, and she covered her mouth in horror at what she had done.

When their nanny—Paige couldn't remember her name, they had had so many—entered the room, Mother sauntering coolly behind, Carter yelled, "She tried to kill me!" Paige cringed, knowing what was coming.

While the nanny cleaned Carter up, Mother whipped Paige with a leather cowboy belt she'd grabbed from the closet. And when Paige cried, she whipped her again. "Stop that crying!" she screamed. "You know I can't stand crying!"

Mother went around the room, picking up a few discarded pieces of clothing, throwing them into the white wicker hamper by the closet. "You've probably destroyed that beautiful face of his, you rotten child! Haven't I told you again and again that temper of yours would be the ruin of you, or of someone else?"

With that, she stalked out of the room, leaving Paige to cry alone and to wonder, with mounting horror, how badly injured Carter was. No one thought to come tell her for hours. The doctor had put in three stitches, almost invisible. And while Paige had been in her room alone, miserable, and fearful she had killed her brother, he had recovered nicely and had been rewarded with an ice cream cone on the way back from the doctor's office.

He came into her room to gloat the minute he got home. "*I* got ice cream and you *didn't*."

She gritted her teeth at the memory, then scribbled through the likeness of Carter and threw down the pencil.

"Sorry, Paige," he said. "I really am sincerely sorry. But he's already invited and he's already coming, and I *need* you."

Paige swore softly. "Sure, sure, Carter, I know. You need me." Lightening her tone, knowing that if she ended the conversation with a cross word, he'd be begging her to forgive him for days, she added, "Don't worry. I'll be there. Just tell me when and what to bring. I do quite understand you need help. This would be a big break for you."

Cheered that she had given in, he chortled, "Can you believe agents are coming to *Wichita?* Do you think they want to experience this backwards place so they can appreciate wild and crazy California even better?"

She laughed. "Probably. And Carter," she added softly, "I do hope you get into that soap. I know it's what you've dreamed of for years."

After Carter gave her his list of food and flowers to order, the conversation ended. Carter seemed mollified and Paige was secretly seething. She hung up and stared at the phone. "I'm a fool. I'm the biggest fool in town." Feeling her anger rising, she gulped and forced herself to calm down. Never again, after that day when she'd injured him, had she allowed herself to lose her temper. Her anger was just too big and dangerous and frightening.

✢ ✢ ✢

Several days later, Paige called the caterer to order food for the big party. Salmon, shrimp cocktail, filet de boeuf roti. Vichyssoise, artichokes, and stuffed avocados. Fresh strawberry tarts with clotted cream and lemon coconut cake. Lots of crusty French bread. As usual, she left the drinks to Carter. She never thought beyond white wine, and now she didn't want to have anything more to do with alcohol at all.

She called the florist to order flowers—huge white poinsettias and armloads of white roses and greenery. Since she hadn't been to Carter's place in a month, she had no idea what the current color scheme was. At least the white and green would be fairly safe. And their coolness might help subdue whatever hot colors he had used this time.

A month before, at that fiasco of a birthday party for Mother, the hot pinks, oranges, and reds had nearly given her heat stroke. Mother had been at her acid best: "Well, Carter, you've certainly outdone yourself this time. Is this how all the best-dressed gay brothels look this year?"

Carter had smiled, a one-sided, self-protective smile, and said, "Yes, Mother, I thought you would know that, having been associating with darling Teddy the way you have recently."

Teddy, Mother's current boyfriend—and he was a boy at just nineteen—had turned white, and Mother had slapped Carter hard. He had just smiled and rubbed the red spot on his cheek.

Chapter 6

H al welcomed Paige into his office, all oak and deep burgundy plush carpet and glass. She sat across from him in the hot seat, where he put his associates to pick their brains for new campaigns.

"This new account sounds old hat, Paige," he said, passing a long bony hand over his face.

The thin man's face looked tired as usual, pale blue eyes dim behind wire-rim glasses. The drained, washed-out appearance was deceptive, though, for behind the pale eyes was one of the brightest, quickest minds Paige had ever known. Hal fooled people by always looking half asleep, until someone said or did something foolish, at which point he devastated the offender with his rapier wit.

The expensively tailored suit, a gray worsted, fit his long, lithe body perfectly, of course, and the subtle burgundy silk tie suited the successful image he portrayed.

"It's not old hat, however," he went on. "It's an oil account—ho hum, you say—but this one is different.

The chief exec is Holder Danton. I'd never heard of him, have you?" he asked in an aside.

She shook her head no.

"He was supposedly a self-made millionaire, but then he made some shrewd investments and inherited some of the Beech fortune—how, I don't know—and he now finds himself a multibillionaire and the darling of the symphony set."

"So what is he doing in Wichita?" Paige asked, wishing too late she could recall the sarcastic tone that would give her away.

"Now, Paige, let's forgive poor little Wichita for being little." Hal smiled briefly, then continued. "I think your style may suit him best, so I would like you to be his first contact." He went on to give her preliminary instructions.

He dismissed her some thirty minutes later with a nod, then stopped her when she reached his door. "Oh, and Paige, I hope his scars won't put you off too much. He assures me they're temporary."

She stared at him. "Scars?"

"Yes, some accident on the Autobahn. I guess it was pretty gruesome. Danton's had plastic surgery to correct some of the damage. But he'll heal up soon and be pretty as a picture, I'm sure." He waved her on out.

She scowled as she left Hal's office. She hoped the scars weren't too recent. She didn't much like being made aware of human mortality.

On the other side of the door, Hal looked pensive and pulled on his lower lip. *I don't feel right, not telling her Danton asked for her specifically,* he thought. *But a big prospect like that—you want to humor him.*

He reached across the desk to pick up the phone,

then hesitated, holding the receiver in his hand as he assured himself: *Someday maybe he'll let me know why he doesn't want her to know that.*

✛ ✛ ✛

Paige arrived a little early for her appointment with Holder Danton. His office on the eleventh floor of the Epic Center was richly furnished, but to Paige's eyes, without taste. She sat back, waiting for him to see her, spending her time critiquing the French provincial and Early American hodgepodge that someone must have thought passed for style. She looked up to find the receptionist staring at her. The stare wasn't hostile, but it wasn't friendly, either.

Paige returned the plump redhead's gaze steadily, with a slight smile tacked on. The message was clear: *I'm friendly enough, but don't mess with me.*

The receptionist dropped her eyes and went back to buffing her nails.

Paige set herself to reviewing mentally what Hal had told her about Holder Danton. She wanted to be prepared for this meeting.

He had already kept her waiting twenty minutes, a power play on his part, she was sure. She smiled a little to herself. *He thinks he's pretty hot stuff. Probably plans to pull a few tricks on a small-town gal. We'll see about that.*

The receptionist sent her into the office with a smirk. The office was decorated with the same heavy Early American touch as the reception area, but at least the white and gilt French provincial stuff was missing.

Paige was not prepared for the man's face. The scars were much worse than Hal had intimated. The jagged, angry red slashes were beginning to fade some, but the skin was taut and shiny where it was healing. The tissue around his eyes was puffy and bruised, his eyes nearly disappearing in the swollen flesh.

Sizing up the situation, Paige decided to be frank. "Your accident must have been quite severe," she said softly, consciously checking any sentimentality in her tone.

He let out the breath he was holding and smiled. His appearance was gruesome, but Paige had not flinched. "Yes, it was."

"I'm sorry," she said simply.

"So was I, so was I." He waved his hand in a gesture of dismissal and indicated the chair across from his desk. "Let's get started. I think you and I are going to get along just fine."

Paige wasn't sure she was pleased with that thought. Something about him put her off. She hoped it wasn't just the scars. Surely she wasn't that shallow. She couldn't deny, however, that physical beauty was important to her. Still, she doubted whether Holder Danton had had any of that even before the accident.

He held himself awkwardly, like a junior high boy uncomfortable with his changing physique. He was of medium height, a little too beefy for the Brooks Brothers suit straining across his shoulders and gut. His sparse, sandy hair was plastered across a bullet-shaped head. In the back of her mind, she could see him as he must have looked ten years ago—a brawny cowboy wearing polyester after it had been passé for years.

Something about his hazel eyes intrigued her, though. There was a power in them that made her squirm a little. His eyes held her gaze a little too long, and that made her uncomfortable.

The meeting was short. Holder went over his needs and said, "I want an outdoorsman image for this campaign, something rugged and individualistic."

Paige knew better than to argue with him. The Marlboro man with an oil twist—which was what he had in mind—would be trite and maybe unwelcome, especially now in this increasingly environmentally aware society.

Finally she said firmly, "I'll draw up several different ideas to present, including some that might not have occurred to you. We don't want to close off your options too early." She looked straight into those strange eyes and smiled. "You want to get your money's worth of the creative talent at Fitzpatrick's."

Danton didn't respond right away. He realized she disapproved of his idea, but he was smart enough to give her some room to maneuver. "Sure," he said slowly, "we'll look at several options."

Paige left his office feeling uneasy, but she couldn't put her finger on the reason.

✛ ✛ ✛

Late that afternoon, Paul dropped by Renee's apartment. He knocked as he had several nights earlier and felt he was in instant replay when she called to him to come in.

"Shouldn't you keep your door locked?" he scolded.

The room was dark except for the flickering images on the screen. It was furnished sparsely, with garage sale finds, he was sure. The TV, large-screen, was new, though. "Renee! Renee, can you hear me?"

She sat staring at the picture, barely reacting when he spoke, then turned slowly to face him. "Yeah, I can hear."

"Turn on that lamp." He crossed the room and flicked off the TV. "Are you on something, Renee?" He sniffed for marijuana smoke, but didn't detect any. He didn't want to name what he could smell though, like neglect and dirt.

"The doctor at the clinic gave me some tranquilizers." She shoved her mouse-brown, straggly hair off her face. She looked pale, her eyes almost blank. "I think I took too many."

Paul sighed, then knelt in front of her to look into her eyes. The pupils seemed large, but it was dark in the room.

He got up to turn on more lights. Her eyes, when he checked them again, seemed normal enough. "I'm going to make you some coffee."

She shrugged. He could feel her apathy and hopelessness rise like a night-time swamp fog in the room. He wanted to shake her, yell at her to evoke a response, any response.

While Paul fixed the coffee, he straightened up a little in the filthy kitchen, running hot water into the sink and scrubbing the few dirty dishes. When he opened the pantry, he found it nearly empty. He shook his head. She broke his heart.

It seemed he collected broken women—Marianna and Renee and Paige, although Paige functioned so much better than the other two. *Dear God, so much pain in this world! Help us all.*

He filled a chipped mug with steaming coffee and

took it to her. "Do you have any idea who's been hanging around?"

"Oh, Reilly, I'm sure."

Paul heard crying in a back room. "A child?"

"Yeah. Reilly thinks he's going to get him back, but he's not." She sipped from the mug absently, as if unaware she was drinking.

"Reilly's . . . and yours?"

"Yeah," she repeated. "My mom's been raising him, but she sent him back. He's getting to be too much trouble for her. He cries a lot."

Paul left her and went to the bedroom. The stench of unwashed clothes and dirty diapers was overwhelming. A small boy, perhaps ten months old, lay huddled in a corner of the filthy crib, whimpering. When he saw Paul, he struggled to stand. "Unh unh unh," he said, reaching his arms out to be picked up.

"Hi, fella," Paul said quietly, careful not to alarm the baby.

The boy wrapped his arms around Paul's neck and squeezed hard. "Dada?"

"No, I'm not Dada." Paul felt sick to his stomach. He took the baby into the living room. Renee looked up at them, but said nothing. "This child is skin and bones, Renee. Are you feeding him?"

"Oh, he's such a picky eater. I feed him what I eat. If he refuses it, I figure he'll eventually get hungry enough to eat what I give him."

"You have no food in your kitchen." Paul's anger was rising, and he wanted to scream at her. "I'm a total stranger, and he acts like I'm his long-lost buddy! Renee, how long has it been since you've fed this child?"

She shrugged and lowered her eyes.

"At least you know enough to feel ashamed. What's his name?"

"Michael," she said glumly. "Look, I didn't want the kid. Well," she corrected herself, "I did, at first, but then he cried all the time." She doubled over, covering her ears with her hands. "I couldn't stand it!"

Paul looked at her in disgust. He grabbed a faded afghan off the couch and wrapped it around the baby. "I'm pretty sure I've got some crackers in my car. I'll get them, then clean him up, then we'll go shopping."

Michael ate the crackers with as much relish as if they were ambrosia. He grinned a lopsided grin at Paul.

Paul melted. "Let's clean you up, buddy."

The bathroom was no cleaner than the kitchen. Paul cleared a spot on the counter where he lay the squirming baby. He was wearing only a filthy diaper that looked as if it had been soiled, dried on its own, then refilled. Paul gasped when he saw the bruises on the thin bird legs. The child was scrawny, but amazingly he kept smiling and wriggling, just like a normal kid. Paul smiled back. He was pretty cute.

"Where are some warm clothes?" he called to Renee in the living room.

Paul heard her exaggerated sigh and lumbering movements as she rose from the couch and made her way to the bedroom. She didn't take long to bring a red, white, and blue sweat suit. It was so tiny! She disappeared right away. He wanted to ask her, not too kindly, whether she had any interest in this small person.

He paused and looked at the baby. He could tell the signs, that he was making a big mistake. He was getting entangled in this messy person's messy life. He knew he had to guard against rushing in to rescue stray pups like Renee. This time, he resolved to stay impersonal, objective, rational.

Once he had Michael dressed, Paul returned to the living room where Renee was once again on the couch, staring at the TV. Again he flicked it off. "I'll need his coat. We're going to the store to buy groceries."

Paul spent the next two hours shopping, careful to buy two large packages of disposable diapers, then returning to Renee's to stock the pantry, feed Michael some nourishing food, and finish the job he'd started on the kitchen. He fed Renee, too, some spaghetti he'd thrown together.

"I'm a good cook," he bragged to Michael, and the child nodded and grinned his toothless grin. He settled the baby down in a now clean crib with a bottle of milk, then tackled the bathroom.

After she ate, Renee wandered off to the bedroom. "I can't stay up. I'm so tired."

Paul was sure she was in no danger of a drug overdose, so he let her go. "I've got Michael in bed, so I'm going to run home and wash some sheets and towels for you. You'll listen for him, right?"

"Sure."

"Renee," he said seriously, "you've got to get some help. I don't mean just with this," he said as he gestured around the messy apartment. "I mean with your life. I don't think anyone showing signs of depression like you are should be on tranquilizers."

She waved one hand in dismissal. "Oh, who cares?" Then her voice grew cold. "I appreciate your help, Paul, but don't start telling me what to do. I'm fine."

He laughed. "Yep, you sure are fine."

That enraged her. "Just get out!" she screamed,

face purplish-red and distorted with rage, neck veins popping out.

Startled by his mother's outburst, Michael began crying. He reached out to Paul to pick him up out of the crib.

Paul had not meant to get involved, but he realized he had to protect Michael, at least until Renee got help or until someone—preferably family—turned up to take care of him. "I'm sorry, Renee, but I'm not leaving this child here. I'll take him with me while I do your laundry, then bring him back."

"Keep him, I don't care." Her lifeless shrug spoke volumes.

He stared at her. "Okay. I'll keep him tonight, then bring him back in the morning. Give me a key so I can get in."

Paul was dead tired, but his anger was energizing. He rummaged through her closets for pajamas, a play-pen, and blankets.

"Come on, Michael." Paul bundled the now-sleepy child up and took him out to his car. He had to make two more trips to collect all the dirty clothes.

Getting into his car, he glanced back at Renee's door. *Pitiful, God, just pitiful.*

Paul got to bed late, after running five loads of laundry and checking several times on Michael, who was sleeping in the playpen he'd set up in the living room. Moses had been very interested in the spaghetti-and-milk-smelling bundle when Paul brought him in. She checked him out, then lay down next to the playpen.

Michael whimpered from time to time, but he slept through what was left of the night and woke Paul in the morning by chirping to Moses. *How can a kid with such a life be so happy?* Paul thought of the resiliency of the human spirit and thanked God for it in this small child.

After diapering the baby, Paul redressed him in the sweat suit he'd worn the night before and fed him two soft-cooked eggs. Michael scarfed them down, along with a banana, cut in chunks, and some toast and milk.

"I hate the thought of taking you home, pal. I'd like to just keep you forever." Paul picked the child up and hugged him. Michael squeezed his neck, and it took all Paul's resolve to load up the car and return the baby and the clean laundry to his mother.

"Get some help, Renee," Paul said firmly when he reached her apartment. "I'm not kidding. This is dreadful."

"Yeah, yeah."

He left her in the living room, in front of the TV, Michael clean and happy with some toys in the playpen. He hoped he hadn't made a huge mistake.

Chapter 7

The minute Paige walked into her apartment that evening, the phone rang. She didn't want to answer, but she willed herself to do it.

Fortunately it was Jenny Parker. "Paige!" she said breathlessly. "How are you?"

Paige smiled when she heard Jenny's voice. She couldn't help liking Jenny—she was like a warm puppy. "Can you meet me for lunch tomorrow? I'd like to start making plans for the reunion, and I thought you'd have some good ideas. How about the Art Museum?"

Paige sighed softly. She didn't want to be roped into helping with this reunion, but she figured she had no choice. She had toyed briefly with the idea of leaving Wichita soon, but she knew she wouldn't. "Sure, Jenny. When did you have in mind?"

They settled on a time, and Paige hung up. She'd wanted to discourage the old gang's friendly overtures, but she just was not succeeding at it. The phone rang again as she stood there, wondering how to get out of the appointment with Jenny.

The voice on the other end of the line was so different from Jenny's. "Paige, Paige . . . it'll be soon now," came a husky whisper.

It was the same man calling, she was sure. With shaking hands, she hung up the phone and unplugged it. She turned off the answering machine, too, just to be sure he could not reach her.

Then she changed into sweats and, putting his harness on him, led Marmalade to the elevator and down into the basement where the exercise room was located. The basement was sparkling clean. Even the water and sewer pipes overhead were freshly painted in spring green, yellow, and pale blue. Paige worked out for over an hour, pushing herself to her limits so she could forget that filthy voice. Marmalade wandered around the room, sniffing out whatever interesting smells he could find. After a long hunt, he tired of that and jumped onto the billiards table and fell asleep.

When her legs and arms were shaking from oxygen deprivation, Paige finally let herself quit.

✝ ✝ ✝

That night she had her old nightmare—of the man with the big, cruel hands and her basset hound, dead in her bed. She woke up screaming. It was the first time she'd had that nightmare since her first year of therapy.

Paige walked shakily to the kitchen and made herself a cup of coffee, hands trembling so she spilled some on the counter. She drank it in the dim light of the clock on the range.

It was his eyes that were so frightening, she remembered. He'd laughed when she found Beau dead in her bed. He always laughed in her dream, watching her all the while.

✝ ✝ ✝

The lunch with Jenny started out badly. Paige felt uncomfortable with the young woman. Short and curvy, with curly light brown hair cut short around her face, Jenny had been head cheerleader in high school. She had been cute and bouncy then, and she was cute and bouncy now.

After they finished their spinach and bacon salads, Jenny gave Paige a searching look. "How are you doing . . . *really?*" she asked softly.

From the way she asked, the warm look of concern on her face, Paige knew it wasn't just an empty social pleasantry. She was tempted to tell her everything—the nightmares, the calls, the scare in the parking garage—but she could imagine the shocked recoil if she dared to breathe a word of her sordid life. So she turned her attention to her croissant sandwich after breezily answering, "Oh, fine."

Jenny stared at her, then lowered her gaze. Mercifully, she changed the subject and started talking about the reunion.

After lunch, before they separated at the parking lot, Jenny put one hand on Paige's arm. "Paige, I don't want to pry, but you look like you're hurting. If you don't want to talk to me, I can give you a name."

"A name?"

"The name of a counselor at our church. She really helped my cousin when she was having problems with her husband. He was an alcoholic, and their life was a shambles. He'd started slapping her around, and she didn't know what to do."

"I'm all right, Jenny," Paige said more harshly than she meant to. "Really," she said, softening her tone, "I do appreciate your concern. You're a good friend." She smiled shyly. "I—I'm a little upset right now, but things will work out."

Jenny colored slightly but said nothing. She didn't want to press Paige. It would mean she thought Paige was lying.

When they parted, Jenny stood watching her go, then shook her head and got into her own car.

✟ ✟ ✟

That night Paige arrived at Carter's apartment fifty minutes before the party was to begin. She knew he would be flitting around, doing a good imitation of the proverbial chicken with its head cut off.

At his door, she took a deep breath to steel herself for the onslaught. Between Carter's omnipresent nervous energy, the wild colors he used to decorate his apartment, and the large numbers of incompatible people he was sure to have invited, Paige knew the evening would be trying. Paul would be there, and she wasn't sure she could face him, since she'd spent the last few weeks hiding from him.

Carter flung the door open with a flourish. "Paige! You're here! Come in, child," he greeted her breathlessly. He was wearing a tan Armani silk suit and looked appropriately successful and creative. He also looked, Paige thought, beautiful, although a trifle gaunt and gray. She wondered if he'd been ill.

"And yes, Mrs. Ziegler," he called to someone behind her, "Carter is having another party!"

When Paige turned to see who he was talking to across the hall, a head of silver curls disappeared behind the door frame, and the door slammed shut. He threw back his head and laughed.

"Carter!" Paige admonished, laughing a little in spite of herself. "Are you tormenting that poor woman again?"

"I keep asking her if she wants to come to my parties, but she just says 'Hmph!' and turns away." He laughed again, a not very nice laugh.

Paige shook her head. The sleek hair moved like a glass curtain, and Carter reached out to touch it. Then he stepped in close to hug her and give her a kiss on one chilled cheek.

"Give me your cape, Paige." He took it from her and hung it up, then took the packages she held in her hands, mostly candies from Cero's. He registered approval of her slim ivory silk sheath with raised eyebrows and a smile.

Paige finally got a breath and turned to look at the living room. "Carter! You've redone it. . . ."

"Of course," he said, pleased with her observation.

". . . and it's wonderful!" The spacious room was now a pale blue, with gray and mauve touches that were, for a change, elegant instead of gaudy.

Carter smiled proudly, his grin nearly splitting his finely chiseled face in two. "You like it, this time?"

"I love it!" She wandered from the lovely rosewood table in the foyer, centered with a sterling vase filled with some of her roses, to the two couches in a mauve and blue floral print, to the Queen Anne tables and large wing chair by the fireplace. A Monet hung over the fireplace, the pastel tones in the picture matching those in the room.

"I figured the gay-brothel effect was out for tonight," he quipped.

Paige nodded, smiling at him.

Jamal arrived next. He and Carter made interesting friends—it would be hard to find two more dissimilar people. Jamal, a hulking 6'4", had been guard on the Southeast football team and, not infrequently, Carter's bodyguard at school. Carter's slim beauty had invited ridicule from the jocks who doubted his sexual orientation, even before he came out. Only one of them had dared to suggest that perhaps Jamal himself was less than manly, and that one regretted it, after the karate moves Jamal demonstrated to him off the school grounds. Soon after Jamal had taken on Carter's cause, the jocks took pains to hide their scorn. Jamal hadn't approved of Carter's sexual orientation, Paige knew; he just gravitated toward defending the underdog.

Tonight, in a pale beige suit and stark white shirt, Jamal looked particularly striking. His face lit up when he saw Paige, who gave him a hug.

"Where's Sherry?" she asked.

"Home with the kids—they have bad colds. I can't stay long, but Carter asked—no, *commanded* me to be here tonight." He shrugged. "He wants me to meet these guys from Hollywood."

Carter came to greet him, slapped him on the back, then peeked around the door. "Did Mrs. Ziegler register your arrival?" he asked gleefully. "A big, handsome hunk like you would give her a charge, *n'est-ce pas?*"

Jamal laughed, shaking his head at Carter's exuberance. Paige stood and chatted with Jamal for a few minutes, enjoying the light banter.

Paul arrived soon after, with the agents from California. He had offered to help Carter out by picking them up from the airport. Paige felt her face freeze; she didn't want to acknowledge him.

When the agents filed in, Jamal was standing just inside the foyer. The first agent in the door—a short, tubby, balding man—handed Jamal his coat. "Here, take care of this, will you," he ordered, assuming Jamal was hired help.

Jamal did not react. He stood like a huge stone statue there in the large foyer. Paige's heart sank. This was a poor beginning for Carter's big night.

Fortunately, Carter thought fast. He laughed his silvery, tinkling laugh. "Oh, no, let *me* have it," he said, taking the overcoat. "Jamal is a guest."

The man flushed, then glared at Jamal. Paige decided he held Jamal responsible for his gaffe and would never forgive him. She smiled over the man's head at Jamal, who gave her a slow wink.

The other two agents were chatting to each other and somehow mercifully missed the exchange. Paige stood waiting until they noticed her. Then, steeling herself, she offered her hand to each in turn, welcoming them to Wichita. This was going to be a long night, a very long night.

Chapter 8

Paul stood in the alcove at one end of the foyer. There was no avoiding him. Sooner or later, Paige knew, she'd have to acknowledge his presence. Forcing herself to relax, she lifted her head and looked at him, willing a smile to her face, one that would seem genuine to him.

He had been waiting for her to look at him. He grinned and winked.

Paige felt her cheeks grow hot. She couldn't help liking Paul, even if she resented his attention. For one thing, she liked his looks, even if they weren't all that striking. He was tall and slim, relaxed and loose in his posture, like a stand-up comic. His dark hair curled crisply around his square face. He wasn't even thirty, but laugh lines were etching paths around the corners of his brown eyes and his full, gentle mouth.

Tonight, as usual, he was dressed too casually— gray worsted trousers and a heavy gray sweater. He appeared, however, so comfortable that everyone else looked silly in their stiff, too fancy clothes.

As he approached her, Paige's stomach lurched a

little, and she was surprised by the power of the attraction he held for her. Surprising, since she knew—without a doubt, without a doubt!—that she didn't want him.

He leaned over her and smiled. "I've been trying to reach you, Paige." She ducked her head so he wouldn't see the guilty secret on her face—her fear of hearing from the caller again, as well as the fact that she was avoiding Paul himself. "I was getting worried, but I told myself you were just really busy right now."

She nodded, relieved. The man's innate courtesy refused to admit her discourtesy. "How are classes going?"

"Fine. They're out for the semester now."

"I appreciated your card, Paul."

He acknowledged her compliment with a slight bow.

"I haven't sent any cards," she went on, "but I send you my wishes for the season, right now."

Before Paul could answer, Carter bustled over. "Paige, I want you to meet my guests."

Paige was kept busy for the next two hours, being the perfect hostess for Carter's big-shot guests. With the thirty people who eventually showed up, the apartment was full. Whenever there was a break, Paul was at her side, cracking one joke or another.

Now, when one of the agents tripped a little over a table leg, Paul said out of one corner of his mouth in a child's voice, "'Kinda wobbly, isn't he? He doesn't walk very good, does he?'"

In a mock-stern voice, Jamal played his part, falling easily into their old pattern, "'Thumper, what did your father tell you?'"

Standing pigeon-toed and swaying a little, Paul replied shyly, "'If you can't say somethin' nice, don't say nothin' at all.'"

Paige laughed. "That's an easy one . . . *Bambi*, right?"

"Well, of course!" He acted shocked, a hand at his chest.

She laughed again.

The food was a success. The tubby little agent seemed to appreciate it most. He had platefuls of the salmon and kept his glass filled with champagne.

About halfway through the evening, Paige noticed small flat dishes of a powdered substance, like sugar, appearing on the tables around the room. She had been so busy, she hadn't noticed them at first, until they were everywhere, like tiny lethal mushrooms after a storm.

"Cocaine?" she said in a pained voice to Carter. "I thought you were clean." She shot a glance at Jamal. Here he was, Carter's guest and friend, an ex-cop headed for law school, in a situation that could jeopardize his future. Jamal returned her look, a resigned, closed look on his face. His mouth was tight, the muscles in his neck strung like a bow.

Carter shrugged. "Jamal won't snitch on me."

Paige was furious. How like Carter to see things only from his own perspective. "But you're putting him—and me too, for that matter—in a bad position," she hissed through clenched teeth. "It's not right—not to speak of the damage you're doing yourself." She raised her hand to her head which was starting to ache. Carter patted her on the cheek and drifted off.

She watched him walk away, struck by how bad he looked in a certain light. The chandelier in the dining room had cast a cold, bright illumination across his features. His color was bad, and the skin around his mouth and eyes was drawn. Her stomach contracted with fear. Was he all right? She'd have to have a good heart-to-heart talk with him. The cocaine would kill him, if some other aspect of his lifestyle didn't finish him first.

She looked at him more closely. Maybe it was something else. Maybe . . . but no, not that. She couldn't bring herself to think of AIDS in relation to Carter. Someone else maybe, but not her brother.

It wasn't a great party. Paige was the only female among the thirty or so men, and as the evening progressed, it became obvious to the three agents why that was true. They didn't seem to care whether an aspiring actor was gay and used cocaine, or even if he lived in a backwards place like Wichita, as long as he had talent.

She walked around nervously, watching the agents, watching Jamal, watching Paul. Jamal was leaning against a wall, his arms crossed over his chest. She thought she could see the wheels turning in his head. He shifted uneasily, a spasm of what looked like pain crossing his face. He exchanged a look with Paul.

Paul seemed aware of the snow in the bowls, but he registered no concern about the situation, nor did he seem to be critical of Carter. *Paul, Paul,* she agonized, *you're too good for us.*

Paige couldn't tolerate the availability of the cocaine. Finally, she approached Carter, who was in the corner talking to the short, tubby agent. "Please pardon me for interrupting."

The man straightened, smiled an oily smile, and bowed slightly. "Any time, little lady."

She didn't like being called a little lady, but she let

it pass. "Carter, may I speak to you?" She heard and detested the quaver in her voice.

He was disdainful. "Can't you see I'm busy?"

"It's the cocaine, Carter. You're going to have to get rid of it."

He started to protest, then halted when Paul and Jamal joined them. "Why?" he said with bad grace.

"You're jeopardizing both Paul's and Jamal's reputations, besides ruining your own health!"

Jamal moved in a step closer. "Let's get rid of it, Carter," he said without hesitation.

Paul and Jamal began gathering up the bowls. Carter hurried after them and took the bowls away. "I'll do it, I'll do it. Don't spill any of that—it's worth a fortune."

Jamal snorted, and Carter darted a look at him, then scurried out of the room.

Paul took advantage of the opportunity to start up a conversation with Paige, but she brushed him off. Since she seemed preoccupied with her worry over Carter, he gave up and crossed the room to lean against the fireplace mantel so he could watch her. She was so beautiful. He could see in her vestiges of the young girl he'd first fallen in love with in grade school, the leggy junior higher he'd taken to their first dance, the laughing teenager at swimming parties. He'd loved her then, and she'd loved him too.

Then, around their junior year, she had changed. She had become distant and cold. And one fall day, when Paul had tried to slip his arm around her, she had turned and screamed at him, "Get your hands off me!"

In his shock, he'd done just that. Then, as though she'd realized she was talking to the wrong person, she'd apologized shakily. "I—I'm just upset these days, Paul. I'm sorry."

It seemed that, after that, there were lots of apologies. She had disappeared for two weeks at Christmastime—"a family trip to Kitty Hawk," she'd said—though Carter was in town. Then Paul had heard gossip, from Renee Wentworth and Reilly Hoskins, that Paige had had to get an abortion.

They'd leered a little at him. Reilly had nudged him knowingly, and Paul had drawn back in horror, feeling as if he'd been kicked in the teeth. He'd been raised by a mother who had taught him that he was responsible for his sexual behavior, that he was to treat a woman with respect, with moral uprightness. He'd never even *tried* anything with Paige.

When she had come back home, she'd refused to talk about where she'd been. She let him try to re-establish their friendship, but something was missing.

She kept him confused all the time, one day warm, the next day cold as ice. The Ice Goddess, the guys at school called her. And it hurt him to admit it, but it was true.

He'd asked one evening at the school Valentine's Day party if there was anyone else. She'd looked him in the eye and said, so seriously, "No, and there never will be. I love you, Paul, and only you." Then she'd turned away and added softly, "But you shouldn't love me."

He had grabbed her and kissed her hard. "I love you, Paige. But something's wrong. Tell me!"

She had remained silent. After graduation, she had gone away to college, then on to New York for her modeling career, where she'd written him a "Dear John" letter.

He'd held on to his belief that she loved him, since she'd never said she didn't. He finally gave up, though, and married Marianna his senior year in college. His marriage was the most miserable two years of his life. Marianna was so delicate and fragile, an alcoholic, he later learned.

He was eager to start a family. But she didn't want kids. "They'll be so much work," she'd whined, "and I don't have the strength."

"I'll help you," he'd offered nobly.

"You'll help me be pregnant and go through labor? Don't make me laugh!" she'd said bitterly.

But he had insisted. She hated being pregnant, hated what it did to her body. "I feel so fat and ugly!" she would wail.

Irrationally, she decided she was an invalid and bought herself a wheelchair. He'd find her sitting in it when he'd get home evenings. He waited on her patiently, a saint in his guilt.

Then one day he had come home from class and discovered her on the floor, unconscious. She'd fallen out of the chair and was near death. Close to term, she'd drunk herself into a coma. He called the ambulance, but they came too late. She died before they could get her to the hospital. The baby too, a little boy.

The doctors had tried to comfort him. "The baby was severely deformed. Fetal alcohol syndrome. He wouldn't have been able to live a normal life." They'd gone on, accusingly now, "Didn't you know how much she was drinking?"

Paul had felt guilty. He was the one who had insisted

she get pregnant. Had he forced her to her death? He went for counseling for a while and that had helped. "Did you force yourself on her?" Dr. Zimmer had asked.

"Of course not!" He'd been offended by her question. "Marianna sent such mixed messages—one moment, flirting with me, seeking out my loving; the next, pulling back in disgust. Whenever she welcomed my attentions, I thought all the problems were solved and things were finally falling into place."

"Well, she's not here for me to examine," Dr. Zimmer said, "but my hunch would be that her problems were biochemical. Your behavior, good or bad, couldn't make her well. You can't *fix* someone else, you know."

"How do I make sure I don't fall into that trap again?"

"I don't know—self-awareness, talking to your friends, listening when they try to warn you that you're headed for danger. They will, you know."

He'd laughed then, a nervous laugh that eased a little of his tension. "Jamal sure tried to tell me. He kept asking, 'Are you sure you should marry so soon after Paige left? Are you sure Marianna is right for you?' And the best questions: 'Have you prayed about this? Have you waited for God's answer?' I hadn't, of course."

"Then he's a good friend. Listen to him."

"I was so sure I was doing the right thing. She needed someone to help her."

"Your wife needed medical help and extensive counseling. Did you pick up those degrees when you got your Ph.D. in English?"

Of course he hadn't. He got Dr. Zimmer's point.

Chapter 9

Paige could feel Paul watching her, although she was trying to dismiss him from her mind. It was difficult, more difficult than she expected. His presence, his steady, warm gaze—she fought against a rising desire to be near him, to renew the old closeness they'd had before. To forget him and to amuse herself until this boring party was over, she focused on the other guests.

Two of the agents seemed indistinguishable from each other. Of average height and coloring, and with bland personalities, they were dressed like highly paid lawyers in a big firm, wearing their conservative gray suits like protective armor. She had pictured them in ascots and pastel suits, with much more flamboyant personalities since they had come from California. Instead, they could have passed for Wichita accountants.

The third one, Daniel Littman—El Tubbo in her mind—fumed the whole evening over Jamal's presence at the party. Paige couldn't decide whether it was simple racism or Littman's embarrassment over his mistake.

She guessed he would never be likable under any circumstances.

The agents, especially Littman, were interested in themselves, not in the other guests, or even in Carter, and it showed. Their eyes continued to roam around the room whenever anyone tried to engage them in conversation.

Paige was conscious of their reaction to her. She suspected that each one hoped for a chance to get her alone at some point in the evening, and the air was charged with electricity. It was confusing—were they gays, or were they straight? She decided maybe some of them were bisexual. They didn't make her feel any more comfortable, though, than did straight men who lusted after her. She was used to sensing a sexual aura around her, but she didn't like it.

She was conscious, too, of their trying to hide their attraction to her. Men, whether fifteen or fifty, were all the same. Only Abe, Jamal, and Paul made her feel like a human being instead of a piece of meat slobbered over by dogs outside a butcher shop.

Trying to ignore the tension her appearance created, Paige floated around the room, speaking to each guest, urging more food and drink on them. As she went from group to group, she overheard conversations that would have left Emily Post cold. Each guest seemed to be talking only of himself. In one group of three, she heard, "My Beemer" from one, "My condo in Aspen" from the second, and "My broker" from the third. No one responded. No one was being heard.

At nine, disaster struck. The doorbell chimed, and Carter looked around bewildered. "Who could that be?"

"I'll get it," Paige said, glad for an excuse to get away from the huddles of men who were talking but not listening.

When she opened the door, Reilly Hoskins was standing there. Reilly stepped into the foyer. "Carter havin' another party?" His eyes raked her, and she recoiled. Paige had always detested him with his weasel-like features, his unwashed, spiky hair, and his greasy black clothes. His hands were always filthy, nails and knuckles edged in motorcycle oil.

She watched as he marched into the living room, shoulders hunched and hands clenched, ready to fight. "Hey, Carter, you didn't tell me to dress up."

Carter paled at the sight of Reilly among his sophisticated guests. He was about as welcome as a scorpion at a pool party. Carter swallowed, his eyes sweeping the room to gauge the others' reactions, and welcomed Reilly in a manner that would have frozen the River Styx. But Reilly didn't seem to notice. Instead, he made himself at home, plunking down on one of the pale blue and mauve sofas. Paige felt like spreading drop cloths around him so he wouldn't get anything dirty. He waited with ill-concealed impatience until she brought him a small whiskey and a plate of food.

He leered at her, with what she supposed was his idea of a sexy look. Her skin crawled. He held up the small glass. "You don't expect this little bit of booze to hold me, do you, Paige? Doesn't Carter have any real glasses in this fancy joint?" he asked, indicating something in a mason-jar size.

Paige didn't answer. She went into the kitchen and got a tumbler out of a cabinet and filled it with whiskey. She shuddered at the thought of this expensive stuff sliding down his throat. Something a lot cheaper would have served.

Jamal spoke briefly to Reilly. They, too, had known each other in high school. Jamal tried to find something to talk to him about but soon gave up. Even Paul searched for a topic of conversation, but Reilly's disdain for Paul's old-fashioned manners soon drove him away.

Poor Paul, Paige thought. *First I ignore him all evening, and then this example of the lowest form of human life cuts him off.*

Through it all, Paul remained pleasant. She noticed he offered whatever help he could throughout the evening, refilling plates or glasses, being inconspicuously kind and gentle with all the mismatched and uncouth humanity in the room.

Others stayed well away from Reilly. He sat alone in his own black circle of belligerence. He plunked the empty glass down on the wood table in front of him, and Carter moved quickly to remove the wet glass and wipe at the ring it had left. *He must be watching Reilly closely,* Paige thought.

By about ten, she was tired of the party and ready to leave Carter to his fate. She doubted he had a chance with these agents now that Reilly had arrived.

She approached her brother when she caught him between groups and hissed at him, "What in the world is Reilly doing here? You can't still be in contact with him!"

He ignored her. She stared at him, then told him she was leaving soon.

Panicked, he grabbed her arm. "Not yet, Paige! You

can't leave me. They haven't made up their minds yet, can't you see?"

She didn't have the heart to tell him they had. She shook him off gently, then kissed him on one cheek. "It's been a long week," she said firmly, "and I am leaving."

"Well, you can't have Paul," he said pettishly. "He's promised to take them back out to the Hilton so they can make their flight in the morning." The pout on his face reminded her of the times he had gloated over getting the bigger cookie when they were children.

She didn't want Paul. Right now she appreciated his kindness, and she truly wished things were different, but she knew he was too good for her.

Paige told Paul good-bye and again wished him a merry Christmas. He helped her on with her cape, his fingers brushing hers briefly, and a surge of emotion jolted her from the pit of her stomach to the edges of her brain. Her eyes met his, and she knew that he knew. She flushed and dropped her gaze.

As she walked out the door, Paige felt his eyes on her and the longing in his heart. *It's not to be, Paul,* she said silently. She felt rather disgusted with Carter, with some of his friends, even with herself. Most everyone at Carter's party were messes. Everyone except Paul and Jamal. They were like diamonds, valuable in their rarity.

The cold, dry air outside the apartment complex was welcome after the stale air inside, and it helped clear her head. The cold bit at her nostrils, and she tucked her head down into the collar of the cape.

Behind her, she heard the door open and close. Her heart stopped. Who was it?

She stood frozen by her car. A big man came out on the concrete apron and stood silhouetted in the feeble light next to the walk. She gave a sigh of relief—it was Jamal.

"Paige, wait up," he called.

"Sure thing, Jamal. I'm right here." She twisted her keys in her hand. When he reached her, she spoke quickly, apologetically, "I'm sorry about the drugs in there. I really believed he was clean again."

He shrugged. "You have to feel for a guy who's so blind. Someday maybe he'll wake up. I can only pray so. So what are you up to, other than playing nursemaid to Carter—still?" he asked, a big smile on his face. "Doin' okay?"

"Yes, really well. How're Sherry and the kids?"

He beamed. "Just great. Those kids are growin' like weeds."

"You're keeping busy?"

"Yes." He walked a few paces as he spoke quietly. She could hear excitement in his voice. "I'm back in school, planning to go to law school. I've left the force to set up my own private detective office for a while, to finance the schooling."

"Great, Jamal, that's wonderful!" Paige knew he'd wanted to go to law school when he graduated from high school, but as the youngest of ten in a poor family, he hadn't been able to swing it then.

"The force is okay, but I'm ready to move on." He looked off down Central toward the Christmas lights at Normandy Square.

"Bad hours?" she asked, laughing. Jamal had been known as the kid who stayed up all night in high school.

No one could figure out what he lived on, since he didn't eat much either.

Paige remembered Mr. Case, their chemistry teacher, asking him how his parents grew him so big, when he didn't eat or sleep. Jamal had laughed his easy, deep laugh and said, "There's no room in the bed or at the supper table. I gotta live on air."

Now he shook his head. "No, it's not the hours, it's the families." Paige could hear a heavy sadness in his voice, see it on his face.

"Families?" she asked, mystified.

"Yeah, the ones who beat and starve and throw out their kids. The husbands who bash in their wives' heads for the fun of it, and the wives who take it until the day they put a bullet through the jerks' hearts—if they have hearts."

The anger and pain in his face made her want to comfort him. "I know," she whispered, thinking of her own family.

He turned and looked at her, and his face softened. "I know you know, and I'm sorry."

She shivered. He was so caring and compassionate, even now in his anger. The words "righteous anger" came to her.

Then the thought crossed her mind: *Maybe I could tell Jamal about the man who's been calling me, about the sound in the parking garage. Maybe he could tell me what to do. But no*—she quickly dismissed the idea—*he'll think I'm an hysterical female.*

Jamal took her keys and opened the car door for her. "You'd better get in. You'll freeze out here." He helped arrange her cape so it wouldn't get caught in the door, and then he mashed down the lock. "Take care."

"You too," she said as he closed the door. She knew his parting words were sincere, not just a social amenity. She drove off, feeling the comfort of his concern around her, as warm as the wool cape.

✛ ✛ ✛

When Jamal returned to the party, he looked for Paul. His friend had mentioned earlier that he wanted to talk.

"What do you think about Carter?" Paul asked, getting right to the point.

Jamal shook his head. "He's pushed the self-destruct button, that's for sure."

"The cocaine. Aren't you worried? If there's a raid, it would affect your being able to practice law."

Jamal hung his head, shaking it from side to side. "I can't worry about my own skin when he's so close to destruction. Let's pray about it, okay?"

They withdrew to a corner, away from the crowd inside Carter's apartment. Jamal prayed briefly. "And, Lord, bind the evil that abounds in this place and surround Carter with your angels. He needs you so much, but he doesn't know it."

Paul put an arm around Jamal's shoulder. "Thanks, pal." He frowned, then shifted uneasily. "I'm confused."

"About Paige, right?"

"Right. I can't figure her out."

"Makes sense. She sends lots of messages at once."

"Do you think a person can lose her salvation?"

"You askin' me? I'm no theologian."

"No, but you know the Bible."

"Can't say. Why don't you ask Paige what she thinks?"

"Are you joking? She'd bite my head off."

Jamal flashed a smile. "So maybe we should both talk to her. She won't be bitin' my head off, man!"

Chapter 10

When Paige got home that night, Chester was waiting for her. "Some man came by earlier to see you."

"Who?" she asked, mystified.

"He didn't give his name. He just wanted to know when you would be home."

"You didn't tell him, did you?" she said, feeling unreasonably panicked.

"No, no," he reassured her. "I'd never give out any information like that, Ms. Brookings," he said earnestly, looking hurt.

She hastened to apologize. "I'm sorry, Chester. I've just been so nervous lately. Please forgive me."

He nodded, waved a hand. "Oh, that's okay. I could tell you've been a little worried." He handed her the mail. "He wanted to ask you about Charlie Keegan, he said."

"Charlie Keegan!" she responded, shocked. "Who would want to ask me about Charlie Keegan? He's been missing for ten years!"

He shrugged skinny shoulders.

"What did he look like?" For some reason Paige felt alarmed.

"Just average, Ms. Brookings. Average height, average weight, kind of mousy brown hair. Nothing special."

She scowled, wondering who it could be. He certainly didn't sound menacing, but could you tell by looking? *You could in the movies,* she told herself cynically. It was the music on the soundtrack that gave it away.

As she entered her apartment, she thought of Jerry Keegan, an old friend from high school. His wife Susan was her friend too. And now they had a little daughter, Stacy, a typical kid. Chester's description—average everything—brought him to mind.

Why would Jerry want to ask me about his creep of a dad?

✢ ✢ ✢

Jerry Keegan fumbled for his key. "Why the heck didn't Susan leave the porch light on for me?" he fumed. He'd had to remove his gloves to find and use the key, and his hands were frozen.

Once he finally got inside, he dropped his coat, keys, and loaded briefcase onto the couch and heaved a sigh. It had been a long, tiring day. He wished he was returning home to a welcoming family, instead of this dark, empty house. But Susan had gone to Winfield to see her mother and had taken Stacy with her.

On his way down the hall to the bedroom to change into something more comfortable, he took a look around. *Who would have thought a nobody like me from a family like the one I grew up in could end up in Brookhollow with a spread like this, and a wonderful wife and a neat kid like Stacy? I'm a lucky man.*

He thought back to his attempt to talk to Paige earlier that day. He was sorry he'd missed her. She might know what Charlie was up to, coming back like this. *I sure don't want him around Stacy, even if he is my father.*

When he passed the bathroom, Jerry heard a dripping sound. *I'll bet Stacy left the water running again.*

He smiled, thinking of her charming nine-year-old grin encased in silver braces and long, curly blond hair. Then he thought of the new Nintendo hiding in his workshop for her Christmas present. She'd been begging for a Nintendo, so she could play Super Mario Brothers or some such foolishness. He warmed at the thought of how excited she would be on Christmas morning.

He followed the sound of the dripping. *I'd better fix that faucet. It drips too easily.*

He could see the bathroom light under the door. *That's funny,* he thought. *Maybe Susan and Stacy got back early and someone's taking a bath.* He knocked, in order to avoid frightening her. "Stacy?" he called.

He got no answer.

"Stacy?" he repeated, louder. He pushed open the door. The sight before his eyes horrified him. The tub was full of water. Stacy was there, under water, eyes wide. She was dead.

He took a step into the bathroom, hands stretched before him, beseechingly. "No, God!" he screamed. "It can't be!"

He never saw the curving blade of a jungle machete. He fell to the floor and died there. Nor did he see the five curled paper matchsticks behind the door, concentric circles turned back on themselves.

Paige didn't hear the news all weekend. She holed up in her apartment and kept the television turned off. She was tired of the world outside.

She started a big, fat historical romance, and when she was tired of reading, she cleaned closets. They didn't need cleaning, but straightening things always helped her relax.

She spent two hours on both Saturday and Sunday using the Nautilus equipment in the exercise room in the Skycrest basement. She pushed and pulled, stretched and shortened muscles. The sweat pouring down her face was cleansing.

Not for the first time she was grateful for the castle-like impregnability of the Skycrest and the comforting old-age decrepitude of the other occupants. They probably averaged over sixty-five years of age. She reveled in riding up and down in the old elevator, Chester at the controls. She was as safe here as a person could be. Inside its walls, she could forget the dangers outside.

Liz Barsolo was the first to let her know, the moment she stepped into the office Monday morning. Ever-cool Liz was shaken. "Oh, Paige, have you heard?" she asked, tears in her dark eyes.

"What?" The question jarred her. Hal? Carter? Who was sick or hurt?

"Jerry . . . and Stacy." Liz burst into tears. Jerry was married to Liz's sister Susan. He'd been Hal's accountant for six years. "Someone got into the house and murdered them both," she cried.

The news hit Paige like a tidal wave. She blanched. "No," she whispered. Stacy, the red-faced, wailing infant at her christening nine years ago, the coltish tomboy who loved to show off her diving at the pool. Open-faced, friendly-as-a-puppy Stacy. Jerry—neat, methodical, meek Jerry—who never failed to be thankful for his blessings, especially Susan and Stacy.

She thought of the man who had dropped by to see her Friday night. Had it been Jerry? And now he was dead? She shivered.

At last she said, "How?"

Liz, sobbing, told Paige how Susan had found them. Susan and Stacy had started off to Winfield, then just blocks from home, Susan's car blew a tire. The two of them changed it, and Stacy got black smudges on her new clothes. Susan took her home to change, then ran to the service station to get the tire repaired. She couldn't make it to Winfield on the small donut tire.

She'd returned home to horror.

The police had found no clues at all, just the physical facts of the murder of the child and the vicious blow that had killed Jerry. There had been no signs of forced entry. No fingerprints or strange objects left behind.

Later Paige couldn't remember any details of that morning, how she reacted, how Liz coped. She asked herself how Liz had even managed to drag herself to work. That was Liz, conscientious to a fault.

Hal kept watching Liz closely. At ten, he said, "You're wandering around, reeling like a drunk. You can't concentrate on anything. Why don't you go on home?"

Liz only nodded, unable to react beyond that.

He took Paige aside. "I'm concerned about Liz. How about going with her?" Picking up the phone, he called his doctor for a prescription so she could sleep.

Susan was under sedation, blessedly, but no one had thought to take care of Liz, supercompetent, sturdy Liz. And she was too dazed to ask for help.

Paige took her home, thankful in a way for this task that would help keep her mind off the horror of what had happened. She tried not to picture the grisly deaths.

As she pulled in to Liz's driveway and turned off the car, an image from her nightmares came to her—a man carrying a machete, the machete she wrenched out of his hands and used to kill him in her dream. She felt again the aching in her arms and shoulders, as though the swing she took to behead him was real.

She gasped at the ferocity of the memory and covered her face with her hands. It was too much like Jerry's and Stacy's deaths.

"Paige!" Liz spoke up beside her. "Are you all right?"

Paige straightened and forced her hands down onto the steering wheel. She could not face Liz. "I'm sorry to frighten you. I'm all right. It's just so . . . so awful. Who could have done it?"

Liz shook her head, long black curls bobbing around her face. "It couldn't be anybody they knew. You know what they're like, what Jerry was like. They couldn't have known such a person. They were so nice."

Paige angrily resisted that idea, but she didn't voice her resistance to Liz. She couldn't. She knew nice people's lives were touched by the vicious, the insane, the

wicked too. Hers certainly had been, even as an innocent child.

She sat up straight, surprised by the connection she
was making between these deaths and her own life.
Where did that come from? she thought. *Why am I dredg-
ing that up?*

She expressed none of these questions to Liz, though.
She couldn't add to Liz's burden. But Paige couldn't
shake the conviction that this senseless crime was somehow related to her, to her nightmares, to her childhood
horror. Why? It didn't make sense.

She mentally shook herself, trying to dismiss self-
involved thoughts from her head. *It's time to worry about
Liz, not me and my craziness.*

Hesitantly, she got out of the car to help Liz into the
house. She was afraid to go into the neat three-bedroom
ranch house on this quiet street, the house where Susan
and Liz had grown up, the house where the group of
high school friends had met after classes to talk, to eat
pizza, to tell secrets—some secrets, not all of them.

When she opened the car door for Liz, who was
slumped in a daze in the front seat, she raised her head
and looked at the house, then turned her panicked-filled
gaze on Paige. "What if . . . ?"

Paige gestured her to silence, shaking her head no.
"Don't even think it. It was such a crazy thing to do,
it had to have been some random attack."

Liz still sat there, unmoving.

A police car pulled up in front of the house. The
two women shot relieved glances at each other, and Liz
smiled through her tears. "We don't have to go in
alone."

Chapter 11

The police were there for two hours, taking Liz over and over her recollections of Jerry's and Stacy's last day. Paige used the first few minutes to contact Hal's doctor's office to be sure they had called in the prescription for Liz. She then called the pharmacy to ask them to deliver the sedative right away. "It's urgent," she explained. "She's had a shock and needs the medicine as soon as possible."

While the officers questioned Liz, Paige made Liz's bed, did a load of wash, and stacked the breakfast dishes in the dishwasher.

Then it was her turn to be interrogated by the police. She twisted the opal ring on her finger around to the inside of her palm and ran her thumb over the warm, curved stone. When she was anxious and had to hide her anxiety from unwanted scrutiny, rubbing the opal helped her retain her control.

She knew nothing about the murders, but her initial reaction to the sergeant's first question—"What can you tell us about this situation?"—was a secretiveness that served to raise their suspicions. Both officers gazed at her with an interest that differed from the male attention she was used to. She was sure they thought she knew more than she did.

She clenched her fists so hard her nails cut into her palms. Detective Wopat, a heavy, dark, brooding man, gazed levelly at her. The brown eyes were slits in the tanned, lined face, strange lines that went down his cheeks instead of across his face. She guessed that they hadn't etched their paths from smiles or frowns, but more likely, from harsh grimaces.

Feeling as helpless as a rabbit in a trap, Paige gazed back, terror in her wide eyes, her breath rasping, tearing out of her body. The doorbell rang, and Liz got up to answer it. Paige's eyes flickered across her friend's retreating back. She relaxed a little. If they accused her of the crime, Liz wouldn't be there to hear.

The other officer, a young blond hulk named Johnson who looked fresh off the farm, said gently, "You got something you want to say?"

She froze, then nodded. In that split second, Paige decided that appearing to bare her soul to them was the best way to proceed. Hesitatingly, she started to explain. "I know you're thinking I know something . . . but I don't. It's just that . . ." She got up and started to pace across the green and gold living room.

Wopat sighed and leaned back in the armchair he was sitting in. Paige flashed him a glance. His lips were stretched tight and he looked thoroughly disgusted. The look made her nervous. *He doesn't believe me, and I haven't said anything yet.* She twisted the opal with the thumb and forefinger of her left hand.

She stopped when she got to the couch, where Johnson was sitting ramrod straight, notepad on one knee. She was doing her best to ignore the doubt radiating from Wopat. "I really don't know anything," she said earnestly. "I've just been so jumpy lately." She described in a rush of words the episode in the parking garage and then her obscene caller. She flushed. "This probably sounds like silly feminine hysterics to you. . . ." At that, Wopat gave a slight nod and Johnson shook his head no.

Paige increased her concentration on Johnson, the one who might believe her. "I've been scared out of my wits lately. This just seemed related to the . . . uh . . . to the threat I've been feeling. These phone calls—they just make me feel wild."

Wopat snorted. "Have you reported these calls?"

Paige's heart sank. *He doesn't believe me.*

She shook her head, then held her clasped hands under her chin, forefingers steepled at her lips. "This can't be related to my nerves, I know," she said, turning to look away from the men, "but it seemed to me, for a minute that it was. Maybe my caller was the person who . . ." She couldn't finish "the person who killed Jerry and Stacy."

Wopat shook his head, just slightly, again denying her words.

She dropped her hands to her sides, feeling hopeless now. "Jerry and Susan are wonderful people. I don't know how such a thing could happen to them."

Johnson gave Wopat a look, then shut his notepad.

Wopat sighed again, stretched and got up, heavily, from the chair. "Oh, by the way, do you know anything about Stacy's diary?" he asked, almost casually.

"Her diary?" Paige repeated. The question confused her. What would the child's diary have to do with this horror? "Why?"

"*We* ask the questions around here," he said curtly.

She flushed. "I gave her a diary last Christmas."

"Describe it."

"It was light blue and lavender and pink, with a unicorn in the clouds on the cover. She loved unicorns," she said to Johnson, a hint of a smile of remembrance touching her lips.

Wopat grunted. "We'll be in touch again. Something might come to you."

Paige wondered if that was a threat.

Once Paige had supervised Liz's medication and had seen the exhausted woman fall asleep, she let herself quietly out of the house, checking twice to make sure the door was locked. Liz's parents were with Susan, but Liz's brother Carlos was on his way to be with Liz and take her to join the rest of the family later.

It felt good to be out of the house. The crisp air was reviving, and the smell of sun-warmed cedar filled her nostrils.

Paige walked, head down, to her car, thinking about the days that lay ahead for them, the unspeakable pain Susan must be going through. When she reached her car, she looked up to see a black Lexus with dark-tinted windows glide by, the driver invisible behind the smoky glass. The Lexus stopped at the end of the drive. The driver's window rolled down noiselessly, and Paige was surprised to see the scarred face of Holder Danton.

"Paige," he called, "strange to see you here."

She shrugged slightly. She had no idea what that

meant. Irritably she thought, *Where does he expect to see me?*

"I heard about Jerry and wondered if there was anything I could do."

"Oh, you knew Jerry?" she asked stupidly.

"Yes, I've known Jerry a long time. He did my taxes, you know, had for a long time."

She put her hand on her car door to open it while he sat in his car, watching her. She looked back, tipping her head a little to one side to encourage him to say whatever it was he wanted to say.

But he said nothing more. Instead, he raised his hand in farewell. "Well, be seeing you."

She nodded. *Odd,* she thought as she got into her car. *He had seemed to want to say something else.* She shuddered.

He's acting a little like he's interested in me, but he doesn't know how to proceed. I wonder if he's married. I hate married men who come on to other women. I'll bet he's a jerk.

Chapter 12

Paige drove up to the Skycrest as dusk was thickening. Chester buzzed for the parking boy, gave her her mail, and took her up in the lift.

"Terrible thing about those people, isn't it?" he asked.

She couldn't answer—didn't want to be part of any discussion of it. She was sure she would scream if he said any more. She blinked back tears. He saw them, then hastily averted his eyes.

When she got out of the elevator, she began to walk down the hall to her door. "That man didn't come back, did he?" she called over her shoulder. "The one who was here Friday?"

"No, ma'am," Chester answered, bewildered.

She entered her apartment a little ashamed of herself for her curtness with the old man. She sank down on the couch, her cape still on, holding her mail. She needed to plug her phone in tonight because she had told Liz to call if she or Susan needed anything. She took a big breath to steel herself for the hours and days ahead, then rose and put her things away.

She glanced at the mail. There were a couple of personal letters, a few bills. The rest was junk. She threw away the junk without even opening it, then opened the bills. Once she filed them in her desk, she sat back down to open the personal letters. One, she was sure, was from a man, the handwriting bold and strong. It looked familiar. Where had she seen it before? She saved it for last.

The other was from Jenny—an announcement of the first reunion planning session, for December 18. *Oh, no,* she thought, her heart dropping to her toes. *Who's going to want to be involved in something like that now, with Jerry and Stacy dead?*

Reluctantly, she got up and marked the time and place in her planner. *Wonder what kind of turnout she'll get. The meeting's at her house . . . I'll bet it'll be brimming with country decor and gingerbread men and kids and toys.* She glanced at herself in the mirror above the fireplace. She wanted to bawl. *What a Christmas!*

Shaking off her lethargy, Paige stalked into the kitchen, carrying the last letter with her. She put a lamb chop into the broiler and made a small salad. She added some cold asparagus to it and then topped it with dressing. She still ate like a model, watching her consumption of fats and sugars. She hadn't given up hope that someday she would return to modeling.

Drying her hands on a towel, she picked up the final envelope and opened it. Once she read the signature— bold dashes across the bottom of the creamy linen paper—she relaxed. Armand Douvier.

She smiled, then lay the two pages down while she

poured herself a cup of tea. Armand was coming to Wichita on the 20th, he wrote. He hoped to see her. She breathed a sigh of relief as she thought of the debonair man she had met in New York in 1988, before she returned, a failure, to Wichita.

They'd seen each other maybe twenty times since then, either in New York or another city. This would be his first time to visit her in Wichita. He was comfortable to be around, comfortable in a world of work and striving for success.

Paige thought of the lazy people surrounding her, her club-joiner mother, her jet-set father, and lazy, charming Carter. She scowled. If people just worked harder, if they just set goals and worked toward them, the world would be a better place, she was sure. For her, work meant morality, an escape from the evil in human beings that threatened to engulf them all, that waited to devour *her*.

If he worked like she did, the man who was her bugaboo wouldn't have time to stalk her, to call her on the phone and frighten her into weakness and mewling, like a newborn kitten. The man she wanted to kill— with a strength of hatred that shocked and yet pleased her—wouldn't have made her life a torment if he'd spent his time more profitably employed.

Maybe Grandmother Frazier was right: "Idle hands are the devil's workshop." With that thought, the image of a man's hands rose up in her mind.

Stubby, freckled hands, ugly hands with coarse red hairs between the knuckles. Hands that had put a poor dead dog's body in her bed. Hands with bitten nails and chewed, bloody quicks. She shuddered. Then her eyes widened, her mouth fell open. *I know who he was.*

I know who did that awful thing, she thought. *It was Jerry's dad!*

He wanted us all to call him Uncle Charlie. Uncle, huh! she thought. *Some uncle!*

She smiled then, a broad, liberated smile. The realization propelled her into the living room.

She fumbled in her purse. *Where is Abe's number?* she asked herself, excited. *I have to tell him.*

With shaking hands, she punched out the numbers for Abe's home. It buzzed, ten long buzzes, with no answer.

She checked her watch. Only 8 P.M. He was probably still at the office.

She tried the office—again, no answer. Disappointed, shoulders slumped, she dropped the receiver down with a thump. "Abe, Abe!" she cried out. "I need you."

She straightened and resolved to busy herself with her usual tasks. She'd try Abe's number later. He was probably on his way home from work.

Returning to the kitchen, Paige smelled the charred lamb chop in the broiler. *Oh, rats,* she thought. *It's burned.* She grabbed a potholder and pulled the blackened meat out of the oven, then sighed and threw the potholder on the counter. *It's not too bad, just a little dry.*

She ate her supper with a lighter heart than when she had first arrived home. Armand was coming, and she had made some progress—on her own!—with her buried memories.

She reread Armand's letter, hearing in her head his deep voice and heavy accent. *Mother would approve of him,* she thought, *although why I care, I'll never know.*

Older than Paige, a serious French businessman who dealt in luxury imported fabrics, Armand was wealthy and safe. There would be no messy complications, no dependent clinginess with Armand.

As she was scraping food scraps into the disposal, the phone rang. She jumped. *Now cut that out,* she admonished herself.

She dried her hands and walked to the phone, hesitating briefly before she answered it.

"Paige?" It was the unmistakable fire alarm clang of her mother's voice.

Paige stifled a sigh. "Yes, Mother."

"I need you to talk to Carter for me," she demanded.

"And why is that?"

"I asked him to help me decorate for my New Year's Eve party, and he refused."

Paige smiled. "Refused?" *How dare he,* she thought cynically. "Surely you don't want to trust him with your decorating anyway, after his last color scheme."

"Oh, *I'm* picking the colors and the materials. I just want him to do the work."

Of course, Paige thought. Aloud she said, "Did he say why?"

"Yes. He's got some bee in his bonnet about going to Hollywood over the holidays. Some agent asked him to come." The whine in her voice was mounting.

Paige straightened. "He did? An agent wants him? Did he say who?"

"Oh, I can't remember. Paige . . ."

"Was it one of the agents who came to his party?" Paige asked, excited.

"I don't know. I can't keep track of his 'friends,' you know." The tone her mother was using signaled to

Paige that Mother thought this was a new homosexual relationship. Mother always displayed mixed emotions about Carter's homosexuality. On the one hand, she asked for constant accolades for her "openmindedness" about the issue, but on the other, she never failed to aim a few darts of disapproval his way. And she didn't seem to mind if a few of them missed and hit Paige. With all the influence Paige had over Carter—more than their mother ever had, that was for sure—she could surely get him to come to his senses and "act right."

Paige ignored the implied criticism. "But, Mother, this could be a break for him. You don't know any details?"

"No, and I don't care. Paige, this is important. He has to help with the streamers and balloons and flowers."

"I'll call him, Mother. Maybe he'll have good news."

"Paige, wait. Tell him . . ."

"Right, Mother," she said into the phone before she replaced the receiver.

She called Carter's apartment and got a busy signal. "This is not my night," she sighed.

Hanging up, she reached for Abe's card. "I'll try Abe again. He ought to be home by now."

Abe answered this time, "Finney here."

"Oh, Abe, am I glad to hear your voice!" she said breathlessly. "This is Paige."

"Paige, Munchkin, how are you?" Fatigue seemed to pull his words back into him as he attempted to force them out.

"Are you okay, Abe? You sound tired."

"I am, but it's nothing. Just a long week." He struggled to sound more alert. "Now what's on your mind?"

"I—I figured out who the man was, the one . . . well, you know." She could feel herself flushing with embarrassment. *He's going to think I'm so dumb.*

"The one in your dreams, right? Is he tied in to the dog?" Abe was perking up a little, interested in her insight.

"Yes," she said, excitement returning. "I recalled Beau being dead in my bed, and someone, some man, putting him there. Tonight it came to me who he was."

She went on to explain about "Uncle" Charlie. "Do you think that this memory came back because of Jerry's death?"

"Jerry? Oh, you mean the Keegan murders. You knew him?"

"Oh, yes, we were in . . . well, I guess it was a clique in high school. There were nine of us, if you count Jenny. She was always there on the sidelines, it seemed." She listed Carter, Jamal, Reilly, Susan, Paul, and Renee Wentworth.

"You know what else?" Paige said, as her vision of the old image grew. "I think he must have been messing around with most of them."

"'Messing around'?" Abe wanted clarification. "Do you mean what I think you mean by that?"

"Yes, yes!" she cried into the phone, tears now streaming down her cheeks. "I think he must have been molesting us." She lowered her head and put one hand over her face as the tears flowed.

Chapter 13

"Can I come see you, Abe?" Paige asked hesitantly. "I know you said two weeks, but I have to see you now."

"Surely, Paige. This is a real breakthrough. I'll meet you at the office. Thirty minutes?"

She dressed hurriedly and grabbed her purse, searching for her keys as she strode out of her apartment to the elevator. She buzzed for Chester, tapping her foot with impatience as she waited. "Come on, come on!"

She sped out of the porte cochere after Chester bowed her into her car, leaving a strip of rubber as she rounded the corner of Oakland, then roared up Hillside to Abe's office building.

The parking garage was dark, with no attendant in the booth at the entrance. Cold mercury lights failed to illuminate the shadowy corners of the interior. She braked, tires squealing, as she realized she had to park in the garage and walk to the elevator.

Beads of cold sweat sprung up on her brow and upper lip. *Why didn't I remember the garage? I have to get in to see Abe, but I can't. I just can't go through that garage alone.*

She picked a tissue from the holder under her dash and wiped the sweat from her forehead. "I can't live like this," she said aloud. She eased her foot onto the accelerator and entered the chilled underground space. She drove as close to the elevator as she could get. At least at night there were lots of places to choose from. She parked and turned off the ignition. Lights of a car swung into the garage and pinned her there against her steering wheel. She watched as it approached her space.

It was a black Lexus—Holder Danton again? Surely there were not that many Lexuses in Wichita!

The driver edged his way into the space to the right of hers. The door opened and Holder Danton's balding head emerged. He squinted his eyes to peer into her car.

She sighed with relief. "Holder!" she said, opening her door to greet him. "We seem to frequent the same places," she said lightly, to hide her anxiety.

"Seems so, doesn't it?"

"I hate these garages, so I'm glad to see a familiar face, especially at night. Can I follow you to the elevator?"

He held her gaze for a long moment. "Sure, Paige," he finally said, "I'll keep you safe." Then he smiled, a strange, twisted grimace. It was so menacing that Paige was chilled. But, she realized, it would be difficult to look warm and charming with those scars healing on his face.

Holder put one hand under her left elbow. "I guess, for a gal, a place like this would be kind of scary."

She nodded, a grin dimpling her cheeks. "Yes, just

the other day, I scared myself silly. I thought someone was stalking me in here." She laughed.

"Silly of you," he said flatly. "What floor?" he asked once they entered the elevator.

"Five," she answered, reaching out to punch the button herself.

He stopped her hand in mid-reach and pushed it for her. Then he turned to look at her, not speaking. After an uncomfortable pause, he said, "I have to see my plastic surgeon."

"Oh." She hadn't really wondered why he was in this doctors' building at this hour of the night, but he seemed to want her to know.

She didn't explain that she was going to see her psychoanalyst. She never shared that information with clients or other professionals in her work. *It's none of their business,* she thought sternly.

Holder moved closer, too close. His arm grazed hers, and she pulled back from his touch. He didn't look at her, nor she at him. *Don't try to make any moves on me, buddy,* she thought, as the elevator lurched to a stop and the doors slid open.

" 'Bye, Holder," she said as she exited. "I guess we're meeting Wednesday?"

"Right." His mouth was tight—anger or pain from the scars?

She was used to reading other people's body language—did it all the time. With his face so mutilated, however, it was hard, and so she wondered whether she could trust her reactions. She tried to shrug it off as she went down the hall to Abe's office.

✛ ✛ ✛

Abe sat by the lamp on an end table between the two matching Queen Anne chairs. The light was low, and his profile was just out of the circle of illumination the lamp provided.

Paige couldn't quite see his face. She pulled her chair a little closer to his. Somehow his distance seemed more than physical to her, but maybe she was dreaming that.

Am I always imagining things? she wondered. *Not this about Jerry's dad, though, not this.*

She leaned forward, earnestly explaining to Abe the awakening memories. "It seems that, little by little, I'm finding new puzzle pieces."

Abe was forcibly aware of the energy emanating from Paige, a living force he warmed to, like the sun. She presented such a calm, serene exterior to the world, but the dynamic power within roiled beneath the surface. He leaned toward her then, unconsciously, trying to soak up her radiance.

At that moment, his face, lips curved in a slight smile, was lit by the lamp. Paige then saw the changes one short week had made in him—the lines of pain around his mouth, the gray, drawn skin.

"Abe!" she gasped. "What's wrong with you?" She propelled herself out of the chair and over to his side. He pulled quickly back into the shadows.

She knelt beside him and covered his hand with hers. "Are you sick?"

He ducked his head. "It's just this blasted ulcer. Sometimes it gets pretty bad."

"An ulcer?" she asked, unbelieving. "It must be quite an ulcer, to make you look like this."

He nodded. "But we're not here to discuss my ulcer," he said, waving her back to her chair. "I'll be fine," he lied.

She shook her head, knowing it wasn't true, but she didn't argue with him. She just sat and watched him out of the corner of her eye.

"Go on, go on," he urged. "Tell me about Charlie Keegan." He pulled at his lower lip. "Didn't he disappear about ten years ago?"

"Yes—but how did you know?" she asked, puzzled.

"It was all over the papers at the time. 'Charles Keegan, small businessman, ideal family man,'"—at that, Paige snorted—"'pillar of the community, disappears from the face of the earth.'"

"I was away at college then," she inserted. "I missed the coverage."

He nodded. "I remember when he disappeared with all the family's savings as well as his hardware store's assets. Some neighbor who was interviewed by the TV stations said he couldn't believe Charlie could be involved in anything unsavory, because he kept his house and yard so obsessively neat." Abe guffawed. "I could have told them that meant abuse, somewhere down the line."

Paige stiffened. Was Abe sending her a message, that her compulsiveness was a sign to the observant onlooker? *No,* she thought, *I've hidden all the abuse well,* she told herself firmly, to convince herself of its truth.

"Either he was abused as a child or he was abusing someone," he continued. "Too much control is inhuman."

She dropped her head, and he softened his tone, "Yes, for you too, Munchkin, for you too. That's why I wanted you to give up some of your extreme concern for order, but I never knew how to help you." He shook his big shaggy head sorrowfully.

She stared at him, wide-eyed. She thought about how soothing it was to clean closets or organize kitchen cabinets when her anxiety was rising, how claustrophobic she felt around any kind of clutter.

"It seems they go to one extreme or the other—these victims of abuse—either extreme neatness or filth." He waved his hand in the air, dismissing the topic. "But that's neither here nor there. You've had a big breakthrough. That's what's important right now." He reached for his pipe from the interior pocket of his jacket, then remembered he wasn't smoking anymore. He sighed. "They won't even let an old man have a pipe."

"You're not old," she countered. "Aren't you fifty-eight or so?"

He nodded. "Tonight that feels old." He shifted uncomfortably in his chair. "Tell me some more about Charlie Keegan."

Gently he led her through the memories she could dredge up, the times, beginning when she was nine, when Keegan would separate her from the group of friends that hung around together. "I liked his attention, until he started doing dirty things," she admitted. "I think he must have been doing the same thing with all the others." She tugged at a lock of hair. "Charlie was the good guy—or so everyone thought—Scout troop leader, organizer of softball games, the parent who was willing to take all the kids to the zoo or help them with their homework." She twisted her ring around to feel the smooth warmth of the opal. "The biggest hit there for a while was his video equipment. He'd let us use it to make videos for class projects."

"Videos?" Abe's interest increased even more.

She nodded. "It was about that time that Jamal and Jerry started fighting, with Jerry hurt because Jamal always left the room when his dad entered it. Jamal refused to go anywhere if Charlie was along, so Jerry was insulted."

She frowned, thinking back to the day, a Labor Day weekend, just before their senior year in high school. They were all excited about being the hot shot seniors, the stars of the high school now. It was big stuff.

It was a Friday, and Charlie had planned a weekend trip to Lake Cheney for sailing on his Hobie Cat and fishing. They were all standing in a group outside the school, and Paige remembered saying to Carter, "Where does he get all this money for the sailboat, the video equipment, and all the trips he takes? He never seems to work."

Carter shrugged thin shoulders, fine blond hair falling across his forehead. "I don't know . . . does it really matter?"

Her brother liked nice things—cars and boats, stereo systems and video games. He wore the designer-label clothes their mother dressed them in with much more relish than Paige ever did. She'd been happy with just enough outfits to get her through the week, while Carter had wanted piles and piles of clothing.

Even then, he'd squirreled away funds—not through working, of course, but through his considerable charm—to buy what he wanted, when he wanted it. If he couldn't wheedle it out of Mother, he begged Dad for it. And it seemed, increasingly, that Charlie too, was slipping him pocket money. Paige disliked seeing the man hand Carter ten dollars here or there, and when she tried to talk her brother into refusing it, he had flushed angrily and said, "Mind your own business, Paige."

Charlie had bustled up to their group and clapped a hairy hand on Jamal's shoulder. "I talked to your mother, son, and she said it would be fine for you to go along." His face was split in a big grin.

Jamal knocked the big hand off his shoulder. "Don't touch me," he growled under his breath, "and don't ever ask permission for me to go on one of your 'outings.'" He spat out the word. "If I want to go, I'll ask permission for myself. And keep your filthy hands off me!"

Charlie stepped back, registering shock. Paige noticed that his eyes scanned the group, inspecting each of the other faces. Had they noticed the interchange?

Paige assumed they had all averted their eyes, as she had. The man's fear tainted the air. But guilt forced Paige to swallow hard, to force back the rising sensation filling the back of her throat.

She blinked, realizing she was in Abe's office, not back in 1985. "That was the weekend that he . . . raped me," she whispered. "That was when I got pregnant and had to have the abortion." She stood up and walked over to Abe's desk to pluck a tissue from the box there. "Mother just hustled me off to the doctor and never asked me who it was." Paige covered her mouth with tissue, to still its quivering. "She said it didn't matter who. She didn't want to know. But I wanted so much to tell her how horrible it was, how he hurt me—she wouldn't let me."

Abe's gentle face softened with pain for her.

"I never let him get me alone again," she said, voice turning to steel. "I never let him touch me. But I'm sure Carter was seeing him regularly." She sighed. "I think now Charlie was making sex videos and selling them." Abe nodded because he guessed she was right. "He had made tapes of me from age nine on, but they were just supposed to be 'grooming' for later modeling jobs. The filming always made me uncomfortable, but I went along with it, until that fall."

She looked earnestly into Abe's eyes. "Mother was there for the first ones. Even those made me uncomfortable—they weren't dirty or anything, I wasn't nude—but his eyes . . . they weren't quite right."

She dropped her head suddenly, hands hiding her face. "You know what I just remembered?" She removed her hands, and Abe could see the fury in her eyes. "After he raped me, he said, 'There's something about you that made me do it.'"

Abe grimaced, then shook his head. "Molesters always try to blame their victims."

She started pacing the room with long strides, stiletto heels punctuating her words. "I hate him. I *hate* him!" She twisted her hands. "I wish he was here right now so I could kill him."

Abe nodded. He was a nonviolent person, but he could only agree with her in this.

"There is no punishment bad enough for him, nothing!" she hissed.

She left Abe's office feeling drained, but curiously refreshed, too, washed clean of her fear. She half-wanted to come across her tormentor now, while she still had the strength of a righteous rage in her muscles and bone.

Abe had encouraged her to call Dr. Lake. When she had mentioned the church counselor Jenny had recommended, he'd surprised her by saying, "That's not a bad idea. Try it."

Paige said she'd consider it.

She stopped when she reached her car and looked around the deserted garage. She wanted to scream at the top of her lungs, "Come out, Charlie Keegan! I'm ready for you." She smiled at herself. *What an extremist you are, Paige Brookings.*

Opening her car door, she looked around her, then slid into the seat. She locked the door and checked behind her. "Just taking precautions," she teased herself aloud. "I want to be ready for him."

She felt wonderful. The rage she had experienced in Abe's office was somehow purifying. It was preferable, at least, to depression and fear. She knew because she had lived through both.

If it wasn't so late, she'd go to Chisholm Creek Park and run. But the gates would be closed this time of night. *In the morning,* she promised herself, *I'll go run this energy off.*

Paige smiled as she turned on the engine and upped the volume on the radio. The Spinners were singing "Workin' My Way Back to You, Babe." It reminded her of Paul, back before Charlie hurt her, and she joined in, belting out the lyrics.

Chapter 14

Paul sat at his desk in a patch of fading sunlight and stretched. He'd been grading finals for days, it seemed. At last he was finished. He shoved the papers aside, then stood up. "December 14. I'll deliver these to campus first thing in the morning."

Moses looked up from her place in the sun next to his desk. She thumped the floor with her tail.

"Come on, old girl. Let's go for a walk. We can both use the exercise."

Paul went into the kitchen to get her leash from the closet, and she waited for him by the front door. She started barking before he returned.

"Someone here?" Paul called when he reached the door. There was no knock or ring of the doorbell, but there was a scrabbling noise outside, as if someone were trying the knob.

He pulled the door open to find Renee Wentworth standing there, holding Michael. She looked as hangdog as ever.

"Renee! Come in." He took Michael from her. The

baby smiled and grabbed his nose. Paul smiled back. This baby felt awfully good in his arms. He hitched the child up a little, to settle him more comfortably on his arm. Michael put his head against Paul's shoulder and sighed.

"I can't hold on anymore, Paul," Renee said. "I have to have help. Can you keep him until I get myself together?"

Paul hesitated. "I'd like to, Renee, but I don't think that's a good idea."

"Paul, you've gotta help me!"

"How, Renee? I'm not set up to take on a baby. I don't have a wife to help me."

She turned her back on him and leaned her head on one hand against the door frame and began to sob. "And I don't have a husband to help me. I can't do it on my own."

The accuracy of her words struck him. He was ashamed he hadn't realized it before. It must be hard to bring up a child alone. He put a hand on her shoulder. "I'm sorry, Renee. You're right. You do need help. Promise me you'll go tomorrow to get help."

"Where?" she wailed.

"Go to my pastor, Dr. Jessup. He'll help you, I'm sure. I'll take care of Michael until I find a better situation for him. I don't mind watching him. It's just that he needs a mother."

She shrugged. "Who doesn't? I can't give him what he needs. I don't hate him or dislike him. I just don't have anything left to give." Her shoulders heaved from her sobs.

Michael reached out to pat her hair. "Mama?"

"Mama's going to be all right," Paul said. "Call

me later, when you've reached someone, okay? I'll call Jenny Parker. She can give me some direction on how to take care of him." She might even take Michael on for a while. She did that from time to time, to help out young mothers who felt trapped.

He watched as Renee's woebegone figure trudged down the walk to her car. *Help her, dear Lord. Help us all.*

It seemed to Paul that his generation was infected with a rapidly-spreading poison, an evil spell that shrouded everything. So many people hurting, unable to function, even on the most minimal personal level.

The next morning Paige got up early. The weather report on the radio had said it was a balmy sixty degrees out, a mild, slightly overcast morning. A cold front was due to move in, though, in the next day or two. She stretched, arching and twisting her back, like a cat. *I think I'll go run,* she thought as she pulled on ivory sweats and laced up her New Balance shoes.

The doorman was someone new—Chester wasn't on the morning shift. This man was younger, with a fox-thin face and the unease of long years of social ineptitude.

He smiled shyly at her. "Out for a run?" he asked softly as he ran the elevator down to the first floor.

She smiled. "Yes, it sounds like we're in for a weather change—so I'd better get out while I can." She flipped her hand back at him as she climbed behind the wheel of her car.

A soft mist surrounded the car as she drove up Hillside to Chisholm Creek. It muffled all sound and drew halos around the headlights of the few cars out this early. She rolled her window down to smell the air, but closed it again quickly. The air was full of refinery gases and the tang of sulphur, held down by the cloud cover. There was no wind or high plains sky to blow the pollutants away today.

At the park, however, the air was clear. The odors of dying sunflowers and bluestem grass bit at her nose. She stretched a little at the picnic tables under the pavilion, to loosen her muscles. She had the park to herself, for the parking lot was empty.

As she began running down the first small incline and rounded the curve, she spooked a herd of deer feeding at the Osage orange trees by the creek. They dashed in fright to her right and then doubled back and raced across her path, where she had stopped, transfixed by the beauty of the one buck and the seven does. She wanted to reach out and touch their heaving sides, the magnificent shine of their coats enticing her.

When they disappeared across the prairie toward the windbreak on the north side of the park, a chasm of silence fell before her. She was amazed at the amount of noise the deer made, thundering right across her path. Deer looked so fragile, but at close range—just an arm's length away—she was struck by their muscled heft.

Paige continued her run in a daze, happy to have seen them. It was a rare gift, in the city, to see deer like this. She was fortunate this morning only because she had dared to leave the fortress of her apartment and take the risk of running alone, early, before other people came to the park and frightened them off with their "civilized" noise.

She ran once around the trail and then started her second round. When she reached the huge pond at the other end of the park, she stopped to gaze at it.

Since there was no wind, the pond—probably a hundred yards across—lay still, wrapped in the cottony mist of the fog. She could see steam rising from the surface of the water. As she watched, three white egrets flew diagonally across the pond, about five feet above the motionless surface. The birds' reflections were perfectly mirrored in the water. The beauty of it took her breath.

She stood still until they were gone. When she resumed her run, slowly now, musingly, she wondered what would happen to the egrets when the cold hit. Wichita in December could be eighty degrees out or twelve below zero, with a forty-below windchill. And it was possible to have both extremes in a twenty-four-hour period. As the old-timers said, "If you don't like Wichita's weather, wait a minute."

When Paige finished her run, she stopped in the parking lot and leaned against her car. She drew in a big breath of the smell of cedar warming in the sun, the smell of dried horseweed and thistle. The contrast of all the expanse of sky and trees and wildflowers around her to her usual enclosed, safe world struck her forcibly.

"He's reduced me to a prisoner," she said. "I'm not going to let him get away with that anymore. I'm fighting him, tooth and nail."

She took one last, long look at the scene around her and climbed into her car. She felt full of health, refreshed and strong. She drove back to the apartment with her car windows down, Pachelbel's *Canon* on the tape deck and a smile on her lips.

Paige went into work for an hour, to touch base with Hal and to look over her schedule for the day. There was a message to call Holder Danton. She grimaced. She did not want to work with the man. She didn't even want to be in the same room with him.

She sat staring at the phone. *I don't want to talk to him right now. I'll call later.*

She thought of Jenny's offer to recommend a counselor at her church. Jenny's cousin's life sounded almost as sordid as Paige's. Maybe this person wouldn't be too shocked to hear her story. Impulsively she dialed Jenny's number.

When Jenny answered, Paige could hear a baby crying in the background. "Am I getting you at a bad time?" Paige asked, a little embarrassed now at her rashness.

"No, no. I'm watching a baby for someone, and he has a little cold. He's crabby today, that's all."

"I was calling to let you know I'll be at the planning session."

"Good! I know you'll have some good ideas about where to hold the reunion, stuff like that."

Paige could hear the warmth and encouragement in Jenny's voice. "And Jenny," she said hesitantly, "about that counselor's name? Maybe I will call her."

Jenny rattled off the woman's name. "I think you'll like her, Paige."

"One dumb question, though . . ."

"What's that?" Jenny asked with a chuckle.

"She won't try to . . . proselytize, will she?" Paige dreaded the thought of getting hooked up with some wild-eyed Bible-thumper.

Jenny was silent for a moment. "I don't know, but I don't think so. I'll call her for you and ask, if you want me to."

"Would you? I'd appreciate it." Paige hesitated. "What time is the funeral tomorrow?"

"Liz said it's at ten."

The conversation ended after Jenny begged her to call back if she needed someone to talk to. For some reason, Paige believed Jenny—her warmth wasn't phony. When she thought back, Paige realized the young woman had always been warm and compassionate, even back in their teens. *I don't think Charlie Keegan ever molested her,* she mused. Somehow Jenny had never lost the innocence and sweetness of her youth.

The funeral service was held in the sanctuary of the Church of the Servant, a great stone Gothic cavern on Broadway. The stained-glass windows softened the vastness of the sanctuary. Light shone through the multihued panes, casting jeweled tones across the faces of the people who had come for the service.

Paige rarely entered church, except for weddings or christenings. She felt a little uncomfortable in this place with the religious trappings all around her, but as she sat there, her discomfort eased. The organist was playing something that sounded familiar. She couldn't come up with its name though. Something baroque, she was sure. *Maybe I'm missing something,* she thought, *avoiding church all these years.*

Paige's mother had always criticized the hypocrites who went to church, and in spite of her own early faith in God, Paige had accepted her mother's view. With a jolt, she realized she probably shouldn't have. *I don't agree with much of anything else she thinks.*

The flowers arranged around the two closed caskets

scented the air with an overpowering fragrance of roses. A pall of lilies and carnations blanketed the two coffins. Stacy's casket looked so small.

All the old group was there. Paul and Jenny stood in back, engaged in earnest conversation—he, tall and lean; she, petite—with her short, softly curling brown hair and rosy cheeks and the perennial sweet smile on her heart-shaped face. They both looked so intent, talking quietly when a third person joined them, a drab older woman. Paul seemed to be explaining something to her, and Jenny was nodding and smiling. Then she stepped forward and hugged the woman, who looked about as responsive as a rag doll.

Renee Wentworth! Paige hadn't laid eyes on her in years. Seeing her now, it was hard for Paige to believe Renee was the same age as the rest of them. She was dressed in a dowdy brown knit dress, its hem hanging unevenly. Her posture, shoulders rounded into her concave chest and head bent, begged for anonymity. Paige recoiled inside. *Why would someone deliberately make herself so unattractive?* she thought. It wouldn't take much for Renee to fix herself up. She hated to see any woman let herself go like that. She thought Renee must work hard to make herself look so bad. She had been pretty enough in high school. With a snort of disgust, Paige dismissed her from her mind.

Jamal was standing alone at the back, looking for a friendly face. When Paige lifted her eyebrows in greeting, he smiled and made his way to her pew. Carter and the grotesque Reilly Hoskins came in next. Paige decided Reilly had cleaned up for the occasion, after a fashion. He was wearing a black denim jacket, and his hair looked combed for a change. She frowned, seeing the two of them together.

"They really look like the odd couple, don't they?" she whispered to Jamal. Carter was in a dark gray suit, the white shirt setting off his fair hair and delicate coloring. "I can't figure out why Carter continues to see Reilly!"

"Why don't you ask him?" Jamal whispered back, a mischievous grin on his face.

"Ha! Very humorous," she answered. They both knew she would get nowhere asking her brother to account for his tastes, especially in friends. He was a strange mixture. He wanted Paige, and others too, to approve of him, but he tolerated no questioning of his actions.

"I hope they sit somewhere else," she muttered crossly. "I can't stand that Reilly."

"Well, don't look now," Jamal said quietly as Carter and Reilly filed into their row.

Paige had to console herself with the fact that at least Carter was sitting between her and the despicable man.

Carter shook his head in disdain as he looked around the sanctuary. "You know you're really in a *church!*" he said, emphasizing the word with a smirk. "This place gives me the willies."

"Maybe it's you and not the place, have you ever thought of that?" Paige snapped at him. She didn't want to hear him criticize the church, although she didn't know why. She knew it was special to some people, even if it wasn't to her, and she was too polite to intentionally offend their sensibilities.

Carter flushed, then glared at her. "Since when have you been religious?"

"I'm not, you jerk. Just be quiet and meditate or something, would you?" she hissed. "This is a funeral."

Carter pursed his lips and looked away. *Oh, brother,* Paige thought, *now he's mad, and I'll never hear the end of it.* She shifted in the pew, turning slightly away from her brother. She was getting heartily sick of trying to be everything to Carter, to her mother, to whomever. She folded her arms across her chest and scowled. *And I'm going to quit, beginning right now!*

Paul and Jenny, who had been sitting near the back of the sanctuary, now moved up to join the others. Paul took a seat right behind Paige, and she sighed. *What does he want?* Then she scolded herself. *I need to quit being so ugly to him—at least he's a world away from Carter and my mother and the rest of the crazies.*

✛ ✛ ✛

How lovely Paige looked today, Paul thought. His heart constricted, realizing he could lose her forever. His gaze fell on the cross above the altar, and he was moved to pray. *Dearest Father, I give Paige up to you now. I give up any claim to her. I only pray that she finds solutions to her problems, and that she returns to you. I pray she will feel your loving arms around her now and forever.*

A shaft of sunlight struck the brass of the cross, and it gleamed brightly. Suddenly he was filled with peace. He felt an assurance that it was all right to continue his pursuit of Paige, yet he knew he must face the possibility that it might not work out. *Okay, Lord,* he conceded. *I'll wait on your leading.*

Susan, Liz, and the rest of their family filed in and took their places in front. There was no one present from Jerry's own childhood family. Paige thought back to the boy he had been in school—skinny, with glasses that were too big for his narrow face, mouse-brown hair, and pants always pulled a little too high above his waist.

He had an eager, overanxious manner that put people off and made him the butt of jokes, until his dad started being buddy-buddy with the gang of kids who played together. It was then that Jerry began to be accepted, little by little, as part of a package deal.

Tears stung Paige's eyes. So sad. Too, too sad. Jerry had always seemed so pathetic. Then he and Susan had clicked and had gotten married, and his life had finally become worth living. Now this. *Why, God, why?*

The minister started talking. Paige tried to listen, but she was having a hard time concentrating. "'"Comfort, yes, comfort My people!" says your God,'" he read. "'"Speak comfort to Jerusalem."'" She tuned in then. He was reading from the huge Bible on the lectern. The words were majestic. "'The voice said, "Cry out!" and he said, "What shall I cry?"'"

Paige wanted to know where she could find the words again and scanned the program. Ah, there it was, Isaiah 40. "'"The grass withers, the flower fades—"'" she looked up at the heavy blankets of lilies and carnations— "'"but the word of our God stands forever."'"

A sob rose in her throat and choked her. The tears gushed out, and she could not stop them. She was conscious of Carter recoiling from her. Any strong display of emotion brought out his snidest reactions. Mother had trained them well never to cry, especially around her. Paige could hear those acid tones now. "Don't blubber, Paige, it makes you look ugly. Your skin blotches so."

Jamal covered her hand with his. Paul leaned forward to slip Jamal a folded white handkerchief. He pressed it into her hand. She nodded, then smiled ruefully. "Sorry."

"Sorry for what, Paige, for caring?" Jamal asked softly.

The service ended. Carter turned to Paige and sneered, "Get a grip, will you?" He stalked out of the church, Reilly in tow, trailing an aura of decay.

Paige sat there for a long minute. She realized she had been waiting for the minister to say, "Ashes to ashes, dust to dust. From dust we are made, to dust we shall return," but he hadn't. She thought all funerals ended that way. Didn't they?

Chapter 15

As Susan, Liz, and the family left the sanctuary, Paige felt a growing rage at Carter. Fists clenched, she rose and grasped her purse under one arm. Her brother didn't know how to behave, leaving before the family did, not waiting to speak to them, passing judgment on another's grief. Jaw tight, she thought of Abe's assurance that Carter would take good enough care of himself if she were to leave. *Huh!* she thought. *See, he can't!*

Paige remembered his solicitousness when he wanted her help with the party. *Aha,* she thought, *there's a new lover in the picture.* He always acts ugly when there's someone new waiting for him. Probably because he didn't feel he needed her as much, that this new relationship would last forever. But of course it wouldn't—they never did.

Paul approached her and, standing behind her, placed both hands on her shoulders. "Paige, are you all right?"

She jumped. "Oh, Paul, yes, I'm fine." She raised

her head and smiled at him. "The service was . . . moving, wasn't it?"

He nodded. Out of the corner of one eye, she saw Jenny approach Renee to speak to her. Renee flinched and drew back, twirling one lank of stringy hair around a finger, her usual gesture when she was anxious. Jenny put one arm around the girl and led her off to a small room next to the sanctuary.

"I like the church," Paige said. He nodded again. This was his church, as well as the Barsolos' and Jenny's. He'd asked her to come with him to special functions many times, but she'd always found some excuse not to attend. "The passage the minister read—I liked that."

"Isaiah," he said. "Isaiah is so powerful, but then, so are lots of other passages."

"Yeah, like 'Behold, God is my salvation, I will trust and not be afraid,'" Jamal spoke up. "That's Isaiah 12." His deep voice resonated theatrically, and he stood in a declamatory stance, one hand on his chest, the other outspread. He grinned. "My mamma wanted me to be a preacher. Greatest preachin' in the world in a black church—but this guy did all right today," he added expansively.

"Considering he's not black, right, Jamal?" Paul teased. He still held onto Paige's arm proprietarily.

"Dude cain't help the fact he ain't black," Jamal said in a heavy put-on drawl.

Paige laughed at their antics. "Oh, you two!"

Paul put some pressure on her arm to lead her out of the building. "You mentioned liking those verses the pastor read. Do you have a Bible?"

She pulled back from him, just a little. "No," she said shortly, trying to cut off the direction of the conversation. She knew where it was going.

He laughed. "Oh, come on, Paige," he said softly, "a Bible won't bite you, you know, and neither will I."

Jamal put one hand on her shoulder and gave it a light squeeze, but he didn't say anything.

She looked at Paul's face. A deep sadness lined his mouth as he gazed deeply into her eyes. "I won't try to force this on you, Paige. It's just that I think everyone's better off with a strong faith in a loving God."

She stopped, then looked at him thoughtfully. "I hadn't thought of it like that. I'll have to admit, you and Jamal and Jenny are certainly better off than Carter and Reilly and I!"

He nodded. "The support system of a church helps, too. It really is like family."

Tears welled up in her eyes. *Family.* She sighed.

Paul tightened his grip on her arm to pull her out of the line of people leaving the church. With a wave of his hand, he dismissed Jamal, smiling a little to soften the dismissal. Jamal acknowledged him with a nod, and Paige recognized in the silent exchange a complicity to take care of her.

"Hey, you guys. I feel like a puppet on a string, and you're pulling the strings!"

"You? Ha! What a joke," Paul said, a smile on his lips. "You always talk like you're so helpless, but you're the strongest person I know."

Paige turned to stare at him. "You must be joking. I'm the one who had the nervous breakdown, remember," she said angrily, "and I'm the one who has spent the last five years in analysis! What's so strong about that?"

He shrugged. "It shows more strength than refusing to get help when you need it."

She heard his implied meaning: "Like some people we know." Like Carter, like Reilly, like that poor wretch Renee?

She flushed then, embarrassed by his attention and praise, but pleased too.

"Paige, now don't say no . . . ," he began.

"No, Paul," she said, fearing what was coming.

"No, no, I said don't say no." He was still speaking in his light, bantering tone. "You weren't listening."

She laughed. "Oh, Paul, you're such a clown."

"I know, I know. Humor me." He began to speak in deliberate tones, as though to a dim-witted child, "Paige, I am taking you to lunch. I will not tolerate no for an answer."

She shook her head. "I can't, Paul. I've *got* to get back to the office!"

"As I was saying before I was so rudely interrupted, I am taking you to lunch." He directed her out of the church and to his car, an old blue Honda. She was laughing, shaking her head no, as he helped her into the front seat.

As they drove away, laughing, a man in a dark car fumed as he watched her ride off. *I'll get you yet, Paige. I removed Jerry and Stacy. She was going to blab, and I had to stop her before she could.* A sob tore through his body. *I loved her—I didn't want to kill her—but I couldn't let her tell. And I can't run the risk of you telling, either. You're too close to knowing everything. You're too strong.*

Chapter 16

Paige relaxed enough to enjoy Paul's company at lunch at the Singapore. He talked about his students, telling the stories like a stand-up comedy routine, exaggerating failings and virtues like any good storyteller. "I swear," he said, "I don't know what high school teachers are teaching in English classes these days. They can't write worth a darn. And their grammar—atrocious!"

She smiled at him. How refreshing to hear him rattle on in such a light vein. Things had been much too heavy lately.

The lo mein she ordered was delicious, as were the cups of green tea. When she had eaten about half of her food, however, her old discomfort at being with Paul returned and she pushed the plate away.

"You're full?" he asked.

She nodded and straightened, to gird herself to wait patiently for him to finish. She was anxious to get to the office.

He grinned. "That boring, huh?"

"What?" she asked, embarrassed. "Oh. I must

seem awfully rude," she said apologetically. "It's just that I've been out of the office so much lately, work must be piling up." She picked her napkin up from her lap and laid it on the table, carefully pleating the linen with long fingers as she waited.

Paul reached across the table, placing his large hand on hers to still the nervous movements. "Paige . . . ," he began.

She slid her hand out from under his and folded both hands in her lap. Lips compressed in a thin line, head down, she shook her head to discourage what she was sure was coming.

"I know you don't want me to bring this up again, Paige, but I must." Paul leaned across the table and grabbed her arm. "I won't give up on this. I love you, Paige, and I want us to work things out. Can't we at least try to mend our friendship?"

She jerked away from his hand. Blood suffused her throat and face. Her hands trembled with her anger. "That's not what you're aiming at. You want to talk about marrying. You think you want to marry me. You don't, Paul. You might think you do, but you don't." She picked up her purse and stood. "And I don't want to marry . . ." She paused without finishing the sentence. Taking a deep breath, she continued, "I will probably never marry. So give it up, Paul."

He stood abruptly, knocking the chair over behind him. He leaned the knuckles of both fists on the table and thrust his face into hers. "Paige, I will *not* give it up."

His voice was rising, and other diners were looking their way. Paige darted a sidelong glance at the curious people in the room. Her stomach contracted—she hated public scenes. She wanted to hush him.

"Once you told me you loved me, and you have never since denied it," Paul reminded her. "You just now wanted to say you didn't want to marry *me*, but you couldn't bring yourself to do it."

"Please, Paul," Paige whispered, "not here . . ."

"I'm *going* to say it. I've been patient long enough, Paige."

Afraid he'd cause a scene, Paige turned and marched out of the restaurant.

Once she reached the parking lot, she remembered she had come here with Paul. Her own car was parked downtown, miles away. She stomped her foot, furious. How dare he put her on the spot like this?

Paul sauntered out of the building behind her, a small smile on his face. "Need a ride, lady?" he asked out of one side of his mouth, in imitation of Humphrey Bogart or some other movie tough guy. She wanted to slap him.

He held the door for her, and she slid into the front seat with bad grace. When he had settled himself in the driver's seat and turned on the ignition, he turned to her and whispered close to her ear, "That was fun, let's do it again sometime."

Paige's rage overcame her social facade. It was all too much—she burst into tears.

Paul leaned over and put his arms around her, holding her close as she sobbed like a child. "I'm s-sorry!"

"You're forgiven," he said softly.

"Oh, I don't mean just for crying," she said in disgust, tears stanched, pulling back from his touch. "I'm making such a scene. I'm embarrassed."

He placed his hands on her shoulders and shook her

gently. "Enough of that. You don't have to apologize for having feelings, Paige!"

"But I feel so . . . so sloppy about it all," she whispered, covering her face with her hands and beginning to cry softly.

Paul pulled her hands away from her face and placed them on his chest. Then he drew her close to him and kissed her hair, his hands gently rubbing her back. "Don't be ashamed of your feelings. It's part of being human." She sighed. "I love you, Paige. You don't have to be a perfect ice goddess for me. I love the depth of your feelings. I love your courage, and your will."

She spoke then, voice muffled in the folds of his jacket, "Don't love me, Paul, you'll end up getting hurt. I'm a jinx, and I'll ruin you."

Paul straightened and looked at her. "Excuse me, Ms. Brookings," he said frostily, "but that's the stupidest thing I ever heard." He shoved the gear shift into reverse and backed out of his parking slot.

Paige glanced at his profile. His jaw was clenched, the muscles in his face tight. Her head spun. Why was he reacting so strongly? "Why is it I can insult you and you forgive me, but if I try to protect you from me, you get mad?" She turned and glared out her window. "I don't understand you at all." She crossed her arms and held them, tight, against her chest.

"Paige, I don't need protecting, especially not from you. I don't know why you have to run yourself down. You've got everything in the world going for you—beauty, talent, money, character—but you walk around all the time with your own personal storm cloud hanging over you. Why?" He revved the motor at a stoplight, his anger ringing in the dead air of the enclosed car.

"Why can't you be thankful for what you have, and get on with your life?" When the light changed, he downshifted and took off with a jerk.

Paige felt the blood leave her face. "You don't understand!" she yelled. "You don't understand! You're Mr. Nice Guy, always acting so sweet and kind and considerate, but you don't even begin to understand!"

His head swiveled around. "So explain it to me! I dare you to explain it to me!" His doubled fist pounded the steering wheel. "You've been seeing a psychiatrist for five years! Why aren't you healed?"

She began to cry again. "I don't know. . . . I just don't know." She looked down at her hands clenched in her lap. "I can't remember parts of the past, and I don't know why. I have all these fears and nightmares, and I don't know why." Her head came up with a jerk. "Except I'm starting to remember a little, Paul." A smile flitted across her face.

He looked across at her, waiting.

"It's been such an awful week," she moaned, beginning to relax.

She could feel rather than see his nod of affirmation. Suddenly she wanted to tell him everything. Oh, how she wanted to tell him! But how could she? It was so ugly and dirty, and he was so clean . . . almost pure. How could she share it with him? "Did you see Renee at the funeral?" she asked abruptly.

"Yes, but don't change the subject," he said gruffly. *I'm not, Paul,* she thought to herself. *I don't know exactly how she's tied in to these memories, but she is.* Paige straightened her shoulders, deciding that she'd opened herself up to him enough for one day. No more . . . it was too painful. "I'm sorry, I didn't mean to change

125

the subject. The killings, the funeral—it's been a difficult week. Poor Susan and Liz."

Paul could hear the change in her tone. The ice goddess was back, and the warm, living, breathing, and yes, hurting, woman was in hiding. "You just shut me out again," he snarled.

"Life's hard," she said coolly.

"I'm not quitting, Paige. I'm not giving up on helping you feel and live again," he said through clenched teeth.

"It sounds like a losing proposition to me," she replied. After a brief pause, she added, almost casually, "Armand is coming to Wichita. I told you all about Armand, didn't I?"

He laughed a short, sharp laugh. "Yes, Paige, you told me all about Armand. Do I get to meet Mr. Smooth while he's here?"

Surprised, Paige turned to look at Paul. He was willing to meet his rival? "Well, yes, if you want to," she said uncertainly.

"Oh, I do, I do." He smiled sardonically. *If she really wanted to marry Armand, she would have done it long ago, wouldn't she?* "I'd love to meet any friend of yours," he said, willing himself to sound confident but quailing inside. *I love you so much, Paige.*

They parted, feeling strange and distant again. Paul accompanied Paige to her car, but before he opened the door, he pushed her back against the car and kissed her—a long, lingering kiss. She tried not to respond, but one hand betrayed her and found his arm and touched it, hungering. He ended the kiss and looked deep into her eyes. Then he smiled. *I'll win you over yet, Paige.* "Don't forget . . . I love you." She stiffened and turned away to unlock the door. "I'll call you," he said softly, letting her go.

Paul returned to his car and sat there for a few moments. *I'll wait on you, Lord. But waiting's hard. Please guide me.* Bowing his head, he sighed deeply. He was so tired.

Suddenly he was filled with peace as a voice spoke into his heart, *Have faith. I have chosen her for you, and you for her.*

Paul was dumbstruck. Blood rushed from his head, then back again. He didn't know whether he wanted to laugh or cry. Either way, he felt breathless. He'd heard of people hearing God's voice, but this was a first for him. It sounded like his own voice in his head, but with an authority he could not doubt. *Trust me and be obedient. That's all I ask.*

This time he spoke aloud, wanting to seal this moment for all time. "I'll trust you, Lord. I'll trust you."

✠ ✠ ✠

Paige returned to the office the next day. She tried to clear her head to reenter the working world. Here life was orderly, calm, controlled. Liz had not returned yet, and the temporary secretary hired to take her place was young and nervous. Paige pushed down her irritation with the girl and tried to be extremely patient with her. That helped her forget the murders, Charlie Keegan, and Paul.

The girl, in a severe gray suit and with her hair pulled in a bun, was dressed all wrong for her age and coloring. Paige could see her in a feminine pink suit, her soft brown hair curling around her oval face. When Paige took time to show her the different office procedures, the girl, whose name was Julie, acted as grateful as a puppy. Paige couldn't help smiling a little.

Julie cut off a caller for the third time, and Paige painstakingly showed her, again, how to work the telephones. When she figured the girl had finally mastered the intricacies of the system, she returned to her office to work on the Danton Oil file. Just as she was succeeding in orienting herself to the account again, her phone lit up.

Paige wanted to rip the intrusive instrument out of the wall. These interruptions were ruining her productivity. When she finally answered, grimacing at the usurper of her time and energy, her irritation mounted to a boil to hear Carter's voice on the other end.

"Paige," he said, reminding her of the Tar Baby oozing all over Brer Rabbit, "who is the imbecile in your office?"

"Oh, it's a temp," she started to explain, but he cut her off.

"I *know* she's a temp. Anyway, I've been trying to reach you."

"Yes, Mother told me you had some news. I tried to call you the other night." Controlling her anger with some difficulty, Paige kept her voice as normal as possible. Any emotional response would make this conversation drag out more than it would anyway.

"I'm going to L.A. That agent, Littman, wants me out there as soon as possible."

"Oh, you mean the tacky little fat one?" Paige couldn't resist one gibe.

"Tacky?" Carter said on a rising note. "My dear, sweet, benighted sister, that man is brilliant, and he may well be my bread ticket for the rest of my days."

"Fat chance," she said. Feeling a little guilty now that she'd wounded him, Paige asked, more kindly, "Carter, did he actually say he could get you a role?" Silence greeted her words. "Carter?" she repeated.

"No, he didn't," he admitted begrudgingly, dragging out the words. "But I just know that if I go, things will work out so he'll use his influence for me."

"So what exactly was his proposal?"

He chuckled obscenely. "Do you really want to know? I didn't know you had such prurient interests."

Paige's heart sank. "Oh, Carter, not another lover," she whispered. "Don't you get tired of being used by these people?"

"Has it ever occurred to you that maybe *I* am using *them?*" he answered coldly.

"Do you think that makes me feel any better about these situations?" She paused, took a deep breath, and plunged in, opening up to him. "Carter, I've started to remember some things about our childhood that I've been trying to bury for all these years. Could we get together and talk?"

She heard his sharp intake of breath. "What things?" he asked, suspicion welling in his voice.

"About Charlie Keegan."

"Charlie Keegan!" Carter wiped his face with the flat of his hand. He was glad Paige was not in the room to see his reaction. He couldn't allow her to become involved in the issue at this point. Steeling himself, he went on, "I'm not interested in talking about Charlie Keegan. He was just a dirty old man who was dumb enough to try to pay us for what he could get for free."

Paige's stomach lurched. She could feel the blood drain from her face. "Carter, don't," she moaned, pain filling her. His view of the horror of Charlie's invasions nauseated her.

"Paige, you are not some innocent little girl in Sunday school. You know what the world is like."

"It's not a world I like very much, Carter," she said haltingly. "It's sickening. And it's poisoned you and me, and Renee too, and Jerry . . . poor Jerry." Her voice broke.

"Oh, quit your bawling. You used to be tougher, Paige. What is this new delicate flower act?"

"Maybe it's not an act, Carter," she said, her voice full of anger now. "Maybe now I'm starting to thaw out, to open up like Paul wants me to, to become human."

"What a load of bull. It hurts, doesn't it? And do you have time for the luxury of it all?"

"Oh, it hurts, that's for sure. And I'm not sure I have time not to grab it while I can. I want a full life, not this pallid, secure, lonely existence."

"Oh, so take some lover. Maybe even Paul would volunteer."

She cringed at his tone. "You can be so despicable, Carter."

"Yeah, but at least I'm living, really living."

A laugh of derision escaped her. His idea of "really living" didn't match hers.

He changed the subject. "I called, Paige, to tell you I'm leaving. You'll have to deal with Mother—she's throwing tantrums—which, by the way, is probably what you're doing. Did you want some favor from ol' Carter too? Is that why you don't want me to go?"

"Carter, I don't think you've ever done me or anyone else a favor, unless it was to get something you wanted." Paige controlled herself again, clenching the fist that held the phone as she did so, knuckles white. Changing her tack, she said, "I'm sorry, Carter." In spite of everything, he was her brother. "I do wish you the best."

She felt phony saying that, considering how angry she was with him, but long years of training in superficial manners won through. Then, unable to control her impulses to honesty, "It can't hurt, I guess."

"Such a caring, graceful farewell," he sneered. "Good-bye, Paige." He slammed the phone in her ear.

✝ ✝ ✝

Carter sat staring at the phone for a few moments. *You'd better not mess this up, Paige,* he thought. He picked up the phone again and jabbed at the buttons in the receiver, scowling in concentration. "Reilly," he said, when he heard a mumbled hello, "it's Carter again. We're going to have to move our plans up. She remembers now. We've got to move fast."

Reilly swore. "Sure, Carter. Name the date. This is going to be a real pleasure." He hesitated a long moment, and added, "You're sure you can cover our tails? And you've got enough dough for me too, right? You'd better not leave me here to face the music alone."

"Reilly, I've told you and told you!" Carter snapped. "Why don't you trust me?"

Reilly said something profane, then, "Gee, man, I don't know why I don't trust you."

Carter could picture the sneer on the man's dirty face. "You do realize, don't you, that I know if I betray you, you'll put the finger on me. Now just forget the garbage and let's move. I don't have much time left," he said as he ran a finger over his protruding ribs and the growing numbers of bruises on his skin. He gingerly touched the sore in his nostril. The coke or was it finally full-blown AIDS? He didn't know, and he figured it didn't really matter. One or the other would get him before long.

He ended the conversation. "We have to be careful. Nobody must suspect us."

Chapter 17

Paige was shaking when the conversation with Carter ended. She was furious with him, and with herself. What a tangled web she was in, with him, with their mother, and with Paul, and now with this double murder. She felt so strongly—and the conviction was growing, not lessening—that somehow Stacy's and Jerry's deaths were related to her memories of Charlie. But how?

She hid her face in her hands, elbows propped on her desk, shoulders hunched to squeeze out the pain in her body. She wanted to throw herself on the floor and kick and scream. Maybe Carter was right. Maybe she was just indulging in a tantrum. Right now, though, she could strangle Charlie Keegan with her bare hands. He was responsible for Carter's messed-up life.

But so was Mother. Mother had known what Charlie was like, she had to have known. Paige almost hated her mother more than she did Charlie. She had to have been almost an accomplice, although not—surely not!—consciously. She couldn't have sold her own children out to a worm like Charlie Keegan, could she?

What inhuman monsters! Paige gagged on her own thoughts.

She took some time to compose herself, then put away the Danton file and straightened up her desk. *This is hopeless,* she thought. *I can't work today.* "In the timeless words of that great philosopher, Scarlett O'Hara," she spoke aloud, " 'tomorrow is another day!' " She smiled ruefully at her weak attempt at humor.

✝ ✝ ✝

Wopat and Johnson dropped by the office later in the morning to ask Paige again about Stacy's diary. At least she no longer felt quite so paranoid at their questions. Wopat was positively rude in his disdain of her, but Johnson was sweetly solicitous. He asked her to try to buy a diary just like the one she'd given Stacy—the lab wanted to do some tests on some half-burned paper fragments they'd found in a pile of litter that had blown up at the side of the Keegans' garage. She promised him she'd go to McLeod's to find an identical diary.

Julie looked heartbroken when Paige said she was leaving for the day. Paige uncharacteristically rushed to explain herself. "It's been such a difficult week, with the deaths. I just can't work," she said, begging for this young, callow stranger's understanding.

"Oh, I understand," Julie said, her face soft with sympathy, reaching out to pat Paige's hand. Curiously, Paige did not draw back for once, but allowed herself to be comforted.

Before she left, she gave Julie some correspondence to copy on letterhead and get into the mail. The young woman nodded her willingness to do the job, but Paige could see some hesitation written across her face. "Is there a problem?"

Julie blushed. "I hate to bother you. But I don't know where the copy machine is. . . ." Her words trailed off in confusion.

"Oh, why didn't you say so?" Paige laughed and gestured for Julie to follow her. "It's in this small room down the hall."

The long hall was quiet, all sound muffled from the offices down at the other end of the corridor. Paige shivered involuntarily. She was glad she wasn't alone right now. She wondered if Liz had ever felt afraid down here.

Paige demonstrated how to use the copy machine. "This isn't a very convenient location for this machine. I never realized just how inconvenient. I'll have to speak to Hal about it. It must drive Liz nuts." She waved as she left the young girl there alone to do the work.

✢ ✢ ✢

The weather was perfect. Indian summer had strayed into the month of December. The brilliant Kansas sky shimmered like enamel on pewter. The air was cool, the sun heating it gently. Paige rolled down her car windows.

At an intersection, a new cherry red Mustang pulled up next to her, its stereo booming. She glanced at the young man who was driving and registered curly blond hair and a neatly trimmed red-blond beard. Noticing her reaction to his music, he grinned sheepishly, straight white teeth gleaming, then leaned over to turn down the volume. Before he did so, she could hear the lyrics, "Our God is an awesome God!"

Christian rock? That was a new one on her. There

was a whole world she knew nothing of—a cleaner, brighter, happier world. How she longed to know more of it, and of open-faced people like the kid in the car next to her.

The light changed, and he drove off. She could see the Wichita State University sticker in the back window. Just a college kid. She ached for a chance to be young and innocent again.

Paige drove to McLeod's to buy the diary, then decided to take advantage of the nice weather and do some shopping. It would be nice to drink up some Christmas atmosphere at the mall. That might rest her mind a bit from her obsessions.

✦ ✦ ✦

When she arrived at the Skycrest, Wopat and Johnson were there, talking to Chester in the lobby. The slight old man looked frightened.

"Ms. Brookings," he sighed in relief when he saw her, "these gentlemen want to talk to you. Seems there was some accident at your office. I was so afraid it might have been you. . . ."

Wopat interrupted. "That will do," he said curtly. "We'll need to interrogate you, Ms. Brookings."

"Interrogate?" she exclaimed. "Accident? What on earth is going on?" Her eyes scanned the faces of the three men staring at her, but she could read nothing but confusion in Chester's, hostility in Wopat's, and embarrassment in Johnson's. The fair-skinned young officer's apparent sympathy for her somehow made the whole situation seem more threatening.

"Can we go to your apartment?" Wopat continued in a gruff tone. She nodded, numb and silent.

Chester beetled around the high desk where he stood guard and over to the elevator, where he held the door open for the three of them.

Inside, Paige stared at the walls to avoid the policemen's gaze, zeroing in on a familiar burl in the paneling. What next?

When she entered the apartment, Marmalade came to greet her. Once he realized, however, that there were strangers with her, he removed himself from the room, tail held high, switching crossly from side to side.

She offered the men coffee which they refused. Wopat glared at her as he began, "When did you leave your office today?"

She glanced at the gold Rolex on her wrist. It was 4:30. "It must have been about noon. Why?"

"You know a Julie Sanger?"

"Why, yes. She's our new temp. She's standing in for Liz because of the Keegan murders." Paige looked back and forth between the two men for some clue as to what had happened.

Johnson seemed to take pity on her. "She was attacked, Miss, in a small storage room down the hall from your office."

Paige blanched. She moved to the couch and sat heavily on one end and covered her face with her hands. She straightened then and looked at Johnson. "By whom?"

"We don't know. We thought you might. She was copying some correspondence from you."

"Yes, I'd left her there with work to do." Paige thought of the sweet, eager young girl. "Is she all right?" she asked, dreading the answer.

"She was choked and then hit over the head with a

137

blunt object," Wopat spoke up. "She's at the hospital. Her condition is serious. We won't be able to talk to her until tomorrow. Her desk . . ."

"Liz's desk," she corrected woodenly.

"The desk was rifled. Would this Liz know what might be missing?"

"I'm sure she would. But why?"

Wopat ignored her question and went on. "Then whoever it was went through *your* office." He seemed to relish telling her the grim news. "He sure left a big mess."

She sat and stared blankly, searching her mind for some reason, any reason, why someone might want to go through her files. "Was it robbery?"

"Do you keep money in your office?" Wopat asked, surprised. He didn't seem to have considered that motive.

Again she shook her head. "It must be related to the murders of Jerry and Stacy, it must!" she said forcefully. "Maybe it's all tied in to the man who's been calling me. There must be some connecting link, something about me, about that man. He must think I know something." She stood up and started pacing the room.

"Well, do you?" Wopat asked. His hostility softened little as it dawned on him that she was a victim herself, of what, he didn't know yet.

She stopped her pacing and turned to face them both. "Is there any way to trace a man who disappeared ten years ago?"

"KBI records, if he has a record, I suppose," Johnson answered.

"KBI?"

"Kansas Bureau of Investigation."

"Oh, it sounded Russian or something. Well, can you try to trace him?"

"Trace who?" Wopat asked, hostility returning. This broad seemed to think they were magicians who could pull a murdering rabbit out of a big hat.

"Charlie Keegan, of course," she said. Her voice was strong and firm. "Jerry's dad. I think he must be back."

Wopat curled his lip in disdain. No way could the solution to these crimes be so easy some emptied-headed blonde was going to come up with it!

Chapter 18

Friday night—Jenny's planning meeting for the reunion. Paige had not been able to accomplish much at work since the funeral and the attack on Julie, but at least this horrible week was nearly over. Julie was recovering nicely. But she didn't know anything about her attacker—she'd seen and heard nothing.

When Paige had visited her in the hospital, she had been cut to the heart by the wounded look on the girl's face. Julie had probably never been betrayed before. No doubt she believed everyone was her friend. Paige hated the fact that someone had disabused her of the notion.

Paul called Renee early, asking her to meet him at Jenny's before the reunion planning meeting. "We need to talk about you, about Michael."

"Why?"

"You have to get help and you need a semi-permanent home for your child. You can't just kick him around from pillar to post!"

"Oh, Paul," she whined, "I can't handle him, but you can. I can't think of anyone else I'd want to have him."

"Renee . . ."

"No, I mean it. It'll take me a while to get myself in shape."

"Did you call my pastor?"

"Not yet, but I will, I will." She spoke quickly to cover his protest.

"Be at Jenny's at 6:30," he said, his tone allowing no arguments.

✛ ✛ ✛

Paul arrived first. When he walked in, Michael beamed and leaned toward him, arms outstretched. "It's frightening how willing he is to accept anyone who is the least bit decent to him. Aren't most kids this age afraid of strangers?"

"Yes, but remember—his mother and father are both strangers to him, for that matter," Jenny said. "You're the most positive thing he's experienced. That makes you okay in his book!"

Paul nuzzled the baby's warm, fragrant neck. His voice broke as he said, "He's okay in my book too." Michael giggled and tucked his head down to escape the tickling.

"I told Renee to come . . . doesn't mean she will," he told Jenny. "I don't want her taking advantage of you."

"Oh, I don't mind. You know I'm involved in counseling young women with crisis pregnancies. This is just helping them a little further down the road. Besides, he's no trouble, really. His cold was bad the first day, but he's fine now."

"How can he be so cheery? He's incredible."

Jenny laughed. "He's warm, dry, and full. What more could a little guy want? Of course he's happy."

At that point Renee arrived. She looked a little better to Paul than she had the last two times he'd seen her, but there was a funny brittleness in her manner. When Michael saw her, he pulled away from her and hid his face in Paul's shoulder.

Renee blanched. "So you've already turned him against me?"

Paul was dumbfounded. "We did no such thing. All we've done is feed him and keep him clean."

"And hugged him," Jenny added softly. "Babies need lots of hugs." She directed at the child that goofy smile adults reserve for babies, and Michael smiled back while snuggling safe in Paul's arms.

"Have you called our pastor?" Paul asked again.

"No, but I will!" Renee shouted. "Leave me alone!"

Michael whimpered, and Jenny's children entered the room, wide-eyed, wondering about the strange lady who was yelling in their house.

"Enough, Renee," Paul said, fatigue in his voice.

"Come with me, Renee," Jenny said gently. "Let's put your coat in the bedroom."

Paul sighed as he watched them leave. He put Michael on the floor and sat on the couch near him. Michael, then Jenny's Jarod, began playing at his feet. "Such an easy baby," Paul said, more to himself than anyone else. "Why can't she manage?"

Paige dreaded the thought of this meeting, but she decided to make the best of it. It would be a chance to get out of her apartment, and to see old friends and acquaintances. She resolved too, very firmly, that she would bring up the subject of Charlie Keegan. The man was dangerous. She suspected that he had killed Jerry and Stacy, attacked Julie, and stalked her.

She dressed carefully, putting on a peach sweater and slacks and adding a peach and ivory Oriental print scarf. Then she slipped onto her ears a pair of smart lion's head earrings Carter had given her on their birthday. With a hoop through each lion's mouth, they looked like door knockers, she thought. She wondered whether Carter would be there tonight. He'd never said exactly when he'd be leaving. *Oh, he'll tell me,* she thought sardonically. *He'll need a ride to the airport.*

When she arrived, only two other cars were there ahead of hers—Paul's Honda and a Ford she didn't recognize. A light breeze lifted her hair as she exited her car. She had to step around a small pink bicycle with training wheels and a red wagon on the sidewalk, left there earlier at the end of Jenny's children's play. A Raggedy Ann doll leaned drunkenly over one edge of the wagon, with a large silver robot next to it. Two whiskey barrels, filled with dusty miller and red geraniums, stood sentinel on each side of the small, well-swept front porch. They were still in bloom this mild December. A peace rose by the front door held two large, tight buds.

A gray long-haired cat, followed by four mewing kittens, approached, meowing softly at Paige. The old mother cat wound herself around Paige's legs, soliciting attention as she did so. Paige smiled—the kittens were adorable. She knelt down to scritch the cat behind one ear. One of the kittens, a little ginger tom, stood on his stubby little back legs and attacked her hand with great kittenish ferocity. She laughed. Here was a miniature Marmalade. Maybe she ought to get him a playmate. She shook her head. The older cat would terrorize a kitten.

As she straightened, she looked around her at the tableau spread before her. It all looked so homey and—safe. She shuddered to think of Charlie Keegan close by, perhaps at some dreadful moment violating this innocent scene. Inadvertently she looked around her, up and down the street. She saw nothing that threatened, but then that meant nothing.

The inside door stood open, and Paige could see three small children tumbling around the floor at Paul's feet. They were dressed in fleecy footed pajamas—pink, red, and pastel blue. Paul had a big grin on his face as he helped a small boy of about three do a somersault. A girl—probably five and the likely owner of the pink bicycle—waited her turn impatiently, jigging from one foot to the other. A baby, old enough to crawl, put one of Paul's shoelaces in his mouth and gummed it. She watched them for a few seconds, a tentative smile struggling with a vague discomfort. Was it an appealing sight, or was it just too corny for words? She didn't know how she felt about it.

The decor was just as she expected—all rose and blue and mauve, country charm up to the eyeballs. There were fat bear designs on wreaths and pillows, stuffed bears in rockers and on low maple shelves on the walls. A large, old-fashioned Christmas tree filled the alcove between the living and dining rooms. Red and green, blue and gold ornaments—many of them obviously made by chubby, incompetent little hands—hung on the tree. It was all so "cute" that Paige felt uncomfortable. She just didn't fit here.

If she put up a tree this year, it would be tastefully decorated, not a hodgepodge of colors and shapes like this one.

Jenny crossed the hallway and noticed Paige standing there. "Oh, I'm sorry, Paige," she said breathlessly, a friendly smile on her face. "I didn't hear the door."

"No, no, it's all right. I just got here."

Jenny motioned her into the living room. The noise of the children's laughter was deafening. Jenny clapped her hands lightly. "Okay, okay, gang, that's enough. You're going to wear Paul out."

Paul looked up, saw Paige, and smiled languidly. When she and Jenny entered the room, he rose slowly from the low couch done in a blue and mauve print. He looked like a kindly giant surrounded by midgets hanging on his legs. Paige felt the depth of his yearning for children just like these. He'd so much wanted the child that had died with Marianna. And she knew he wanted children now—his children, her children. *I can't, Paul!* she wanted to scream. He lowered his gaze, then bent over and tickled the boy, who fell on his back in a fit of giggles.

"Don't get too wound up, Jarod," Jenny warned her son.

The pink-pajamaed girl turned to study Paige. Her look said imperiously, *Who are you to be interrupting our fun?* Then Paige's looks seemed to register with the child. She smiled broadly and wandered over to take the beautiful woman's hand and lead her to the couch.

"Ashley, don't bug Paige now," Jenny said nervously,

watching Paige for her reaction to the children. "I know you aren't used to children," she said apologetically.

"No, I'm not," Paige answered honestly. Jenny seemed to want some approval of her brood. "You certainly have three healthy-looking specimens, though," she said lightly.

Jenny gave a sigh of relief. "Oh, they're certainly that!"

"Who all is coming?" Paige asked, fighting a desire to push away the child's hands. Ashley was now fiddling with the silky scarf around Paige's neck, and she wanted to scream. She hated to be handled like this.

"Renee is here already. She's putting her coat in the bedroom. She'll be out soon. Carter, Jamal—they're not here yet—Paul, you and I. That's about it. I knew Liz and Susan wouldn't be interested right now."

Paige nodded. No, they wouldn't be interested in a silly class reunion. They were still mourning. Jenny hadn't mentioned Reilly, either.

"Since we all still live here," Jenny went on, "we're the likely candidates to plan the reunion." She smiled, her face lit up by the sweetness of her smile. She looked now, as she had ten years before, open and happy and warm in her rose pink sweater and rose and blue plaid skirt.

"Well, should we do this like a formal meeting?" Jenny asked with a little laugh. "You know, with Robert's Rules of Order and all?" She pretended to bring a gavel down on the arm of the couch. "This meeting will now come to order," she ordered playfully.

Renee entered at that point, coming from the bedroom wing. She pushed her hair back from her face and, seeing Paige, said breezily, "The class star is here! Great of you to join us."

Paige stared at her, bewildered. She couldn't tell whether Renee was trying to be funny or just deliberately rude. Her voice was too loud and sounded brittle.

The biggest shock, however, was her appearance. Her eyes were too bright, and her face had a high, unnatural color, not at all like Jenny's pastel prettiness. Her makeup was too heavy and in the wrong shade, so that her blush and lipstick stood out on her face like clown paint. Her hair was swept up on top of her head and was falling messily out of its pins. Instead of the browns she had worn to the funeral, she was wearing a fire-engine red dress. Paige struggled not to show her surprise. Renee was like a different person compared to the one who had attended the funeral!

Truthfully, though, this person didn't have any better taste than the dull, drab Renee. Paige fought the desire to rip the ugly dress off her and wash the makeup off her face.

"What's wrong, Paige?" Renee asked. "You look like you swallowed a cow."

Paige ran a hand across her face. For some reason she felt like laughing. She dared not look at Paul—one glance at him would set her off, she knew. "Hello, Renee," she said when she had regained control, "how are you?"

Renee answered at length, but Paige had a hard time following her conversation. It was disjointed, skipping from her job to high school days to a parking ticket she'd just received. On top of the confusion of Renee's garbled words, Ashley continued to pat Paige's face and hair. When the doorbell rang, Paige scowled, feeling a sense of unreality.

Mistaking her expression, Renee took offense. "Oh, I know, I don't interest a big deal like you," she said bitterly.

Paige felt she ought to apologize, but she didn't know how. Paul moved closer to Renee, and Paige wondered why—to keep them separated, perhaps? It was all getting stranger and stranger!

Little by little, Renee seemed to wind down. The young woman was obviously suffering from some slight—what, exactly, Paige couldn't name.

The atmosphere lightened when Jamal entered. Paul entered into a lighthearted banter with him, as naturally as in high school days, and the attention shifted from Renee. *Paul is protecting her from me,* Paige thought wildly. *How odd, I thought I was the one he wanted to protect.*

Carter arrived soon after. Paige had half-expected him to bring Reilly along, but mercifully he hadn't. He spoke to everyone but Paige, merely nodding in her direction, stiffly. *He's still in a snit,* she thought.

Renee darted occasional glances at Paige as the others chatted together. Paige felt that Renee wanted something from her. What? Approval, perhaps, or some special favor? Renee's glances reminded her too strongly of Carter's never-ending demands. She wanted to scream at them both, *What do you want from me?*

Now that everyone was present, Jenny started the meeting over. Paige felt more befogged than ever. It was impossible for her to enter into the planning. She was worrying about how she would bring up the subject of Charlie Keegan.

Ashley had stopped touching her face and hands and clothes and now was snuggled sleepily against her side. The voices of the other people in the room eddied around Paige, but she didn't respond to them. She looked down at the sweep of long, dark blonde lashes across the child's cheeks and felt an unexpected surge of love for her.

Paige could not understand this peculiar reaction, nor the strength of it. It washed over her in waves, like the tide at Galveston Beach, warm and life-giving and strong. She wanted to protect this child from the Charlie Keegans of the world and felt an inexpressible sorrow, knowing full well that she couldn't.

Suddenly Paige had a vision of all her friends from high school—those present in the room and those who were not—as children again. Carter, slim, blond, laughing, crystalline in his delicacy. Reilly, neglected and scrawny, but hanging around the fringes, begging attention. Jamal, silent and strong, a little removed from the group, but always ready to help, to smile, white teeth flashing against warm cocoa skin. Paul, lanky and clownish even then, the smart kid in the class who never flaunted his intelligence. And Jerry—poor Jerry!—and sweet Jenny . . . and awkward Renee. She loved them all then, and she loved them now, for what they had been as children. Again she gazed fondly at Ashley asleep at her side. *I thought I hated children!* she argued with herself and looked up to see Paul watching her, a slight smile on his face. *He knows!* she thought panicking. *He knows what I'm feeling!* She could never marry such a person—she'd never have a moment's privacy!

When Jenny noticed that Ashley had fallen asleep,

149

she walked over to the couch where the two were sitting. "Let me move her to her bed," she said softly.

"No!" Paige said abruptly. "I mean . . . just leave her. She's all right."

"You're sure?"

She nodded, eyes wide, softened with unshed tears as she looked up into Jenny's gentle face.

Renee snorted. "I thought you always hated kids, Paige. What's this, a new madonna and child act?"

Paige flushed. "If you say so, Renee," she said coldly. *I'm not giving you the satisfaction of riling me,* she thought.

"It's Paige's new image," Carter said snidely. "She's giving up success for midwestern mediocrity. That includes liking rug rats, I guess."

"Someday, Carter, you are going to say something like that, and someone is going to tear you apart," Paige said through clenched teeth.

Carter recoiled as if slapped.

Jamal shifted in his chair. "Looks as though you just got a good start on it," he drawled, a big smile on his broad, dark face.

Carter turned and glared at Jamal, who merely returned his gaze coolly.

It struck her forcefully how odd some of the members of their little clique were, and all because of Charlie! Here were crazy Renee, obnoxious Carter, and damaged Paige—all his victims. Jerry and Stacy—their spirits seemed to join them there—perhaps two more.

Nervously, Paige decided now was the time to bring up Charlie Keegan. The mood of the gathering was going from bad to worse, and she feared that if she didn't broach the subject now, she wouldn't get another chance.

Hesitantly she began, "Jenny, could I say something before we go on? I hate to insert this here—since this isn't the purpose of the meeting—but I'm afraid . . . that is, I think Charlie Keegan is back."

Renee made an odd, strangled noise. All eyes shifted to her. In her determination to continue, however, Paige persisted, trying to shut the woman's contorted features from her mind. Renee was white, her eyes bulging, her hand clutching her throat. "No!" she moaned. Then, in front of all of them, she wrapped her arms around herself and doubled, as though someone had slugged her in the abdomen.

"Yes," Paige said softly, "Charlie. I know he's not a pleasant subject, but I must bring this up. I think he's back, and I think he killed Jerry and Stacy!"

All four adults in the room stared at her, dumb-founded. Renee shook her head no, then grabbed the sides of her head with her hands. Paige watched in amazement as Renee seemed to shrink before her eyes, turning once more into the drab person she'd been before.

Sliding out of the chair she was sitting in, Renee crawled around behind it. She looked like some wild animal there on the floor. She drew her knees up to her chest, and hugging them, began rocking, bumping her head against the wall and humming tunelessly.

Paige's mouth dropped open. She quickly shut it again. "Renee!" she whispered, keeping her voice low to avoid startling the sleeping child beside her.

Jenny dashed across the room to try to comfort Renee. She looked back in bewilderment at Paul. "What should I do?" she asked him.

Paul picked up both small boys who were still playing at his feet. "Here, take the boys and take them somewhere safe," Paul said, handing them to Jenny. The baby cried and strained back for Paul. "Dada!" he screamed.

Paul smiled at the baby. "I'll take Michael and get him settled."

"Michael?" Paige asked. "Dada?"

Paul shook his head at her. "Later," he mouthed to her. He strode across the room, Jamal on his heels.

Paige moved carefully, trying not to awaken Ashley. "A sight like this would give them nightmares," she whispered to Jamal. He nodded without turning, full attention on the poor creature now writhing on the floor. Renee's dress was hiked up above her knees. To the horrified Paige, the creature looked like a damaged and forgotten rag doll.

Gently easing Ashley full length on the couch, Paige joined the others, to offer what help she could.

Carter leaned back hard in the chair he was sitting in and snorted. "Well, at least when you had your breakdown, Paige, you were more discreet about it," he said loudly.

"Shut up, Carter!" Jamal barked. "I mean it, man! You kick yourself into shape, or I'll do it for you!"

Carter flushed. "Hey, man, sorry." He changed tack immediately, suddenly anxious to win everyone's good opinion. "I'm not a total jerk, I have some sympathy for her."

"Good!" Paige said coldly. "Should I call 911, Jamal? Will she hurt herself this way?"

"No, no!" Renee screamed. "Stop talking about me like I'm a piece of furniture or a stupid child!" Her face was streaming blood where she'd scratched herself with her long fingernails. Then she covered her eyes with her hands and began sobbing.

Chapter 19

The ambulance arrived and the paramedics took Renee away, hands tied to the stretcher to keep her from hurting herself.

After that, the meeting broke down in complete confusion. Jenny's son Jarod, having wandered back into the room to see what was going on, felt the tension and began crying. The uproar woke Ashley. She gazed from her mother to Paul and then to Paige, trying to read in their faces what was going on. White-faced, she crossed the room to stand by her mother and cling to her hand. Paige, agitated by the children's tears, was contrite. "Oh, Jenny, I'm sorry."

Turning to leave the room, one arm around Ashley and the other holding Jarod's hand, Jenny shook her head. "Why are you sorry?" she asked gently, bewilderment on her face.

Paige started wringing her hands. "I feel responsible. I started her off." Paul walked across the room and put one arm around Paige, while she looked anxiously at the others in the room. "I didn't know she would get so upset." She stretched out her hands in supplication, for forgiveness, for understanding.

Carter sneered. "It's just your inimitable charm, Paige."

Paige's face drained of blood, and she wove a little, one hand against the side of her face. Paul tightened his hold on her and led her to the couch. "No fainting, now," he said lightly, trying to conceal his concern.

"You ought to get the kids out of the room, Jenny," he said swiftly. "Maybe we should just shelve the meeting for the time being." She nodded in assent.

Carter, stung by the palpable disapproval in the room, looked a little abashed by his growing unpopularity among the people who had always been his friends. As he stood to leave, he thought, *I wish I were capable of expressing my feelings for these people. Someday it'll be too late, and they'll never know I love them, in my own way.*

Glancing at her brother, Paige was momentarily shocked by his appearance. His skin was paler than usual, purple smudges and tiny lines underscoring the beautiful blue eyes.

"Please call me, Paige," he said softly. "I need to talk to you again before I go."

"Sure, Carter." She watched sadly as he hurried out of the house with a backward wave to the group. She sighed.

Paul tipped his head to one side in a customary gesture, returning her gaze with a quizzical look. Then he said, softly but coolly, "Surely you didn't mean what you said about Charlie?"

Her stomach contracted. "You don't believe me!" It hadn't occurred to her that they wouldn't believe her.

It had taken too much effort for her to get up the nerve to mention Charlie. How could Paul think she wasn't serious?

When Jenny came back from putting the children to bed, Paige was sympathetic. "Poor kids."

"They'll be okay," Jenny said, walking over to put one arm around her. "We'll say our bedtime prayers soon, and they'll go to sleep with their special angels standing guard." She smiled her sweet smile. "Twenty thousand for each kid, you know."

Paige smiled back. Jenny's words sounded so child-like, but sincere. "How comforting to have you for a mother," she whispered, a twinge of envy pinching at the back of her mind.

Paige fell asleep after staring for hours at the darkened ceiling, thinking about what it would have been like to have a mother like Jenny, warm and caring and . . . there. A mother who might have known and protected her from things a child should never have to go through. She slept uneasily, then woke in tears from a dream—her aborted baby was crying for her, "Mommy, Mommy!" And she was crying for it. She had never let herself feel anything for her baby, had never allowed herself the luxury. But now she was mourning the child who would never be. "Oh, God, dear God, it hurts," she moaned. She curled into a ball in the bed, hugging her knees to her chest to control the pain coursing through her.

With a jerk, Paige realized she must look just as Renee had earlier. *Oh, Renee,* she thought with growing conviction, *he got you too, didn't he? I'm not imagining things, and Carter and I are not the only ones.* That certainty both hurt her and comforted her.

She willed herself to try to pray for Renee. "I don't know how to pray," she whispered. "I hope you can make sense out of this, God. But help that poor wretched creature. Please, please, help us all."

With time, she relaxed enough to stretch out in the bed. Then she drifted off to sleep.

Chapter 20

Paige awoke feeling curiously refreshed. She lay in bed a few minutes, enjoying the extra minutes spent luxuriating in her silky cocoon. Finally she hopped up and peeked out behind the drapes, to check on the weather. It was a gray, dismal morning, a stiff wind worrying the trees.

"Yuck!" she said. "There goes my resolve to get out and run." She flipped the edge of the drape back where it belonged and marched to the bathroom, grabbing up her sweats as she went. "No, I will run," she said with determination. "I need it, and I'll do it!"

On her way out the door, she heard the phone ring. She broke stride momentarily, then went on. "Not now. I'm not interested, whoever you are."

It was cold. The wind bit at her nose and ears. It wasn't unbearable, though, just brisk and bracing. She'd get warmed up before she'd finished the first half of the path.

As she ran, Paige kept looking for signs of wildlife

in the park. The elemental strength and power and freedom of wild creatures tugged at her heart. The sun was breaking through and the high-arching Kansas sky broadened and lightened her mood.

She felt her lungs expand. At first the unfamiliar pull hurt, and she realized how much of her life she spent breathing shallowly, anxiously, as if someone might discover she was using up some air and would reprimand her for it.

To her left, she saw a few squirrels foraging for walnuts, and then a small opossum looking for crawdads, she figured, down in the creek. The opossum's head was incredibly ugly, endearingly ugly. But no deer, no egrets. She ended her run and did her stretching exercises at the car, feeling a little cheated. Maybe next time.

When Paige pulled into the porte cochere at the Skycrest, she failed to see the man sitting in a car across the street, watching her. *Ah ha,* he thought, *changing your patterns, huh?* He made a fist with his hamhock hand and pounded the steering wheel. *That will make this a little more complicated, but I'll get you, Paige.*

Armand arrived on Sunday from New York. Paige was early to pick him up at the airport. After such a long separation, she felt mixed feelings about seeing him. She couldn't picture him in a Wichita setting. He just didn't fit. Her hands felt a little clammy, and she wiped them, surreptitiously, on a tissue in her purse. Sweaty palms . . . how unglamorous!

Was Armand going to be in her future? She turned

the large opal ring around and started rubbing the stone as she mused, waiting as the plane taxied down the runway. Perhaps this visit would help decide matters. Could she escape this sordid mess she found herself in, or would she discover she would rather face it head on?

Armand was the first off the plane, strolling from first class, she knew, and he smiled when he saw her. The slim man, of medium height and looking so distinguished with silver hair combed carefully across his forehead, wore a beautifully cut gray suit with a bright white shirt and a burgundy silk tie. His urbanity and fashion sense contrasted with the sweatshirts, denim jackets, and lumpy sweaters that followed him off.

Paige could feel herself beaming as she stepped forward into his arms. "Cherie," he whispered as he kissed her cheek, somewhat absentmindedly, she thought. Paul would have grabbed her and given her a big bear hug, embarrassing the life out of her, she thought. Oddly, she briefly wished Armand could be so warmly uninhibited. *How contrary of me,* she chided herself.

She listened intently, head bent toward the man who was just her own height, as he spoke, in his French-accented English, of the project he was working on. Bloomingdale's was planning a Kansas promotion again—the one in the '80s had been a huge success—and he was in town to work up displays using his imported fabrics at the Symphony Showcase House as well as at the Bar Association ball.

He paused long enough to ask, "How are things going for you, my dear?" And when she replied, "Oh, fine," Armand went on talking about his plans. She felt a momentary jolt of realization of his self-centeredness.

But I knew that, she argued with herself. *That shouldn't surprise me.*

As his voice droned on, her mind wandered. She heard the voices of Jamal and Paul turning Armand into a comedy routine. She smiled at the thought.

Looking at her at that moment, he frowned. "Why the smile? What's funny about a lost load of brocades?" he huffed.

Paige blushed. "Oh, I wasn't smiling about that. Sorry." She put her hand in the crook of his arm. "I'm glad you're here, that's all."

He patted her hand proprietarily, then drew away from her. "Here's the baggage carousel. How competent are these rubes about getting luggage out quickly?"

"They do all right," she said stiffly. His assumption of Wichita's backwardness bothered her.

Armand moved away from her and stepped in front of an elderly lady with a walker. Paige watched him. *He's brash, self-contained, and inconsiderate,* she thought crossly. *He must have been the same in New York—why didn't I notice?*

Soon bags and boxes started their circuit around the carousel. Armand moved aggressively to take his own luggage off before others could get theirs, ending up with five matched pieces of gray Louis Vuitton bags.

For some crazy reason, Jamal and Paul and the routine they'd work up came to mind again, and Paige wanted to laugh. What would they make of this spectacle, of this ostentatious little man with his matching luggage? She felt embarrassed to be in his company. How strange that he seemed so gauche now, when she'd thought of him for so long as debonair.

She tried to shrug off her disappointment. Such odd

things had been happening lately that perhaps her view of things was just temporarily jaundiced. She would put these reactions aside for a while, until she could see Armand in a more normal situation. She just hoped he didn't knock the little old lady on the walker over in his haste to do his thing!

On the way back to town, Armand commented at length on Wichita's hopelessly provincial air. Paige eyed the small shops, the weedy verges along Kellogg, the miles of gaudy billboards, and decided he was right. Then the charming tower of Friends University, the Arkansas River with the three arches of the 2nd Street Bridge reflected in its metallic stream, the Epic Center, the Plaza, and the Kansas State Bank building all came in for a snide comment or two. "This is a *skyline?*" he laughed.

She was getting heartily sick of his patter. "Oh, it's not so bad, Armand," she said testily. "It's a place where people can live and work and propagate. What more do humans need?"

"How about culture and variety and drama?" he answered crossly.

She laughed bitterly. "Oh, there's plenty of drama here." She went on to tell him, a little, about the last few weeks—the murders, her concerns about Carter, about ending therapy, about Renee's breakdown. She didn't mention Charlie, however.

He dismissed the murders with an airy wave of his hand. "Surely that has nothing to with you, Paige, my dear. It sounds so sordid. Murder is an everday occurrence in New York—but it doesn't happen to people like us."

"But that's just it!" she replied hotly. "Jerry and Stacy *were* 'people like us.' I went to school with Jerry, and I was there when Stacy was dedicated at church and for some of her birthday parties over the years. That's what's so frightening."

"You probably just need to get back to work. Didn't you say on the phone there was some big, new account you were working on?"

"Danton Oil, yes." She grimaced. "With all this other brouhaha, I've hardly been able to even think about it! It's so frustrating! And I can't stand Holder Danton."

Armand gave her a searching look. "Now that doesn't sound very professional, Paige. It doesn't matter whether you like the wretched little man or not. Just do your work, and don't get involved with these petty little people."

She nodded, then smiled. "You're right, of course. Work is the best antidote, isn't it?"

He reached over and patted her hand. "Of course."

She did not tell him about the phone calls, however. She was sure he'd give her some smug advice, and that wasn't what she needed.

Armand was staying at the Tallgrass Inn for the three weeks he was to be in town. When the bellhop had taken his luggage out of her trunk, Armand leaned into Paige's car window and kissed her coolly on her cheek. "Once I get settled, *ma petite,* I will call. We will spend much time together, *n'est-ce pas?*" he said softly. His raised eyebrows and one-sided smile promised romantic hours together, she knew. She flushed and smiled back, lowered lashes sweeping the high, lovely cheekbones.

She left him at the Inn and drove home. She was disappointed he'd dismissed her, but she realized she felt relief, too. Why did she feel such conflicting emotions? Why was nothing clear or simple? *I want . . . what? What do I want? Everything—or enough of the right thing, with Paul?*

By the time she reached home, she felt headachy. Her head spun with the thoughts chasing around her skull. Oddly, Chester didn't rush out to hold the door for her. She could see him behind the desk, and he saw her, but he did not come to the door. She fished in her purse for her key to the big door.

When she entered the lobby of the Skycrest, she froze. Who was that standing at the central desk? With a start, she realized it was Holder Danton leaning across the counter and talking comfortably with Chester. The turquoise western suit he was wearing stretched lumpily across his wide shoulders and bulging ribs.

She shuddered. *He certainly has crummy taste, other than the Lexus, of course,* she thought.

"Why, Paige," he drawled when he caught sight of her, "I hear from Chester that we are now neighbors."

"Neighbors?" she repeated dumbly. She looked, bewildered, at the old man standing there, grinning foolishly.

"Yep, Mr. Danton here has bought the vacant apartment on the ninth floor," Chester said proudly. "He says you and him are working together. Now isn't that nice?"

She felt her heart drop. Nice? *Of course it isn't nice!*

she wanted to snap, but instead she answered coolly, "Well, yes, it is. Welcome to the Skycrest, Holder." She realized her face felt frozen, the smile wooden. Would he realize how hard she had to work to fake mere pleasantness?

He was grinning, watching her closely. She straightened and returned his gaze. *He knows I don't like him, but we'll both be too genteel to mention it,* she told herself bitterly.

"We'll get to know each other real well, won't we?" he said, continuing to grin.

She didn't reply. She asked for her mail abruptly. Then, with a curt good-bye to Holder, she said to Chester, "I see you're busy . . . I'll use the self-service elevator."

"Oh, I'll run you up, Ms. Brookings!" he protested, but she was striding down the hall by the time he rounded the corner of the desk.

Holder Danton in my building! she fumed. *First I have to work with him, and now I have to live with him!* She scowled and punched the button for her floor, hard. She clenched her fists. *No fraternizing, though, Holder, none at all. So don't get any big ideas.*

Chapter 21

Paige fixed a simple dinner—broiled chicken breast with garlic and lemon, a small salad, and a croissant she'd picked up at Bagatelle on the way home. While the chicken was cooking, she changed quickly.

She removed the contents of her slim leather portfolio onto her desk. She needed to do a little work, since she'd neglected it for so long. A memo fell out of the briefcase that she couldn't remember having put in there. She picked up the small buff-colored piece of paper and stared at it.

There was no logo, nor did she recognize the handwriting. The scrawled words said, "Remember Beau." She blanched and dropped the memo. It fluttered to the floor and under the front of the couch. She heard herself whimper and hated it—the feeling of being the victim of this amorphous torture, perpetrated by some faceless tormentor. She wanted to scream, to howl at the heavens for surfeit, for release, for an end to this madness.

Dropping to her knees, Paige stuck her hand under the front of the couch, trying to reach the note that had landed there. A loose staple tacking the upholstery to the underside of the couch scratched the back of her hand and she jerked it out and saw the blood welling on the long scratch.

Tears started from her eyes as she sat back on her heels and stared at the blood. Hysteria rose in her, and she knew that if she didn't regain control of herself soon, she'd start screaming. She swallowed hard to quell the sobs in her throat. It was time to do something about her tormentor, but what?

The blood was congealing on her hand. She got up and went to the bathroom to wash it off and apply a germicide. It didn't look so bad now, with the blood washed off. Still, the thought of Beau sickened her. She realized she was shaking. Tell Jamal, or Paul? Tell them what? It wasn't really a threat, was it?

She walked slowly, tentatively, back to the kitchen. She removed the cooked chicken breast and looked at it. It would make her vomit if she ate it. She couldn't eat now.

She suddenly saw an image of herself as fragile, weak, limp. She couldn't bear the thought of herself becoming a recluse, lying curled on her bed, unable to plan or move, spending hours in fear and helplessness. *I won't turn into an invalid, I won't! If I don't eat, I won't be able to fight him. I won't give up!* She clenched her teeth and brought one hand, doubled into a fist, up to her chin.

Resolve hardened, she made herself eat most of the food she'd prepared. She tore some of the meat off the chicken breast and fed it to the cat. He chewed at it savagely, growling to warn off any possible predators to his food. She smiled at him. "That's the way, Marmalade—let's be tigers!"

After cleaning away the remains of her dinner and changing the cat's litter box, she put on her exercise clothes. She then put Marmalade's harness on him, picked up a towel, and headed down to the basement. Holding him close, one hand tight on his harness so he couldn't wriggle away, she took the service elevator at the back of the building, to avoid running into anyone. She just couldn't make light conversation tonight.

Marmalade was talkative enough for her. He yowled and squirmed the entire ride to the basement. He was a cat of mixed emotions, so she felt they suited each other. He hated the ride in the elevator, but he loved being allowed to roam loose throughout the basement while she worked out. He gave one heart-wrenching yowl just as the elevator stopped at the bottom floor. "Oh, hush," she said crossly, "you'll wake the dead. I didn't get that Siamese at the pet shop, if you'll recall, Mr. Marmalade, because I did not want a vocal cat!"

He ignored her, leaping from her arms the minute the door opened. He darted here and there, smelling in the corners for interesting things to be discovered. There were no mice allowed in the Skycrest, so he never found anything interesting.

Paige turned on the radio in the corner of the room and began warming up. It didn't take long for the adrenaline the memo had started pumping through her veins, to be dispersed with the physical effort she was exerting. After about twenty minutes, she began to feel the stress drain away and a pleasant ache fill her muscles as she upped her bench presses.

Marmalade had returned from his explorations and

was now stretched on his back on the pool table. She had registered his return at the edge of her mind, but she really wasn't paying him much attention.

Suddenly the cat rolled over. He lay sphinx-like, paws in front, body stretched flat on the table, head alert and ears pricked forward. Hair stiffened along the ridge of his back. Then he hunched his body together, lowered his head, flattened his ears, and growled. Paige grew alarmed. She stiffened and turned to follow the cat's gaze, to a patch of shadows behind the door, which stood open perhaps twenty feet away from the bench press.

He leapt down from the table and began to stalk whatever he had heard and seen there. Paige shivered as the sweat cooled on her back. She struggled, as noiselessly as she could, to get to her feet, to prepare to run, surprised at the shaking in her legs.

She sidled over to turn the radio off. When the sound died, she strained to listen. At first nothing, then the squeal of metal against metal. She heard a faint click, then the room fell dark. She let out a scream when the lights went off, then smothered it quickly. She wouldn't give whoever was there any bearings on where she was.

She moved quietly, purposefully, around the room, to keep the Nautilus equipment between her and the door. She waited to allow her eyes to adjust to the dark, but she realized with alarm that no light at all penetrated into the black cavern of the room.

Soft footfalls strode to the door, then stopped. Marmalade hissed, then was silent. Paige covered her trembling mouth with one hand. She felt the cold concrete wall behind her back—there was no way to retreat. She wanted to find a hole to climb in, to stay in forever.

Eyes wide with terror, she watched as the person at the door flicked on a huge flashlight and played it briefly around the room. Its bright circle did not find her. She crouched behind the large exercise bike and tried to scoot, duck-like, over to the pool table. *He'll find me. I'm trapped!*

She knew it had to be Charlie, but how could he have gotten in? The security in the Skycrest was so strict that someone who lived here had to give permission for any stranger to enter. Who knew Charlie? Who could have let him in?

She doubled over in pain and terror. The man was venturing into the room, taking small, shuffling steps. Terror forced her blood into her ears, and she heard its rushing, like a torrent about to drown her. She whimpered and immediately hated herself for it.

Her stalker chuckled. He continued his slow progress into the heart of the room, ever closer to where she crouched, hidden, under the table.

Marmalade yowled. She couldn't see where he was, but she could hear his claws skittering on some hard surface across the room. She knew he had jumped up on some object—what she didn't know—and was trying to gain purchase. Discordant music tinkled. The piano! He had jumped onto the piano. She felt relief. At least he was out of this monster's way and wouldn't be injured.

The flashlight glared into her eyes, blinding her. The man was at the other side of the table, squatting to get on her level. She had to make an attempt to get away. She straightened quickly and nearly stumbled, her muscles and joints stiff from having crouched so long. She put her hands out to catch herself and fell forward against the bike, cracking her chin on the handlebar.

The man stood then and sought her out again in the beam of his light, then turned it off. She knew she had to keep trying to get away, she had to! Running her hands over the bike to get its shape in mind, she knelt quickly and started to scramble away on all fours. He could see her in the brief spurts of light from the flash, toying with her, increasing her panic. She knew it was hopeless, that she could not escape him. It seemed to her that he was dragging it all out, playing with her like a cat with a wounded mouse. She wanted to scream, to bite and kick.

As she progressed across the room, Paige put one hand on a barbell. A weapon! She crawled quickly behind the rack of weights and ran her hands over them until she found one of about fifteen pounds. It was light enough to wield easily, heavy enough to inflict some damage. She stopped to wait for him.

She knew her plan would fail if he turned the flashlight on again in the next few moments. *Please, God,* she prayed fervently, *please don't let him use the flashlight!*

She heard his approach. He wasn't trying to be quiet. She hefted the weight in one hand, eager to use it. He was perhaps now only five feet away.

She shifted to get a firm footing. Now he was closer, almost striking distance. Her breath quickened and her heart raced. Her hands itched to get at him. She could hardly wait to hurt him—the man who had hurt her and Jerry and Stacy and Julie, Renee and Carter, too. It had to be Charlie!

He lunged and grabbed for her neck, dropping the flashlight as he did so. He knocked her backwards, but she kept a tight grip on the weight. When he was close enough that she could feel his breath on her face, she struck. She hit him in the side of the head as hard as she could from the awkward position she was in, with his body so close and his hands on her, and he gasped. She struck out at him again, this time in the chest, and felt his hands loosen their grip on her neck. Then he pulled away and ran out the open door.

Softly, Paige called Marmalade to her. She could hear him meowing from across the room. "I wish I could see in the dark like you," she said into the cat's neck when she'd picked him up and comforted him. She knew she had him to thank for the advance warning of the attacker's presence.

She made her way carefully out of the room and to the elevator. After she pushed the up button, she gingerly felt her throat where the man's hands had grabbed her. She felt bruised from the force of his attack, but she was sure there was no injury. She knew she should only feel fear, but she felt pride, confident she had inflicted more damage on him than he had on her.

When she got to the first floor, she exited the elevator cautiously. She had to find out if anyone else had preceded her. She didn't want the young man on duty in the lobby to know what had happened, so she held the cat close to hide any marks there might be on her neck. She stopped to tell him that she thought the breakers had been tripped in the basement. She had to solve this problem herself, so, in an attempt to be casual, she said, "Did anyone come up from the basement just now?" Her voice cracked a little, but she hoped he wouldn't notice.

"No, no one," he replied, but didn't seem particularly curious as to why she was asking.

Fine with her. She could not, would not tell him

about the attack. It had to have been Charlie. But she needed to be able to prove it before she accused him.

She had to gather more evidence first. Then she'd take it to the police. For now, though, she'd handle the situation herself.

The question was, how?

Chapter 22

C arter awoke in a muzzy cloud of pain and despondency. The small leather-encased alarm clock by his bed read 5:45. "In the *morning*," he groaned. He looked around his room and swore. The place stank—he'd been sick again in the night and hadn't felt up to cleaning up after himself. The stench of illness overlay the stink of stale smoke and dregs of liquor in dirty glasses. He knew Maizie's Maids would quit for sure. Maizie herself said last time that her "girls" just weren't interested in coping with his apartment anymore.

"Oh, God!" he wailed as he tried to stand. He clutched his head and swayed a little. Nausea rose in his throat. He thought of Paige, and fury swelled in his fevered brain. *She's going to abandon me,* he thought, panicked. *She's playing a game of new innocence these days, and she's going to decide she's too good for ol' Carter.*

He made his way to the bathroom as quickly as he could. His feet and legs hurt, like he was walking on razor blades and broken glass. He made it into the bath just as the nausea overwhelmed him and he vomited bloodstained bile into the commode. There was nothing left in his stomach to heave up.

He fell on the floor then, writhing in pain. There were a million flames, all the fires of hell, in his stomach. Oh, the pain! He lay on the cold tile floor a few minutes to wait for it to pass. Cold sweat stood out on his forehead and upper lip. He started to chill, lying there in wet, stained navy pajama bottoms.

He reached up for a towel from the closest towel rod and wrapped it around himself. *The fat, fluffy maroon towel went so well with his navy pajamas,* he thought, *but who gave a darn anymore?*

When the spasms passed, he dragged himself to his feet, straining muscles, gritting his perfect white teeth. Once he was up, he caught a glimpse of himself in the mirror. If he hadn't felt so rotten, he would have howled at the sight of beautiful Carter looking so bad. Kaposi's sarcoma lesions were beginning to appear on the flawless face. He gingerly touched one lesion under his left eye and another inside his nose. He wanted to cry. His face really was his fortune, even if that was a cliché. For him, though, it was the literal truth. He had to get better, fast, so he could get to Littman before it was too late. He had to.

"I've got to call someone, now," he said aloud, his words echoing in the cold tiled bath. "I need help. Paige, Paige," he cried, "why do you have to be such a loss?" He dragged himself into his bedroom, past the tumbled, filthy bed and the piles of designer clothes all over the floor and the furniture. "This place looks like a sty." He reached for the phone. "I'll call Reilly. He's not worth much, but at least he won't sneer at me or pity me. He's lower on the scale of human worms than I am, and that's a point in the wretch's favor."

When Reilly answered with a curt "H'lo," Carter told him he was sick and needed help. Reilly breathed into the phone from his end and didn't answer. "Look, Reilly, I know I probably woke you, but I'm in a bad way, man," Carter said, trying to keep a whining tone out of his voice. "I'm so sick, someone ought to take me out to the back forty and shoot me."

Reilly chuckled. "At this time of day, I'd love to." He then asked, "Why can't your hotsy-totsy mother or sister help you?"

"Good grief, man, I can't let them see me like this!" Carter replied quickly. Sweat poured down his face at the thought, and he rubbed one hand across his eyes. His mother would turn up her nose at him—she hated anything that wasn't perfect or pretty. "I look like death, or worse, and they'd stick me in the hospital or something. I can't go in until we take care of Charlie, man."

"Yeah, yeah. Okay, I'll come, you jerk," he answered, ringing off.

Carter was trembling when he hung up. The small amount of effort it took to get to and from the bathroom and to make the phone call had taken more energy than he had left. He fell across the bed, one arm flung across his eyes. His breath came in short gasps as he lay there. *I've got to get in there and get myself cleaned up a little bit before he gets here. I'm in too disgusting a state for even Reilly to see,* he thought. He couldn't move, however, and he drifted off into a pain-ridden agony of sleep, only to be jarred awake by the doorbell some thirty minutes later.

Reilly leaned on the buzzer for probably ten minutes

before Carter could make it to the door. "First you call me," Reilly stormed, "then you don't let me in. I don't have time for these donkey games." His face was contorted in rage.

As he approached, greasy face thrust forward, Carter could smell his unwashed hair. It made his stomach turn, and he grimaced.

Reilly noticed and bridled. "You don't think much of me, pal, but I might be all you got left."

Carter held up one hand, nodding his head. "I know, I know. Please, Reilly," he begged, "cut me a little bit of slack here, man. I'm dyin'."

Reilly looked at the emaciated, green-hued man cowering in front of him and knew the words he spoke were the literal truth. "You don't look too good, that's for sure."

Carter almost smiled. "That's an understatement." He gestured around the filthy apartment. "You gotta help me get the place cleaned up, and me too," he added as an afterthought. "I'm too weak to move." As if to support his statement, he swayed drunkenly, holding onto the door to remain upright.

"I don't clean my own place. Why should I clean yours?" Reilly sneered.

Carter nodded, eyes closed. "I know I'm asking a lot, Reilly, but I've got to have your help . . . to get Charlie so I can leave town for good."

"You're not leaving me holding the bag, man!" Reilly replied, threatening, his face again pushed into Carter's. Carter shook his head. "You know I'll pay you well. There's not much time," he said with urgency. "Paige . . . it might soon be too late to help her, Reilly."

He swayed. He knew he'd pass out soon. "I gotta get in bed. Please!" he begged.

"Oh, awright!" Reilly stuck his head, hair standing in greasy spikes all around his crown, into the bathroom. It looked like he hadn't even combed it when he got out of bed this morning, Carter thought. *And I expect this pig pen to help me clean up? What am I reduced to?*

"Jeez, man, this is disgusting! You got a shovel and a hose?"

Carter slipped into bed, saying as he slid down into oblivion, "Thanks."

✦ ✦ ✦

Paige looked out the window to check on the weather. In spite of her experience the night before in the basement, she refused to be made a prisoner. She intended to go to the park to run. Rain and a stiff northerly wind drove sodden leaves across the walk eight floors below. Her face fell, and she considered, briefly, giving up her resolve.

She straightened her shoulders. *If Charlie can't keep me in, then a bit of bad weather won't either,* she told herself. The decision made, she felt pounds lighter, freed of the chains of safety, even if only for a few minutes' run in the park.

She dressed and ate a piece of dry toast, then glanced at the clock. *I'm running a little late. I'll probably be late for work.*

The phone rang. She crossed the room purposefully. Just as she reached down to pick up the receiver, she realized how odd it was that she was doing this so willingly. Just a few days' healing and she could answer the phone like other people.

"Paige," the voice whispered. "I'm ready for you."

She gripped the receiver hard. "Who are you? What do you want?" She gritted her teeth.

"Soon, now, Paige . . . you'll join Jerry and Stacy . . ."—here the disguised voice broke, as though the man, unbelievably, were close to tears!—"in a better place. I'll help you along, out of this hellhole people call life . . . soon." Whoever it was replaced the receiver softly.

Paige began shaking. "You rat! You rotten excuse for humanity! I hate you." She sat on the ivory couch next to the phone and lowered her head and closed her eyes, fists clenched on her knees. "It's got to be Charlie, I know it is. Where is he?"

She rose slowly from the couch, like an old woman. As if in a dream, she wandered back to her room and changed out of her jogging clothes. She stood in front of her closet, staring at the neat rows of clothes and shoes ranged before her. *What does one wear to an execution?* she asked herself. *One's own execution, at that?*

The phone rang again. Tears sprang into her eyes. *What? What do you want?* she cried inwardly. She approached the bedside phone slowly. It continued to ring. "Hello?" she whispered.

"Paige? Did I wake you?" It was Paul. His bright tones filled her head.

"Paul?" Tears ran down her face.

"Paige, are you awake?"

How odd for him to be so cheerful. Didn't he know she was going to die? "I'm awake," she answered flatly.

"Did Armand's plane get in all right?"

Armand who? she thought. She realized that she had completely dismissed the man from her mind, for keeps. She sat on the edge of the bed. "Paul, I just can't take it anymore."

Paul's face, at the other end of the line, blanched. *Have I blown it?* he thought. His stomach dropped twenty floors, he felt, in his utter disappointment. *Have I lost her? Is it too late now, for good?*

But Paige surprised him by saying, "Please come over, Paul. And can you bring Jamal?" Realizing he was probably at work, she corrected herself, "No, not Jamal. He's surely gone for the day by now."

✠ ✠ ✠

On the way over to Paige's apartment, Paul thought about Renee. He'd called the hospital to find out about her condition and had learned that she was sedated and couldn't have visitors. "Thank the good Lord, Michael is safe at Jenny's," he said to his reflection in the mirror. What a thing for those kids to go through.

Jenny had assured him that the whole scene would fade to nothing with time, like a scene in a movie that was over their heads. He wasn't so sure, but she'd sounded confident.

He'd go see Renee later, one way or another.

When he reached Paige's apartment, jubilant to be asked to help, but mystified as to the reason, he learned she had already called the office to pass on a message to Hal that she wouldn't make it in today. Hal had called back a few minutes later to try to order her to work. "You're risking this account with Danton Oil, Paige!" he stormed at her. "He keeps calling to ask when you'll be in touch with him. I can't promise your position will still be here if you don't get busy and secure that account!"

Hal had never before yelled at her or ordered her around. She was too tired to be offended, though. "I'm sorry, Hal," she said softly. "I just can't function yet. I have family problems to take care of." They weren't really family problems, and she wasn't used to lying, but this was a special situation.

When Paul entered her apartment, she gave him one long agonized look, then walked into his out-stretched arms. He buried his face in her hair, smelling hints of vanilla and gardenia.

"Help me," she whispered.

He held her at arm's length to look into her face, that beautiful face he'd loved so long. "Tell me. What?"

"It's Charlie—I just know he's back and after me. When I mentioned him the other night, you doubted me, but I know it's true."

He pulled back and stared at her. "Charlie?" he said at last, very quietly. "How can that be, Paige? He's been gone for years."

"Don't look at me like that, Paul, like you think I'm crazy! I'm not crazy! He's around, has been for months." She walked away from him, approached the couch and sat down. She ran her fingers over the cording on the upholstery. "I've been getting phone calls since spring. And I'm sure—or at least I think—he stalked me once in the parking garage at Abe's office." She looked back at him, tears filling her eyes. "Last night someone tried to attack me in the basement here. And he killed Jerry and Stacy, I just know it!"

He strode across the room and sat beside her. He

gently put his arms around her, pain and compassion crumpling his face. "What attack?"

She told him briefly about her experiences the night before.

"Did you see a doctor or call the cops?"

She shook her head no.

"Why haven't you mentioned all this before? You could have been killed! You could still be in danger. . . ."

"I've just felt I couldn't talk about it. I just couldn't. For a long time, I almost thought I was imagining things, you know, like my hallucinations that I'd killed him."

"What hallucinations?" Paul asked. "I haven't heard of any hallucinations!"

Paige bowed her head and covered her eyes, then straightened again. "That's why I came back from New York, that's why I was doing drugs and why I had my . . . breakdown. I dreamed—even when I was awake—that I'd killed a man, but I couldn't see who it was." She turned away to fidget with a small vase on the end table. "Now I know it was wishful thinking, that it was Charlie I wanted to kill," she whispered.

He reached for her hand and squeezed it. "Paige, I'm so sorry." It pained him to think how burdened she was.

"He molested me, you know, and I think Carter too." She hid her face with one hand. "And I don't know who else."

Paul swallowed. He was afraid to speak, for fear she'd hide from him again. But if he didn't speak up, perhaps she would consider him callous. He kept silent for a moment, then said quietly, "Paige, I wish I could carry this for you."

She shook her head.

Paul took her in his arms and held her for several minutes. After a long pause, she lifted her head and ran her hand up over her face to drag back the heavy hair that covered it.

"I love you, Paige. You know, don't you, that what he did doesn't change that?"

Still, she didn't speak. She began twisting the opal ring around her finger, twisting and twisting. He lay one hand gently over hers, holding them until their restless motion ceased. She lay her head back against his shoulder, and he could feel her relax. He gathered her close, praying to his Lord, *Dear God in Heaven, help me help her, I beg of you!* Would continuing to talk about it help her? How could he encourage her to open up more?

"The videos!" Paul said, the memory flooding over him. "That's why he always wanted us with him and why he was always giving us things. He was making pornographic movies, wasn't he?"

She nodded, head down. She felt so tainted and damaged, embarrassed with Paul here next to her. *He* hadn't been molested, obviously, so why had she and Carter?

"And probably Renee too," she added aloud.

"You're right! Probably Renee too!" He turned to her and gently pulled her face around so she would look at him. He could see that the strong Paige was back in control. He could encourage her to take action. "That's why she flipped out the other night! You have to go talk to her, Paige."

"But why?" Paige drew back in horror. "You saw

what happened when I mentioned Charlie. I couldn't run the risk of pushing her over the edge again."

"No, no, Paige, don't you see? She's in the hospital where she can get medical help if she needs it."

"But it seems so cruel, Paul."

" 'You shall know the truth, and the truth shall make you free,' " he quoted softly. "Paige, you have to help her see the truth."

She stared at him, then repeated, " 'The truth will make you free.' " Tears began rolling down her face. "That's what *I* want, to be free of this fear and hate and filth, Paul. That's what I want. You don't know how much like damaged merchandise the hands of a Charlie Keegan can make you feel."

"Tell me, Paige. Why did you run away that year in high school?"

She stood and started pacing. "Oh, Paul, it's so dirty. I don't want to burden you with any more of it."

"If you lived through it, I can stand to hear about it."

Wringing her hands and looking at him from time to time, she paced like a caged lion. "I left to have . . . an abortion."

He nodded. "I'd heard that, but didn't know whether to believe it."

"He . . ." She paused, unable to go on. Paul stood and took her into his arms. "He raped me. Then my mother turned on me, assumed I'd been fooling around. She wouldn't listen, didn't care." She started crying, the sobs racking her body.

He led her over to the couch and gently lowered her, keeping his arms around her. His heart ached for her. Such pain!

"Then she sent me off to North Carolina to have an abortion. My dad has a beach house on the Outer Banks where she could hide me for a while. I was so furious at the way she was treating me, never listening to my feelings about it, that I refused to come back when she beckoned. I sat in that beach house and fumed. I planned all kinds of ways to kill them all." She turned her face away from him. "She made me kill my baby. It was a real baby, not some hunk of tissue! I'd go down to the beach—it was off season so no one was there— and march up and down and scream. I was a murderer too! How could God ever forgive me?"

"Oh, Paige." So young to be so alone.

"I dream about that baby at times. What if . . . what if the abortion ruined my chances to ever have another child? You have to consider that, Paul. I saw the hunger in your eyes for those children at Jenny's. What if you married me, and I couldn't bear you a child?"

"I'd still want you. Yes, I want children, our children, but if we can't have any, we'll . . . adopt or something."

She melted into his arms, the stiffness draining away. "Oh, Paul, you're so good to me. You're unbelievable, really a saint."

"Whoa! Do you mean a saint in the biblical sense— a believer? Or a saint as in a person ready to be led off to the slaughter? I'm not interested in being beheaded or burned at the stake or . . ." He straightened, and a teasing smile crossed his lips. "Maybe Renee will give me her little boy."

"What . . . what are you saying?"

He filled her in on Michael's story.

"So that's why he called you Daddy."

"He's such a cute kid, but I can't raise him for her."

"Why not?"

"Well, I'm just an acquaintance, not family or a parent. What do I know about raising a kid?"

"What does Renee know?"

He snorted. "Not much. Okay, okay, you've made your point. At least he's safe at Jenny's for now." He went on to tell her about Renee's excuse for his being so scrawny. "The kid I fed supper and then breakfast to was no picky eater."

"She felt paralyzed," Paige said. "I know just how she must have felt, so helpless, so hopeless." Her eyes were soft and luminous, her face relaxed now.

He held her and kissed her tenderly, on her eyelids, around her hairline, on her lips. "I'm sorry, Paige. I love you, and I'll stand by you through whatever it takes."

She nodded. "Let's go see Renee now." She glanced at the clock. "Oh, Paul, look at the time! Don't you have class today?"

"No, the semester's over. But oh, shoot, I do have a department meeting." He picked up the phone and began to dial. "I'll call Judy and tell her I can't come."

"No, Paul," she said firmly, depressing the hook on the phone to disconnect the call. "This is something I can do myself."

"But I said I'd help you with this." He tried to lift her fingers off the hook.

She took the receiver from him and smiled gently. "I have to do it alone. It's like exorcising a ghost."

He put his hands on her shoulders and gave her a slight shake. Looking her in the eye, he said, "Paige,

I've told you before that it's your strength I love—among other things, of course." He smiled wryly. "So I guess I'll have to let you function on your own." He hesitated, thinking what was at stake. He then stepped closer and put his arms around her again. "But don't take any chances, Paige," he whispered into her hair. "This is life and death."

"It always has been, Paul. Where Charlie is concerned, it always has been." She took his hand and led him to the door. Plucking her ivory cape from the coat-rack by the door, she said through a sweet smile, "I *will* let you walk me to my car, though. That's the thing that spooks me the most these days."

As they descended in the elevator, Paige turned to Paul. "Do you think we should involve Jamal in this? I keep wondering," she said sardonically, "what I would do with Charlie if I caught him. Maybe it's time for me to admit it's a matter for the police."

"I'll call Jamal after the meeting. Then I'll come to the hospital to be with you. Can you wait until I get there to talk to Renee?"

"I don't know. They may not let me in at all."

He nodded. That was certainly true. "Come with me to campus now. Then we'll go together later," he suggested eagerly.

"No, Paul. I'm a big girl. I'll manage." She tried to soften her words with a smile, but he still wore an injured look.

At her car he kissed her, and she returned his kiss with passion and warmth. "I love you, Paige," he said.

She smiled broadly. "I know. And I'm glad." She gave his hand a squeeze. "I'm glad you haven't given up on me yet. Hang on just a little while longer, okay?"

"To my dying day."

With his choice of words, she grimaced. "Don't say that," she whispered. "No dying for us, for either of us, not yet anyway."

Chapter 23

Charlie watched from his car as Paul helped Paige into her BMW and witnessed the tender kiss they exchanged. He was parked across Douglas in front of the Emporium where a big stuffed gorilla, dressed in a Santa Claus suit for the season, swung on a swing in front of the magic supplies store and smiled his idiotic smile.

Paige drove off, with Paul close behind. They never noticed the man sitting in the car.

Charlie gritted his teeth and punched the steering wheel with his fist, hard. His frustrations were mounting. Things had been going so smoothly for him. He'd gotten her in a state of near panic, he was sure. He'd covered his tracks well and made his plans for an airtight alibi—so now why did things keep getting in the way so he couldn't actually get the job done? A cold fury rose in his head, then turned white hot.

He thought back to that day when he was eight. He'd wet the bed again, and his mother had beaten him with an extension cord, then thrown his clothes out in back with the sodden sheets.

He couldn't go to school. He didn't have any decent clothes. He sat hunched on the front porch and watched his classmates pass on the way to school.

They'd laughed and chatted as they passed his house. He was sure they were laughing at him. The worst was when Mary Ray walked by. Mary was the class beauty—long blonde hair and big blue eyes—his first love, from the first day of kindergarten when he first laid eyes on her, until that day. She laughed the most.

No one came to help him.

Did Mary Ray make sure everyone at school knew about what had happened? He could see her taking others aside and telling them and laughing. He never forgave his mother or pretty Mary Ray.

Charlie came back to the present with a jerk. A cop was stopped at the light, sitting in the lane next to where he was parked and giving him a funny look. Quickly he started the car and pulled out into the lane once it was clear.

Now that he'd missed his chance, he didn't know where to go. *I guess I'll go on to the office. I'd better stop for coffee first, though, so I can get a grip on myself,* he thought. *Tonight, surely tonight. I'll get her to go down to the basement exercise room again. It will be dark and empty.*

✦ ✦ ✦

Paige was ready to confront Renee with the facts about Charlie, even though she had balked at the idea when Paul had first suggested it. Renee would have to face the truth, just as she had to. *It's better that way, I know it is,* she said to convince herself she was on the right course.

A starched nurse presided over the desk on the fifth floor. Somehow Paige supposed the nurse wouldn't let her visit Renee, so she sat in the waiting room for a few minutes to make a plan. She didn't even know what room Renee was in!

She remembered then that the last four digits of each patient's phone number corresponded to the room number. She slipped off to the house phone bank and dialed the hospital operator. It was room 4238—easy enough to find.

She watched as an elderly gentleman came down the hall from the elevators and approached the desk where the nurse sat. He flipped the nurse a wave of his hand and walked on down the hall. Paige felt a wave of relief. See how easy things were for people with no ulterior motives? If she didn't feel so guilty all the time, she wouldn't be standing here making a mountain out of a molehill! She could just go merrily on her way and visit her old friend who just happened to be in the hospital!

She passed the nurse with a sidelong glance, but the nurse didn't even look up.

When Paige got to Renee's room, she saw a pastel patterned curtain pulled around the far bed. The nearer bed was empty, all made up with tight hospital corners, waiting for the next sufferer. The cool white bed looked chilly and hard to Paige, and she involuntarily shivered. She paused at the edge of the curtain, to gather her resolve before she could bring herself to go in and face Renee. *I precipitated this psychotic episode!* she reminded herself. *How can I face her? What if she wigs out again?*

She heard Paul's voice ringing in her head: "The truth shall make you free!" She took a deep breath and stepped forward to pull aside the curtain.

Renee was lying curled on one side, one hand under her head. Her eyes were open, staring out the window at the many-leveled roofs of the hospital. Tears traced a watery path down her cheeks. Stringy hair was matted and twisted on the back of her head where she had lain on it. The grief on her face caused Paige to hesitate. *Can I face this?*

"Renee?" she called softly.

Renee's head jerked around and she scowled. "Oh, it's you," she said with a world-weary sigh. The tears dried up, but the pain in her face deepened. Her eyes slid back to the window.

Paige's hand came up to cover her mouth. She wanted to cry, seeing that face. To think that that person was once a child, a happy, laughing child—like Jenny's Ashley—and now to see the illness in her mind written on her face. It hurt to see it, to think of what Renee had been through. An ice goddess wouldn't feel this pain, she thought. But then, an ice goddess couldn't try to heal some of it, either.

"Renee, I . . . I hope I'm not intruding," she began. "I just wanted to come see you and to tell you I'm sorry, for everything."

Renee didn't look at her or respond.

"I think . . . I believe," she corrected herself, "that Charlie Keegan must have . . . molested you. . . ." At that, Renee started, then curled into a tighter curve, arms protecting her abdomen. Paige stepped around the bed and knelt by Renee's head. She reached out, tentatively, to smooth her hair. "I'm sorry, I know you don't want to hear this . . . I didn't, either. But we have to face it. Together. I'll stand with you."

Renee covered her head with both hands, pulling herself into a ball. A low sob escaped her lips.

Paige's mouth started trembling, and she began to cry herself. How could she add to this person's pain?

But I have to, she shouted in her head. *It's like the surgeon's knife, to cut away the cancer.* "Oh, please listen, Renee!" she cried. "He molested me too."

At those words, Renee seemed to relax slightly, then froze. Paige saw Renee's eyes dart toward her face, listening. "Yes, he messed me up too, and Carter, and I don't know who else. He must have abused lots of kids."

Paige put her hand firmly on Renee's shoulder. "And I think he's back. I think he killed Jerry and Stacy," she added, repeating the words she had spoken at Jenny's the other night.

"No," Renee moaned, covering her ears and twisting away from Paige's hand, "no!"

"Please, Renee," Paige begged, on her knees, hands held out in supplication. "Listen to me. It wasn't your fault—don't hold it all in like this. It was him, it wasn't you."

An odd childlike voice, coming from Renee's lips, lisped, "But he said it was me . . . that I made him do it. It was something about me. He said so."

"No, Renee!" Paige contradicted. "It was him, it was all him. You were a child, he was the adult! It was his responsibility!"

Tears coursed down Renee's face. She started shaking her head back and forth, denying what Paige was saying, what she had wanted to hear for years.

Paige continued to kneel by the girl, not knowing

what to do. She wanted to take her in her arms and comfort her, but she feared Renee would reject her, wouldn't welcome the physical contact.

Then, to Paige's horror, Renee started screaming, her hands pressed hard over her ears.

At that point the starched nurse rushed into the room, scowl and tart words at the ready. "What are you doing in here, and what are you doing to this patient?" she snapped, a drill sergeant wolf in Nightingale's clothing.

Paige stood abruptly, hands pulled back away from the screaming girl. "I . . . I came to visit her. I'm sorry." She backed away another step from the bed, stumbling a little over the bedside table leg in her way.

"You'll have to leave, right now," the nurse ordered.

Paige nodded dumbly and left the room, shaken by the spectacle of Renee screaming there in the bed. She felt sick to her stomach, but the feeling that she'd done the right thing resurfaced.

I need to talk to Paul, she thought, as she waited, trembling, for the elevator to remove her from that horror scene.

Chapter 24

Charlie Keegan walked into Danton Oil's office suite in the Epic Center. He tugged his jacket over his expanding waistline, and then smoothed his thinning, reddish-brown hair.

"Oh, Mr. Danton," the blonde receptionist said, "you're supposed to call Hal Fitzpatrick at the ad agency. He said he wanted to touch base with you."

Charlie—Holder Danton—said something like "hrumph," then corrected himself, smiled broadly at her and said charmingly, "Why, thank you, honey chile. I'll have you ring him up in a few minutes."

He went into his inner office, closing the door carefully behind him. Then he walked over to his desk and unlocked the top right-hand drawer. He ran his hands over the tattered diary, pages torn out and burned, that had belonged to Stacy.

He thought briefly of Stacy—the blonde pigtails, the teeth in braces, the long, coltish legs—like Paige's when she was that age. He'd loved Stacy, really loved her, his only grandchild. He shuddered and ran one hand over his face. Why did these people he loved put him in these situations? Females all—you couldn't trust them, no matter how much you loved them.

I had to kill Stacy because she told about my . . . affections for her in her diary. I had to kill Jerry because he knew about the plastic surgery and my reincarnation as Holder Danton, successful oil man. Jerry—always such a loser—but he turned out pretty well, a success himself, like me, and then so kind to his old dad when I returned last summer to Wichita. But he'd never tolerate me touching Stacy in that way. He'd have killed me.

And now Paige . . . she knows who I am. When she looks at me, I can see that she recognizes me. She'll tell, and she'll ruin me. Tonight I'll remove her too. He thought briefly about how he would kill her. He wanted her to face him and say his name, and then he'd strangle her. His hands and gut itched at the thought. He'd enjoy this one too, even though he had loved her, he really had. But did she love him back? No, she scorned him, just like Mary Ray, just like his mother.

Why did she have to be so cruel to me? he cried.

✦ ✦ ✦

At about eleven that morning, Reilly put the finishing touches on Carter's apartment. He walked over to shake Carter, but he couldn't rouse him. A cold terror flooded him. *He's dead,* he thought. *What am I going to do?*

He felt for a pulse. It was there, just barely. Relief, then bewilderment. *What do I do? I need to call an ambulance or something, but what if they blame me for the condition he's in?*

Reilly knew he needed to avoid contact with the

police. His record—drugs, breaking and entering, armed robbery—would allow no casual contact with officialdom.

He looked wildly around the room. He knew Carter kept his cocaine in an old baking soda box in the refrigerator. He went to the kitchen and removed the box, then stuffed it into his jacket pocket. He went to the front door, making sure to leave the lock off so he could get back in. He darted out to his truck and stuffed the container into the toolbox he kept behind the driver's seat. *Idiot,* he swore at himself, *that's where they'll look first. But not yet,* he argued. *They'll take care of Carter. I'll scram, then dispose of it at home.* He dug under the driver's seat for a flask, which he opened, then held up to his mouth for a long drink. *The thing's empty. I need something to bolster me.*

He raced back into Carter's apartment and checked on him again. Still breathing, but not conscious, that was for sure. He got some whiskey from the liquor cabinet and poured himself four fingers, which he downed immediately. Then he took a deep breath and dialed 911. He couldn't leave Carter uncared for. There is honor among thieves, right? He pulled a face at his reflection in the mirror in the back of the liquor cabinet.

Besides, he might pull through, and we can knock off Charlie. Then he'll pay me, and pay me good, and we'll be on Easy Street.

Sirens screamed, the paramedics came in and ministered to Carter. One shook his head over the unconscious man and then glared at Reilly. Reilly struggled to calm his jagged nerves. *Just get him out of here and into the hospital and let me go! He thinks I have something to do with that mess that used to be pretty-boy Carter. You'd better pull through, Buster,* he said mentally to the departing form on the stretcher, *so you can set them straight.*

✛ ✛ ✛

Driving back to his apartment, Reilly thought back to the day Charlie Keegan had ruined his life. *He's the reason I'm where I am today. I could have been a success, too, like Carter and Jerry.* The irony of the fact that Carter was dying and Jerry was already dead, murdered, escaped him.

That day one summer, when Charlie had made advances to Jamal, and Jamal had rejected him, Reilly—puny little puppy dog Reilly—had tried to make up for what Jamal had said to "Uncle Charlie." Jamal had rejected him and that had filled the man with rage. Reilly didn't really like him, but Charlie was the only person who paid him *any* attention. His dad—who knew who he was, or where—and his mom. . . . He'd wander the streets at night while she lay drunk. No food, no access to a bathroom or soap, no warmth or talk or loving smiles—ever.

But Charlie had been warm and kind. He'd always seemed so nice. Then that day, he had taken Reilly off with him to the boathouse at Cheney, where he'd whipped him. Then, in a frenzy of remorse, he'd apologized and cried and begged for forgiveness. He'd poured him a large glass of whiskey, his first. "It'll help you sleep and forget the pain," he'd said.

The whippings had continued then, over the next few years, but not often, just when someone had put Charlie down or rejected him. The last beating, the day before Charlie left town ten years ago, had nearly killed him.

Carter and Jamal, driving home from a late basketball game one night, had driven by Reilly's house and had seen him lying on the front walk of the drab, decaying little house on Elpyco. They'd stopped and taken him to the Wesley emergency room. *They'd probably saved his life, but for what?* he wondered.

He wouldn't give the hospital, or the police summoned there to interrogate him, any details. They'd had to throw up their hands in helplessness.

But Carter and Jamal knew. They'd begged him to tell, to get Charlie once and for all, but Reilly couldn't. He'd been the only source of love Reilly had ever known—as well as the deepest wellspring of hatred.

The next day, Charlie was gone, for good, they'd all hoped. Reilly couldn't tell what he felt about the disappearance. He grieved for the loss of someone who had filled so much of his life, as well as for the small child who had been used by that someone. He hated Charlie then, but he loved him too.

At least now the love was all gone. Gone for good.

After leaving Renee's room, the angry nurse glaring at her retreating back, Paige was shaken and frightened.

She took the elevator down to the main floor and went to the Building 4 lobby of the huge, sprawling hospital complex. She would wait for Paul and Jamal there. The lobby stank of stale smoke and unwashed bodies.

Paul and Jamal came striding in soon after she'd taken a seat. Two tall, handsome men, one white, one black. They drew the eyes of the others in the waiting room.

It was good to see them—old friends who had stood by her through everything, who loved her unconditionally. She stood quickly and walked into Paul's arms. "Oh, Paul." His arms felt so good around her. Why had she resisted so long?

He held her at arm's length to look into her face. He was stricken to see the pain written there. "What's wrong?"

"I did it—I talked to her. But I went too far, Paul. She ended up in another psychotic fit."

Jamal looked around at the stone and concrete walls of the hospital and quipped, "Good place for it." Paige smiled through her tears, thankful for his light touch in the gravity of the moment. She reached out and patted him on the arm.

"She really freaked out this time," Paige said.

"But she's fairly safe here, Paige," Paul said seriously. "Like Jamal says, this is a good place for her to face up to the specter of Charlie. Now let's go see if we can visit her."

"Not me!" Paige said. "There's a dragon of a nurse up there who'll never let me within a hundred yards of her!"

Paul nodded, realizing she was right. "Then you wait here. There's a snack bar down the hall. I'll buy you some coffee or something, and you can catch your breath."

He turned to Jamal. "We'll go as visitors from the church."

"Oh, good," Jamal said. "We won't have to wear any heavy disguises." The three chuckled.

"This reminds me of high school and our attempts to put one over on the librarian or the English teacher," Paige said, smiling.

"Yeah, that librarian was a witch, wasn't she?" Jamal said. "She kept those sex manuals behind her desk, and Paul and I were bound and determined we were going to get at them."

Remembering the scene upstairs, Paige grew serious again. "I hope you two can undo some of the damage I did to her," she said with a tilt of her head upwards, to indicate the room where Renee resided with her terror of the man who had ruined her life.

The two men sobered. Once they had Paige settled at a small table with coffee and an apple, they left to visit Renee.

Paige sat watching the hall for their return. It always seemed, when you were waiting for someone, that the errand took so much longer than if you were running it yourself.

After fifteen minutes she checked her watch for the dozenth time. When she looked up again, she saw a familiar figure go by. Holder Danton! Why was he always hanging around the same places she frequented? It was weird. She resisted any hints of paranoia. *He's not really following me,* she assured herself.

She jumped up from her chair, nearly knocking it over in her haste, and dashed to the door. She watched as he walked down the hall. His back, his stride, the way he swung his arms—he reminded her of someone. Who?

Someone from high school, she thought, someone she associated with the miseries of her last year of school. Who, who? She raged at herself in the frustration of trying to remember.

Chapter 25

Paul and Jamal rounded the corner of the long hospital corridor as Paige stood in the door of the snack bar, observing Danton's retreat. Their faces were grim.

"Let's go," Paul said, grabbing her arm.

"Wait! My purse!" Paige pulled away from him and ran into the shop to pick up her bag. "What's up?" she asked, frightened now.

"We gotta get outta here," Jamal said, propelling the two out the door. "Renee has told that head nurse up there that someone is coming to kill her. She said she got a phone call." He pushed them in front of him, out of the hospital and into the parking garage. "The nurse called for the cops, and then gave your name."

"*My* name!" Paige gasped.

"Yeah. Guess she was lucid enough to tell the nurse you were the troublesome visitor. Somehow, both crazy Renee and the supposed professional linked you and the threat in their numb brains."

Sirens wailed at the emergency entrance on the south side of the hospital.

"Where's your car?" Paul asked brusquely.

"The green level—over there."

The two men hustled her to her car. After seeing her safely inside, Jamal spoke in an authoritative manner. "You stay with her, Paul. Wait here till I drive around, then follow me out. They'll have your description, Paige, but I doubt they'll think you'd be leaving the garage now since you left the floor so long ago."

"But wait—I forgot to tell you—I saw Holder Danton in there!"

"So?" Paul said, bewildered.

She haltingly explained. "It just seems weird that he has business wherever I do, and at the same time."

Jamal and Paul paused to look at each other. Finally Paul spoke. "Let's process that later. We have to get out of here."

While they waited for Jamal to join them in his car, Paige went on to describe more of her experiences with Danton. "And, Paul, when he was walking away from me, down the corridor in there, I swore he reminded me of someone from high school. But I can't figure out who!"

"Another student, you mean?"

"No, he's too old for that. He's old enough to be your father. . . ." The blood left her face. "Jerry's father—that's who he is. Charlie Keegan!"

"No! That's impossible," Paul argued, trying to encourage rationality.

"I know he doesn't look anything like himself now, but . . ."

"Then how could you have recognized him?" Paul interrupted.

"He's much heavier now . . . by thirty pounds or more," she continued excitedly. "And he's had plastic surgery . . . *that's* why he had it!" She bit her lower lip in the excitement of the dawning revelation. She turned toward him, her face alight. "That's why I started having the nightmares again . . . after I first met 'Holder Danton.' It was his hands, his stance. He couldn't change those."

Long-suppressed images of Charlie's hands, with the red hairs on the knuckles and the bitten nails, flooded back, threatening to overcome her. Tears started in her eyes, and bitter bile rose in her throat.

Paul reached over and placed his hand on her neck, massaging it gently. He felt a depth of empathy for her he couldn't express. Such a helpless feeling—he on one side of a chasm of experience, and Paige on the other. He thought back over his childhood and adolescence. There had been problems and pains, sure, times when he wanted to find a big hole and crawl in and stay for a million or so years, like any kid, but never anything like the traumas Paige and Renee had endured.

His folks—how he'd fought them when they were so restrictive with him. They'd never allowed him to go on the outings with the Keegans, and he never understood why.

When Charlie disappeared, his mother had said through tight lips, "I just never trusted the man, Paul. And I didn't want to scare you or put you off people in any way, you know, never being able to trust others. Most people are okay, but that Charlie—I just couldn't entrust you to his care."

His mother was tiny—barely five feet tall—and softly feminine, but when it came to her children, she was steely firm, a tigress. She would never give in on a matter that she considered harmful to their welfare, and Paul had hated that. "You're so hard," he'd said through gritted teeth to her once. She had refused to let him go to a rock concert where there were rumors of drug use. A look of hurt had crossed her face, but she hadn't budged.

Paul hadn't understood then. Now perhaps he did, a little.

Jamal drove up behind them. He honked lightly and Paul waved in recognition. They proceeded slowly and decorously out of the garage, Paige fighting the whole time her urge to floor the accelerator.

As the two cars headed south on Hillside, toward the Skycrest, an ambulance heading north turned into the emergency parking on the southwest corner of the hospital. Inside the ambulance, two paramedics worked feverishly, purposefully, over their patient. Carter Brookings—once a breathtakingly handsome young man, fashion plate, every status hostess's dream guest—lay near death. Even in his present condition, through the ravages inflicted on his body, the medics could see vestiges of the beauty of his facial structure, the once sleek skin and hair. They could also see the signs of cocaine use and the Karposi's lesions as well. One looked at the other and whispered, "What a waste."

The resident on the fourth floor stood outside the nurses' station and flipped through Renee's chart. Sweat poured down her sides. This could be life or death: Was the woman hallucinating or was there really a person coming to kill her? The diagnosis was messy—a multiple personality resulting from dissociation. The poor thing had willed her mind to leave her body whenever the unknown molester had approached her. Amazing what the human mind could do, the resident thought. And now full-blown paranoid delusions. *But I can't dismiss her fears now, I just can't. I have to believe her,* the young resident thought.

She walked through the door into the small room where computers whirred, printers shot out reams of paper, phones rang, and fifteen or sixteen nurses milled around. *What if I'm wrong?* she thought nervously. *They'll lose whatever respect they might have for me.* She shook herself. *I'd better alert security.*

✝ ✝ ✝

Charlie entered Renee's room stealthily. He looked up and down the hall. This room was far enough away from the nurses' station to give him confidence that once again he could get away with—he chuckled obscenely—murder.

Renee turned to look at him when she heard his laugh. She appeared to be alarmed to see a stranger in her room, but she obviously didn't recognize him. *I think I'll tell her who I am. I'd like to see her reaction then.*

He approached her bed, a half-smile on his lips. She continued to stare at him, curious but not really frightened, yet.

"Renee?" he whispered.

Her eyes widened a fraction. "Who are you?"

With a gloved hand, he took a long knife out of the top of the lizard cowboy boots he was wearing. He picked up her right hand and placed it around the handle of the knife. She struggled a little. "What . . . what do you want?" she asked, beginning to panic. He leaned over to whisper in her ear, a cruel smile on his face. "Why, it's me, your Uncle Charlie. Don't you remember me?" As he said it, he slipped a free hand over her mouth to keep her from screaming, then raised the knife. She shut her eyes and tried to roll away, anticipating the blow.

"Hey," he admonished her, "aren't you going to fight me?"

Her head jerked sideways. No, she wasn't going to fight him. Death was better than this kind of life.

He hesitated briefly. It wasn't any fun when they didn't struggle.

Just at that moment, he heard a noise in the hall. Men's voices and heavy footsteps were approaching this end of the hall. He brought the knife down a glancing blow, missing her heart. She jumped but didn't cry out.

I can't leave her alive, she'll tell! But whoever that is is getting closer. I've got to get out of here!

He walked briskly out of the room and down the hall toward the fire stairs and away from a trio of men— two security guards and the head of hospital security, he was to learn later. When they entered Renee's room, he heard one of them yell, "Hey, stop that man!"

Charlie dashed to the door and crashed through it, racing down the stairs as fast as he could. His body poured sweat as much from the exertion as from the close call. He grimaced when he reached the parking garage where his car was parked. Things were getting too hot. Once he took care of Paige, he'd have to leave town, again, and start over, again. Women were always messing up his life.

✢ ✢ ✢

Jamal, Paige, and Paul pulled up at the Skycrest to find Althea Brookings waiting for Paige in the main floor sitting room. The woman approached the three of them with purpose.

Paige's heart sank. She wasn't interested in dealing with her mother right now. Behind her, Jamal muttered, "Uh oh."

Blonde hair—out of a bottle, of course—perfectly coiffed. A full-length mink coat over a frilly dress in fuchsia, gold, and forest green. High fuschia pumps that made the almost pudgy woman wobble a little as she crossed the carpet. She looked well-fed, well-corseted, and well-heeled. The image Althea projected was one of high fashion bordering on tastelessness. To Jamal and Paul—although never in the twins' hearing—Paige and Carter's mother had always been both daunting and an object of ridicule.

"Paige!" she said in her high-pitched, no-nonsense voice. "I got a call from that Reilly person just as I was leaving the house. Carter's on his way to the hospital."

"What's wrong?" Paige asked, alarmed.

"I told Reilly he couldn't expect me to rush to Carter's side," Althea went on, ignoring the question. "I've certainly told him often enough he was playing with fire with that lifestyle of his. I've got a big bridge tournament today. I told him I'd try to grab you and send you up there."

"You don't want to go see what's wrong?" Paige blurted out, unbelieving. "A bridge game is more important than your son?"

"You know I was never very good with illness," she replied, wheedling now. "I need you to go, Paige. You're so good with Carter. Besides, I think I might be coming down with a cold." With that, she took out a white lace-trimmed handerkerchief that she held delicately to her surgeon-retroussé nose and sniffed.

Paul looked at Paige's face. It was frozen hard as ice, sparkling, crystalline, adamantine—and cold as marble in winter on the steps of a tsar's northern palace. He could feel the rage rising phoenix-like in her soul. It was a frightening thing. He moved in closer to Paige, to signal his presence and support.

"I'll go, Mother." Her words were clipped and sharp. "I'm glad you're at least considerate enough not to take him a cold."

Althea started. She certainly hadn't been thinking of Carter's welfare when she'd mentioned her cold. She smiled smarmily. "Right. You know I'd hate to add to his woes. Now, Paige," she went on, issuing further orders, "I need him to get better fast so he can help with my party. Tell him that, will you?"

"Yes, Mother, I certainly will," she replied, sarcasm dripping from her voice. "He'll be so glad to know you're thinking of him."

"Well, he mustn't give in to his feelings, now, when I need him." She spread the fingers of one hand lightly across her chest and with wide-eyed innocence, said, "I never wanted to raise such a sissy. He can just get up out of that bed and quit acting helpless." With that, Althea gathered her mink coat and swept out the front door.

When she'd left, Jamal let out a snort. Paige's head whipped around and she glared at him, and he raised one large hand to ward off her anger. "Sorry, Paige, I couldn't help myself. She's quite a presence."

Paige's rage died down, and her shoulders slumped.

She rubbed the back of her neck, to massage out the stiffness there. "Isn't she awful?" she asked matter-of-factly. "No wonder Carter and I turned out so badly."

Paul lifted her chin with one hand. "I don't believe you've turned out badly. Hang in there, kid." He smiled at her, and she managed to smile back.

"The hospital! Will they let me in?" Paige began pacing up and down the length of the large sitting room, past the heavy English furniture and over the real Persian rugs. The room looked baronial with its high-beamed ceilings and walnut paneling from floor to ceiling.

She turned her ring around and began rubbing the opal with her thumb. She was caught in a trap. She *had* to get into the hospital to see Carter, but now she might be arrested for setting foot in the building, all due to her attempts to confront Renee. She spread her hands in a gesture of helplessness. "What do I do? They won't let me in now."

"We'll see about that," Jamal said firmly. "Let's go."

Chapter 26

Getting in to see Carter was easy. Jamal used the in-house phone at the hospital to find out what room he was in. Then the three of them found Building 3, took the elevator to the fifth floor, and Paige followed Jamal and Paul, trying to look as inconspicuous as possible as they proceeded down the hall to his room. The labyrinths of the large hospital were convoluted enough for her to be present and never be noticed by Renee's watchdog nurse.

Paige gasped when she saw the life-support systems Carter was hooked to. He was unconscious when they reached his bedside; to her, he looked dead. Only the little blip-blip on a green screen assured her he was truly alive.

She still didn't know what was wrong with him. There were no visible injuries. She could see the lesions of the sarcoma on his face, but they didn't look like injuries to her. "What . . . why do you think he's here?" she whispered.

Paul shook his head. "I'll go check with the head nurse, see if I can find out."

Paige stepped closer to the bed. When she noticed she was holding her breath, she exhaled forcibly. Then she lay one hand tentatively on Carter's. A sob escaped her lips. "Oh, Jamal, look at him."

Jamal put a comforting hand on her shoulder. He couldn't take it, either. The grayed face of his friend, the sunken eyes—it was heartbreaking to see him lying there.

"It's no use," Paul said when he came back into the room. "I can't get any information. I explained that I was visiting from our church, but that didn't cut any ice."

"But how can I find out?" Paige asked. Panic rose in her chest. Somehow knowing the name of what had put Carter here would help her heal him, keep him alive, she was sure. He was part of her, had been from the time of their conception. They'd been aware of a oneness from the first. "He's going to die, isn't he?" she whispered, no longer able to hold back the tears.

Neither Paul nor Jamal answered. There was nothing to say.

Paul pulled up a chair and eased Paige into it. She sat holding Carter's hand.

"Dear heavenly Father," Paul began to pray. Paige's head jerked up in surprise, and she turned to look at him and Jamal. Their eyes were closed, Jamal echoing the soft phrases or agreeing with an "amen" from time to time as Paul prayed on. She closed her eyes, too, and felt the solemn supplications rise above them as Paul prayed for Carter, for his healing, for his soul. Then he prayed for Paige, for strength during this difficult time, and her tears gushed forth. It was so strange—both wonderful and painful—to have someone who cared for her pray for her like this. She felt like a sleepy child whose father was tenderly wrapping her in clouds of fleecy blankets and tucking her safely in for the night.

When a nurse bustled in, Paige opened her eyes reluctantly. She hated to leave the praying—it felt so good. She stood and moved aside to let the nurse take Carter's vital signs.

The young woman, a petite redhead, said breathlessly, "Oh, I don't think Mr. Brookings can have this many visitors at once."

"This is Carter's sister," Paul hastened to explain. "And we're friends from church."

The name tag on the nurse's uniform read "Kelly." Inconsequentially, Paige wondered whether it was the cute, bouncy little nurse's first or last name. She looked Irish, that was for sure, with her red hair, bright blue eyes, and fair skin. Either way, the name suited her. The nurse nodded, a big frown knitting her brow. "I don't know . . . ," she said indecisively.

"Can you tell us his doctor's name?" Jamal asked. "The family doesn't even know the diagnosis yet." He smiled that dazzling smile at her.

Flustered, she blurted out, "Oh, AIDS, of course."

Paige blanched. She felt the words slam into her solar plexus like a solid line drive. "Oh, dear God," she murmured at last.

Kelly—Ms. or not—turned beet red. "I shouldn't have told you. I'm sorry." Conscience-stricken for having made such a mistake, she seemed younger than ever. She stretched a hand out to touch Paige softly on one elbow. "Are you all right? If you feel faint, let's put your head down between your knees."

Paige vigorously shook her head no. "No, I'm all right. I . . . I've been worried about this all along, and I've done a good job of denying it to myself." She took a deep breath. "What are his chances?"

"It's hard to say right now. This is his first crisis, I understand. He may snap right out of it and do pretty well for a while." She hesitated. "You do understand, though, that for the long haul . . ."

Paige nodded. Yes, she understood that her brother would die, and much sooner than he ought to. What a waste. She thought of his talent, his joie de vivre, his style.

The nurse wrote Carter's doctor's name down for Paige. "Call him for more information. I'm sorry. Sorry he's so sick, sorry I told you the way I did." She looked pained, her small face sad and worried. "I'm new at this," she added softly, by way of an apology. "Come back in a couple of hours," she continued in a kind voice. "We ought to know more then. I go off at three o'clock. You can come before, or you might want to deal with a more experienced nurse later." She smiled, her obvious natural good spirits returning. She lifted her hand in a small wave as they left.

When Jamal, Paul, and Paige reached the first floor, Paige swayed on her feet, and Paul caught her. The two men led her to a chair and helped her into it.

She held a shaky hand to her forehead. Her face was white as alabaster. "I'm afraid I'm going to faint," she said. "I'm sorry." She looked around. To her horror, she noticed other people watching her. Her head cleared with the realization that she was being stared at. "Get me out of here," she begged. "Please!" Hands shaking, she gathered her purse close to her body and tried to rise. Jamal put one arm around her and helped her up.

Heads turned to follow their progress out the waiting room door. The beautiful blonde woman, dressed like something out of *Vogue,* looking like she was about to die or coming down off drugs, and two sleek, handsome males, assisting her. Paige could only imagine the stories they might be concocting in their minds about the three of them, but she was sure it would never match the soap-opera unreality of her life.

"I need to get back to work," Jamal said when they reached the car. "Can you stick with her, Paul?"

Paige hastened to demur. She still felt lightheaded but she couldn't keep monopolizing their time and lives this way. "Oh, I'll be all right. You both go on."

Paul shook his head vigorously. "No, I'll hang around for a bit. You go on, Jamal—I'll keep you posted."

"Paul," Paige argued, "this is so embarrassing. I make a scene in there and now you feel like you have to nursemaid me." Her face, brows knit, mouth skewed, reflected the massive problem that had been thrown at her in the last few minutes. Without a word, Paul shepherded her into the car and slammed her door, then walked around and slid behind the wheel. "We're not having any arguments about this. You've had a big shock—on top of multiple other shocks, I might add— and you need some relief."

He drove her to his house in College Hill. The stately house looked quiet and restful to Paige. When he parked in front of the garage, she sighed with relief. Her nerves were stretched so thin she feared she would break in two, that she would start screaming any moment now.

She allowed him to lead her into the house. It was simply furnished, with old leather chairs and overstuffed couches—probably bought second-hand with an eye to comfort only—hardwood floors with a few Oriental rugs, long windows laced with thin white curtains to let in the Kansas winter light, and shelves full of books in every room. At the center of each high-ceilinged room was a fan.

Moses wandered in, tail wagging, to sniff at Paige's hand. "The old girl's afflicted with arthritis, and she's slowing down these days, but she keeps busy checking out my callers," Paul explained. "Now let me have your cape." He motioned Paige over to a big red leather-upholstered rocker by a huge fireplace with an ornate oak mantel.

When Paige sat down, Moses positioned herself at her side. With a sigh and a thump, the dog plopped on the floor next to the chair, tail well away from the heavy curved wooden rockers.

Paul left the room, and Paige could hear the rattle of crockery. He returned soon with a tray of coffee in large, unmatched mugs. Hers had a pig wearing a bathing suit and sunglasses on it. The logo said, "Supigstar." She smiled wanly at the pun. Paul and his sense of humor. She wanted something light and fun too, anything but this concurrently dull-aching and sharp-screaming pain that filled her now.

He placed the tray on the small table next to the rocker. She watched in horror as he put two heaping teaspoons of sugar in the coffee and abruptly covered the top of the mug with her hand, causing him to spill some of the sugar. "Stop! I can't have that much sugar!"

"Always the model, even at a time like this," he teased. "Tsk tsk."

She grimaced. "You actually said 'tsk tsk.' I didn't think anyone ever said that outside of Victorian novels."

"What can you expect from an English professor?" He smiled, then carefully filled the sugar spoon again. "You need this for shock." He stirred the sugar around in the coffee, then handed her the mug.

"Yes, sir." She took the hot mug with trembling hands, surprised at how weak she felt. "This is good. I hadn't realized how cold I was." She rocked slightly, then leaned forward to say earnestly, "What's the next step? Carter, Renee, Charlie? I don't know what to do next."

Paul pulled a wooden side chair over and sat in front of her, his knees almost touching hers. He scowled in thought. "What to do first? Who knows? We'll be like Stephen Leacock's Guido the Gimlet of Ghent and jump on our trusty steed and ride off in all directions at once," he replied with a sardonic wink.

"That's what I feel like." A sob rose in her throat, and she choked it back. She looked down at the steaming coffee in the mug. "Don't you wish you'd never met me, Paul? My life is such a mess, like a soap opera," she said, recalling her earlier impression in the hospital when it seemed everyone was watching her.

He gazed deep into her eyes. "Paige, I'm not even going to answer that," he said softly. He took a big sip of his coffee, from a chipped black Wichita State mug with gold lettering. "*My* first priority is to keep you safe."

She snorted at that. "Fat chance!"

He ignored her comment. "Carter and Renee are in the best of hands at the moment."

She jerked her head to the side. The images of the two of them in the hospital bit at her.

"But Charlie . . . ," Paul went on. "Can we find some evidence that will link him to Jerry's and Stacy's deaths?"

"I need to call him about his account, but I can't bear the thought of speaking to him," Paige admitted. "Hal's on my case about not working the last week or so. He's afraid we'll lose the Danton Oil account."

"If Charlie is Holder Danton, as you suspect . . ."

At that, she bridled. "I *know*!"

He held up one hand. "Okay, okay. Anyway, my point is, if they are one and the same, you're not going to lose the account. Holder—Charlie—wants you as the account exec on this. He's not going to miss a chance to increase his contact with you. And if he gripes to Hal—well, who cares?"

"Huh! Hal will care, and he'll have my hide for it."

"Do this," he suggested, lifting his shoulders in demonstration. "Shrug Hal's demands off, just for the moment. Let's see you do that, just shrug."

She got up abruptly from the rocker. "I don't have time for foolishness now, Paul." She began pacing up and down the long living room, twisting her opal ring and rubbing the stone.

"It's not foolishness!" he stormed, replacing his mug on the table with a thud. "You'd better get a grip on yourself so you can think clearly. Your anxiety will only increase the likelihood of mistakes!" He stood across the room from her, scowling.

She glared at him, then she deflated like a punctured balloon. She nodded. "You're right, of course."

His heart softened at the sight of her. He came to her and put his arms around her. She melted. He ran one hand up her back and tangled his fingers in her silky hair. "I love you, Paige. Let me into your life, your heart, all the way. Now," he said softly.

She whimpered, then returned his kisses with a passion he did not expect. Excitement leapt through his veins. He kissed the tears away from her eyelashes, savoring the salt of them, then led her over to the couch in front of the wide front windows. They sat down together, and he held her until she fell asleep.

Chapter 27

Paige slept all night. When she awoke, she didn't recognize her surroundings. Then she remembered, and she smiled and stretched like a cat in the comfort of a safe place. The old quilt Paul had covered her with, its many colored patches softened by years of use, slipped to the floor as she stretched.

Paul was sitting in the red leather rocker, reading his Bible. He looked up when she stirred. "You let me sleep," she said.

"You needed it. You looked so peaceful lying there, I couldn't disturb you."

She nodded. "I think that was the best rest I've had in months. What are you reading?"

"Ecclesiastes—chapter 4, verses 9 and 10: 'Two are better than one, because they have a good reward for their labor.'" He got up, walked over and sat beside her on the couch, pointing to the words: "'For if they fall, one will lift up his companion. But woe to him who is alone when he falls, for he has no one to help him up.'"

Reading ahead, Paige pointed to verse 12: " 'Though one may be overpowered by another, two can withstand him. And a threefold cord is not quickly broken.' Like you and me and Jamal," she added.

"Like you and me and *God*," he corrected softly.

She pondered for a moment. "So what do we do now?"

Paul smiled to himself. Progress. She had said "we." He gave her his hand, pulled her to her feet, and engulfed her in his arms. "Let's eat first. I've made some breakfast—I'm a downright, absolutely wonderful cook, you know. Even Michael agrees."

She laughed. "He should. He's an expert."

"I've got some croissants and some ham and cream cheese. Surely you can find something suitable for a model to eat."

She tipped her head appealingly to one side and grinned at him. She loved him.

✛ ✛ ✛

They ate in his formal dining room at a small oak table set in the recess of a bay window. Outside was a terraced garden with redwood benches built into the privacy fence surrounding the yard. Three large bird-feeders hung from a locust tree. Goldfinches dined busily on niger thistle seed at one feeder. A cardinal, crest flaming in the afternoon sun, chirruped from a hedge of ornamental quince.

Paige sighed. "So peaceful." She went on to tell him of her experience at Chisholm Creek Park the day she started jogging again, after a six-month hiatus. "The deer and the egrets—I ached to touch them, to be part of them. I felt free for the first time in a long time." She looked away from his steady gaze. "I've been Charlie Keegan's prisoner for too long. So have Carter and Renee. I've got to declare final, total independence from his hold on me, once and for all."

"How?"

"I have to face him, unmask him. I have to tell him I know what he did to us. I have to tell him the damage he's done."

"You can't go to him, not alone anyway! He's dangerous."

"I'll be safe enough, in full daylight, in his office. He won't do anything where there might be witnesses."

Paul shifted in his chair. "Maybe." He paused in thought. "It won't be easy, facing him now."

"No, but it's time. May I use your phone?"

After she made an appointment to see Holder Danton later, Paul drove her home to get her car. On the way, he felt a rising anxiety at the thought of her facing the ogre of all her nightmares. And the man's presence in her life wasn't just the content of dreams—he was a real threat to her. To her sanity, at the very least. And if he had really killed Jerry and Stacy, to her life.

"Can we pray first?" Paul asked when he had pulled to a stop in front of her apartment.

She put one hand in his. "Sure."

Paul prayed briefly, ending by saying, "Keep her safe."

"Thanks, Paul. I feel God with me again, after a long time of being separated from him."

He didn't bother to lecture her. God had always been with her.

"It's like a three-strand cord, isn't it?" she asked.

He nodded, eyes on her face. "Are you sure you don't want me to come along?"

Eyes still closed, as if in prayer she said, "I'm sure."

Once she got into her car to drive to see Holder Danton—Charlie—Paige hesitated briefly with her fingers on the ignition key. Confused feelings flitted through her mind. She was afraid to see Charlie, yes. She couldn't even imagine what the confrontation with him would be like. It wouldn't be easy, that was for sure.

She thought back to the time she had spent with Paul. A feeling of warmth flooded her. She had felt so calm, so secure.

Briefly, she thought just on a practical level, what marriage might mean. *If I were to marry him,* she thought, *life would be easier for me. I would be out of reach in most men's minds. Maybe they would stop looking at me like a piece of merchandise to be bought or a prize to be won.*

Put that way, it sounded so self-serving, so cold-blooded. Was she really an ice goddess at heart, after all these years of acting like one?

Maybe the bonds of marriage, which seemed so constricting at times, really meant freedom for her, freedom at last.

But there was more to the attractiveness of marriage than that sort of protection. She did love Paul, always had. There was never any question about that. She had loved him from the first day she saw him, in kindergarten at College Hill School. Tall for a five-year-old, confident and clownish even then, he'd captured her imagination and her affection. She smiled as she thought of Paul over the years, a collage of remembered images of him at different ages—from five to fifteen to nineteen to today at twenty-eight. It seemed to her suddenly that each person she knew was many different people—infant, toddler, gawky twelve-year-old, adult—all at one time.

She turned the ignition key. Was Charlie Keegan ever a young, innocent, lovable child? She shivered. Maybe so, though she couldn't imagine him that way. Who had done unspeakable things to the child Charlie must have been at one time? Her blood froze. She was trying to make excuses for him. How could she be feeling any kind of empathy for such a monster?

Still, she couldn't believe that some babies were born bad. She could never accept such a notion.

When Paige stopped her car in front of Holder's building, she realized she was shaking. Holding her hands in front of her face, she watched her fingers tremble, then made fists of them and thrust them down into her lap. She took a deep, steadying breath. A cold, refined anger filled her head. *Control, control!* she raged at herself. Control was paramount for this encounter.

Unbidden, the image of a long, sharp knife in her hands rose in front of her. "I wish I could kill him," she whispered to the dead air in the car. She shook her head to clear it. No, never! She could never kill anyone, not even this man. "Be with me, Lord."

When Paige entered his office, Holder rose from his chair, pleasure written across his scarred face. He stretched out a hand to take hers in a warm handshake.

She shook her head slightly, keeping her hands rigidly at her sides.

Holder flushed, then changed his gesture to a wide arc indicating that she should take the chair in front of his desk.

Paige shook her head once more. "No, I'm not staying, Holder—or should I say *Charlie?*" she asked pointedly.

All color left his face, and he collapsed into his chair. "What . . . what do you mean?" Eyes riveted on her face, he took in a big breath and did not exhale.

Paige smiled. "You look frightened, Charlie. Any particular reason?" she asked mockingly. "Surely you aren't afraid of me . . . or any of the other children from the past." She allowed herself to approach his desk, to place her hands on its smooth surface and lean forward into his face. "Like Jerry . . . or Stacy?"

Charlie's face was deathly white, the reddish stubble of his morning shave standing out like spikes of winter grass in the snow. "You have no proof!" he rasped. A hideous purple suffused his face. He leaned forward and pointed a shaky finger at her, rage growing to mask the fear he felt.

She laughed harshly. "You're the proof, the living proof." She turned sharply on her heel to leave.

"You and that brother of yours," he hissed. "You won't ruin my life."

She turned back to face him. "You've ruined Carter's life!" she shouted, then lowered her voice. "You've ruined Renee's. You almost ruined mine, but I woke up in time." She could see the stark animal terror in his eyes, could smell it on his body. "I think you'll ruin yourself, and without my doing anything at all. You're

close to the brink, and you'll fall over the edge by yourself. . . ."

She was speaking softly now, almost kindly. "By
yourself," she repeated, "all by yourself, forever. . . ."
She paused, a sob catching at her throat. "How could
you have killed Stacy? She was such a lovely child."

Again the man blanched. He fell back in his chair
and covered his face with the hands she remembered
from her childhood—short and wide, with freckles and
rust-colored hairs around the knuckles, the nails bitten
to the quick.

He lifted his head to look at her. "What makes you
think I'm Charlie, that I killed Jerry and Stacy?" he
asked, misery and craftiness blending on his face.

Again she paused, thinking, remembering. "It was
your hands," she said at last. "I'd remembered them
putting Beau, dead, into my bed. I've always had nightmares about them, but I couldn't put a face with them
until recently, until you started the phone calls again,
started following me. You ruin yourself, don't you?"
She smiled sardonically. "Just do everyone a favor in the
meantime, Charlie . . . stay away from children so you
won't damage any other young lives. Ruin and failure
seem to follow you around."

"Don't you say that again!" he shouted, rearing up
out of the chair like a phoenix from a funeral pyre. "I'm
a success! I'm a millionaire five times over, you witch!
I started with nothing, from the wrong side of the
tracks—in spades!—and I made something of myself!
And you're not going to spoil it for me!"

During Holder's speech, Paige had opened the door.
Now his secretary, overhearing his tirade, was staring
with open mouth. Three businessmen, sitting in the

waiting area, looked thoroughly shocked. Paige smiled again, realizing he had just admitted everything—and to witnesses!

Then she suddenly sobered, remembering his earlier comment. "What did you mean, Carter is ruining your life?"

Charlie opened his mouth, then shut it, a steel trap. He glared at her, crossing his hands across his chest and smiled, knowing he was going to win on this point, at least. He wouldn't tell her.

Those frantic calls from Carter in the last two weeks, he thought. *He's trying to blackmail me, but I'll see the creep dead first!*

Paige shook her head, then shrugged. "I guess it really doesn't matter, does it?" she purred and left the office as Charlie yelled at his secretary to shut his inner door.

He sat in his chair and fumed. Paige had ruined his power play by not even caring.

It will be a distinct pleasure to kill her, he thought, stretching and rubbing his hands together. *But I'll have to hurry.* He rose from his chair and rushed to the window. He watched as she strode across the parking lot to her car, looking carefree and strong. "Just you wait," he growled.

Chapter 28

J amal sat across the desk from Wopat. "Gimme a break, okay, man?"

His former fellow cop stared at Jamal over steepled fingers. "What do you want?"

"I need to look at that file on Jerry Keegan."

"For personal reasons, right?" Wopat shifted his bulk in the heavy wooden chair. The permanent grimace on his face signaled the permanent pain in his gut. Wopat was never free of stomach problems. Crossly he added, "I don't think that falls within the range of sharing professional information."

Wopat and Jamal had been partners on the force for a short time, but Wopat hadn't been able to deal with Jamal's intelligence and smooth handling of other people. And when Jamal made rank before him, Wopat hated him for it. He'd never been able to accept the fact that this younger man—a black man at that—was his superior. Wopat doubted that there was any benefit to him in helping Jamal. The guy was gone, a private dick now, on his way to becoming most cops' least favorite professional, the lawyer.

Jamal grinned, cocking his head to one side. "If I find in it what I think I'm going to find, I'll give you the info and you can take all the credit for solving the case."

Wopat looked at him thoughtfully, weighing his options.

"It could be a real biggie, Wopat. And you can be the guy to break the case."

Wopat didn't trust him. "If you want to do me a favor, why don't you just tell me what to look for?"

Jamal straightened and leaned in close to speak earnestly, "If I'm wrong, it'll be a bomb. Some big wheels might get egg on their faces when this case breaks. I can't run the risk of pointing the finger at the wrong person."

Wopat grunted, then leaned over to reach into a drawer for the file. "I'll be looking for favors, man. Don't forget this—*I* won't." Jamal grinned again.

"I won't forget."

✝ ✝ ✝

Once he was back in the privacy of his car, Jamal took the file out of his briefcase. His nerves tingled a little, the only sign he usually had that he was excited. Another thing Wopat had hated in him, Jamal recalled with a smile, was his steady nerves.

He flipped through the pages. Toward the end of the fat file on the Keegans, he found what he was looking for, what he needed to prove that Charlie was the killer.

Man, it was an almost perfect crime: Disappear for ten years, then come back as a person as opposite to your original identity as possible. But Charlie hadn't been able to change everything about himself. Plastic surgery couldn't alter the inner man. And Jamal knew him too well.

Well, he could tell Paige she was right. She would be relieved—it wasn't just her intuition. There were facts now. Hard facts.

He started the engine and drove off, whistling, his customary pleasant expression of contentment and solid confidence on his face.

✢ ✢ ✢

A little before two, Paige was back at the hospital to check on Carter. The little nurse Kelly saw her coming down the hall from the elevators, and she bustled out from behind the desk to greet her. She reminded Paige of a little wren, hopping busily about to gather seeds.

"Ms. Brookings! I'm glad you're here. Your brother was awake a bit ago and was asking for you." She led Paige down the corridor to Carter's room. "He seems to have stabilized a bit. Are your parents in town? It would sure be great if they could come while he's so alert."

Paige frowned as she tried to process the implications of that brief statement. Kelly assumed Carter's parents cared about him, assumed that this alertness was short-lived. Paige wanted to scream. Neither assumption was acceptable to her. Their parents didn't care, and Carter couldn't—just couldn't—die!

Carter was awake when they entered the room. He managed a weak smile when he saw Paige and reached a hand out to her.

She rushed forward to grab his hand, and then she

leaned over him gingerly, trying to get through all the medical paraphernalia to hug him. She tried to speak but found she couldn't. A confusing tangle of emotions roiled within her.

But at last one overrode all the others. Love for her brother. "Oh, Carter . . . ," she began, tears trickling down her cheeks.

"Now, no blubbering," he said in a teasing tone. "You know crying is just not done in the Brookings clan." He stopped and took a breath, recovering his strength from the little energy he'd just expended.

Kelly busied herself taking his vital signs and rearranging his covers.

Paige studied his face for a long moment. His color was gray, the flesh shrinking on the high cheekbones. His arms were full of needles connected to plastic tubing. His muscles looked flabby, all tone vanished.

He smiled and whispered, "I look like day-old dog dung, don't I?"

She giggled a little. "Yes, Carter, you do." She straightened and willed the tears away.

Kelly lifted a hand in farewell and left the room. Paige wanted to call her back, to hold as a shield between herself and the reality of Carter's illness.

At last she said, "Have you known for very long that you . . . were sick?" She couldn't bring herself to say "that you have AIDS." Maybe if she didn't label it, it would go away.

"Not too long." He turned his head away and gazed out the window.

"Have you been in touch with Charlie?" she asked softly.

His head jerked a little. If she hadn't been looking

for a reaction, she might have missed it. "Why do you want to know?"

"I just left his office. He mentioned your name, said you were trying to ruin his life, but he wouldn't tell me how. I thought maybe you could tell me, and maybe I could help you ruin *his*."

He looked at her in surprise.

She smiled. "Just maybe, though. Depends on what you had in mind."

"You keep away from him," Carter said coldly. "I don't want you involved in any way."

Paige blanched. His words were like a slap in the face.

A long silence fell between them. At last, Carter said, "Reilly will take care of it for me."

"Reilly! What does he have to do with it?" she asked in alarm.

"Paige, for once I do not want your help. I know I've always asked you to do my dirty work for me, but not this time. Reilly isn't worth much in your eyes, but he's just right for this . . . task."

Paige shivered. His words were cold as marble on a mausoleum floor.

He continued weakly, "I'd hoped to execute him myself, but time got away from me."

" 'Execute him,' " she whispered, terrified. "Carter, what do you mean?"

"Just what I said," he snapped. "Since I'm dying anyway, they couldn't punish me for it. This one act might salvage some meaning, some value for my life."

"But your soul—what would murdering someone do to it?"

He laughed harshly and didn't answer.

Paige started pacing. She ran one hand through her hair. Carter's eyes rested on her briefly, then closed. Wild thoughts raced through her brain, and she couldn't control them. At least in the hospital, in such dire health, he couldn't possibly kill Charlie. At last she bridled her thoughts and turned to face her brother. "Do you want to see Mother?"

He snorted. "Sure, send the old bag up. What do you think she'll say when she sees me looking like this?" A hint of the old devilish Carter returned. "It'll really wreck her day, won't it?"

Paige chuckled. His charm was irresistible to her, always had been. She loved him in spite of himself. She relaxed a little and went to move a chair next to his bed. She picked up his hand and began to rub it gently. "I'll get her here. Is there any way . . . ?"

"Way for what?" he prompted.

"For there to be some sort of healing between the two of you?" She hesitated again, afraid he'd pick up on her assumption that he didn't have much time.

He jerked his hand away from her. "Are you crazy? Do you think I'm to blame for our relationship, or that I can do anything about it now?"

She stood up and laid her hand on his shoulder. "I . . . I'm sorry, Carter. Please forgive me. I didn't mean that at all." She covered her face with one hand, her head bowed. "It's stupid, isn't it," she whispered, "to never give up hope that someday a rotten mother or father will turn into Ozzie and Harriet or the Huxtables? But I never give up hoping she'll someday be the mother I want her to be."

"You're right. It's stupid," he said with finality.

She sat back down. "Carter, I wish we could talk about Charlie a little."

"Why?" he said, expecting no answer. "He's another topic where there's no hope for discussion."

"But I have to deal with the destruction he's done in my life. Don't you?"

"No," he said flatly. He paused, then went on. "He didn't turn me into a homosexual, you know."

Her head jerked up. Her eyes fixed on his face, willing him to go on talking. She believed Charlie had influenced Carter's lifestyle, so why didn't he think so?

"I've done lots of reading on the subject, Paige. And Mother didn't turn me into a gay man, either, so I can't even blame her."

"Well, *I* can!" she snapped.

He shook his head. "I knew from the first that I was different. I honestly didn't choose to be gay. It would have been great to have simpler choices, to be like Paul or Jamal, and date the pretty girls in our class, instead of being the butt of the homophobes' anger and fears, fear that they might turn into a pansy, too, if they got too close to me." The bitterness and hurt in his voice made her want to comfort him, but she knew he'd reject any such attempt.

"But Mother and Charlie damaged you. You can't say they didn't!"

"Of course they did. I don't argue with that. I might not have been such an unholy failure if Mother had done a better job, if Charlie hadn't been hunting for victims of his hang-ups all the time. And maybe I wouldn't have been so . . . loose with my affections, shall we say, if they hadn't done a job on me." His eyes clouded over with grief. "And maybe I could have escaped this fate, dying with AIDS." He sighed. "It's pointless, sugar, to dwell on it too much. What's done is done," he finished softly.

"It's not done. Unfortunately, Charlie is still capable of damaging other children!"

"Not for long," Carter said meaningfully. A wry smile twisted his mouth. "You know, when you think about it, it's a mystery why someone hasn't offed him before now."

Paige sat in silence next to her brother, biting her lip as she tried to process his words. "Please, Carter, call Reilly off. Nothing good can come of an attempt to kill Charlie."

Carter glanced quickly at the clock on his bedside table. "It's too late. The game has already begun."

"What? What do you mean?"

He waved a hand in the air. "Too late." He smiled again. "Now I need some sleep. Come back later, okay?"

✛ ✛ ✛

When Paige got outside, a light drizzle was falling. There was no wind now. The weather forecaster had promised freezing rain, changing to snow—maybe four to six inches overnight—with windchills of forty below. That was a snowfall of blizzard proportions in Wichita. High winds made everything worse in winter here on the plains, and driving would be a nightmare by morning.

She needed to call Reilly, much as she hated the idea. When she got home, she tried his number, dialing three times with no success.

Feeling jumpy, she decided to go to the park to jog

235

before the weather got worse. She took care of Marmalade and gave him a perfunctory scratch behind the ears. Then she changed into longjohns and her heaviest sweats. Next she put on thin cotton socks, then long woolen ones. A peach windbreaker, ivory scarf, hat, and mittens completed her attempt to hold off the plunging temperatures.

✛ ✛ ✛

As Paige drove out of the Skycrest, head down against the bite of the cold air, she failed to see the black Lexus parked across the street. It pulled smoothly out into traffic, remaining three or four cars behind her as she drove east on Douglas, then north on Oliver.

At Oliver and 13th, Jamal, who had just left his administration of justice class at Wichita State and was heading south, saw Paige drive by. He honked and waved, but he got no response. "She didn't see me," he told himself.

When the light changed, he crossed the intersection and glanced to the left again. There was a black Lexus, like Holder Danton's. The hairs on the back of his neck prickled.

He continued on his way, uneasy. The Lexus was not that common a car. Not here in Wichita.

Once he'd reached Central, he was sure it was no coincidence that a car like Charlie's was following Paige. He pulled into the video store on the northeast corner and sped out north. He had no idea where she was heading. How would he find them? He shrugged. He had to try.

When Paige got to the park, there were three cars in the parking lot—a white station wagon with *SPRINT* printed on the side, a gray Accord with a "Williams for Senate" sticker on its back window, and a blue van. She was glad to know she'd have company. That meant, though, that she wouldn't catch a glimpse of the deer. The shy creatures would never come out with that many humans around.

As she stretched, a family of five came up the walk and said hello, then got into the van and drove off. She was sorry to see them go. Today, out here by herself, she felt exposed.

She started to run slowly, to warm her muscles. When she reached the first bridge, she heard a car door slam. She continued on her run, thinking how confined she would feel when the bad weather hit and she couldn't get out to exercise.

✛ ✛ ✛

Charlie leaned against his car for a moment, pulling on heavy leather gloves. He punched the fingers of his right glove down in between the fingers of the left, then looked at the other two cars parked next to Paige's in the lot. Fleetingly, he wondered if it was wise to try to get her here. He regretted, briefly, having such a distinctive car. *I'll hide the body well. No one will attach any significance to my car being here today.*

He was so accustomed to doing what he wanted, legal or not, and getting away with it—getting away with murder, he thought, pleased with his little play on words—that this would be as easy as the other crimes he'd committed. He took a deep breath. *Easy to do,* he corrected himself. Not so easy to think about Stacy and Jerry lying dead at his hands—but what choice did he have? And what choice did he have now?

And why had Reilly called him for an appointment tonight? He'd mumbled something in the phone call that came into Holder's office earlier, about Carter dying in the hospital, about Reilly now having the evidence Carter was holding on him.

Well, he'd just have to remove Reilly too.

Really, all those kids from that class were such losers. He'd be doing the world a favor to remove them all. Carter dying now, Renee crazy as a loon, Reilly a psychopath. God knew he'd tried to do his best with them when they were young. He spent more time with some of them than their parents did, that was for sure. Paige and Carter looked good, but he knew they were pathetic.

He started off down the path. He planned to cut across a field of bluestem grass and wait in the hedgerow near the far bridge for her return. His heart skipped a beat and he smiled in anticipation.

Chapter 29

Jamal skidded to a halt at 37th Street. There were no cars ahead of him on the road. Where had he lost them? He had passed the entrance to the park six blocks back. An alarm sounded in his head. "They're not going to Bel Air." He made a U-turn in the tan Ford and sped back down Oliver.

"Would she be dumb enough to run alone?" He reflected that in her present state, Paige just might do anything to shake off the chains of catastrophe that were tightening around her. She was such an independent spirit, he knew. That was one of her most attractive and most threatening traits. Insecure men like Charlie couldn't handle that in a woman.

His tires squealed as he turned into the park. He drove into the parking lot. Both cars were there. At least he didn't have to guess their whereabouts.

He jumped out of his car and ran down the path. He had to find Paige before Charlie did. This park was small, but you could still miss another person out here easily enough.

His feet pounded down the path. There was no other sound around.

The sun was a rosy stain on the western horizon when Paige rounded the far curve of the path. She was running easily and beginning to feel her second wind. She smiled and increased the pumping of her arms. This was great.

Ahead of her lay the glassy pond, then the field of big bluestem grass, reddish now in its dormant state. Just beyond the field was the darkened line of Osage orange trees that had once been a windrow. On one side, this side, of the hedgerow it was bright and sunny. Once she passed through the opening cut for the path to snake through, however, she would be surrounded by the cottonwoods, walnut, and mulberry trees that grew thick around the creek bed.

The sight of the darkness on the other side of the hole in the hedgerow caused her to break stride for just a moment. She felt she was being stupid for being afraid, stupid for not listening to her fear. Conflict, conflict! How wonderful it would be to be a simple person without all these complex emotions warring in her!

She forced herself to continue on.

When she entered the hedgerow, she increased her speed. Out of the corner of one eye, she saw a shadow dart toward her. A deer? She hesitated briefly to get a better look at it.

"Oh, no!" She tried to scream, but only a hoarse cry escaped her throat.

It was Charlie. The look in his eyes told her his

intention—she would not live to tell anyone about this attack.

His mouth twisted cruelly. He lunged forward, caught her by one sleeve, and jerked her back into the shadows. His hands encircled her throat and he began choking her. His hands, his hands, she thought. It was always his hands that had tormented her in her dreams and now they would end her life.

Fury filled her and she reached up to tear at his hands, to scratch his face, his eyes. *I hate you, Charlie!* The thought exploded in her, but she couldn't utter the words.

The pressure increased on her throat. The crushing of her larynx was excruciating. Red and orange fireworks filled her head, and she could feel herself slipping away. Life was over for her, and she regretted that she hadn't really lived. No Paul, no babies, no simple happiness. She blacked out then, tears burning her eyes.

✢ ✢ ✢

Paige was first conscious of pain, horrible pain. She couldn't swallow. She raised one hand to her throat to ease it. Then she was conscious of being cold.

She frowned. She was alive, but how?

"Paige," a male voice called insistently.

She kept her eyes shut tight, then nodded to let him know she could hear. The voice belonged to someone she knew and trusted. Then her eyes flew open. "Where's Charlie?" she whispered, the effort of making any sound triggering a fresh onslaught of pain. "Where . . . ?"

Jamal was kneeling beside her, one hand under her head to support it. Her body sagged with relief. "Oh, Jamal, thank God you're here," she croaked.

He grinned and nodded. "You hurt pretty bad?" he asked solicitously.

She grimaced. "That's putting it mildly. Where's Charlie?"

"He got away from me." Jamal frowned. "I'll get him, though. I thought it was more important to stay with you."

She smiled weakly. "Thanks." She took his hand and squeezed it. The thought of the danger she'd been in washed over her. "But . . . how did you happen to be here?" She massaged her aching throat gingerly.

"Ask *him*." Jamal gestured heavenward. "I was driving south on Oliver and saw you going north at 13th. I honked, but you didn't see me." She shook her head in confirmation. "Then, not three cars behind you was Holder's Lexus. That alarmed me, but it took me a while to realize that was just too unlikely to be coincidental. I made a U-turn and followed. I almost drove to Bel Air though, before I woke up to the fact you might be in the park and in danger."

"Thank God," she breathed. She closed her eyes again.

He started to lift her. "Let's get you to the emergency room and a doctor." He chuckled. "Pretty soon we can have the class reunion at Wesley—you, Renee, and Carter will already be guests there."

"Ha, very funny." She frowned. "I don't want to go to the hospital. I'll be all right."

Jamal snorted. "That's what you think. You need that throat looked at. You should see the nice bruises coloring up right now."

"What can they do, splint it? No, I'll be fine." She struggled to stand, but her legs were much weaker than she expected, and her head was full of cotton rags. She stumbled, and Jamal steadied her.

"Hey, lady, are you sure you don't want a doctor?"

"I'm sure," she said firmly. "Jamal, we have to find Reilly."

His eyebrows shot up at that. She quickly explained the conversation she'd had with Carter earlier. "We have to find him. I don't understand this execution stuff, or how they think they could get Charlie to trust them enough to fall into their hands, but Carter sounded pretty confident they could pull it off."

Jamal didn't argue with her. He took whatever threat Carter was making seriously. He knew Reilly's record. He was a psychopath, capable of great viciousness. "He looks like a loser," he said to Paige as he steered her to his car, "but he's capable of the worst cunning and violence."

She stopped and pointed to her BMW in the lot that was now empty except for their two cars. "I can't leave my car here."

"Paul and I will come back for it later. Your safety is more important right now." He urged her into his car. "You couldn't manage driving now anyway."

She moved stiffly and slowly. Movement hurt, and she knew she was probably in for a lot of pain and stiffness by bedtime. Once she was in the car, she flipped down the visor to look at herself in the mirror. "Yuck!" She examined her neck, looking at the purplish-red bruises there, then ran her fingers through her hair. There were twigs and dried leaves tangled in the strands of fine gold. A smudge of dirt stood out on one cheek and several long scratches abraded the other. She brushed the dirt and leaves off her sweats. "I'm a mess!"

"Yeah, but you're an alive mess. We can praise the Lord for that." He started the car and drove slowly down the park road. "I'll take you home now."

"No, you won't!" she said emphatically. "I'm not dropping out now to go home and sit and twiddle my thumbs! I've had it with the nice, passive little lady bit."

Jamal looked at her out of the corner of one eye, then nodded and returned his attention to his driving. After waiting three or four minutes for the traffic to clear, he pulled onto Oliver. "When, by the way, did you start thinking of yourself as passive?"

She snorted. "The day I realized I was letting everyone else dominate me. I was Charlie's victim for a while, Mother's good little girl, Carter's patsy. And I have had it! When I realized I was afraid to leave my apartment to go run, when I started seeing shadows everywhere—and they were tormenting me all the time—I woke up."

She paused and looked out the window. "I've tried to control all the tiny details in my life—you know, no mess, no disorder anywhere—but I realize my obsessions were enslaving me." She turned back and smiled at Jamal. "I felt liberated the first time I decided to ignore my fears and come to the park to run again. It was wonderful."

Jamal nodded, a slight frown puckering his brow. "You do know, don't you, that it's Christ who liberates you? I don't want to preach, but I do want to remind you of that. Otherwise, you're running down a dead-end street."

"I know that, Jamal—only Christ frees us. I've been a slave to everyone else, even to myself. Now I'm letting him back in my life. He's the only one who can make sense out of any of this. . . ."

They drove on silently, then Jamal said, "I always knew how strong you were, strong enough to know when you're weak. I'm glad you're realizing it too." Paige's face colored at the compliment. She reached across and squeezed his hand. "Thanks."

They continued down Oliver to the little house on Elpyco where Reilly lived. When they drew up in front, Jamal searched the front of the house before opening his door. "It looks like Charlie isn't here, and neither is Reilly. Let's see what we can find inside."

"But what if it's locked?" Paige asked.

He grinned and held up a set of picks. "What if it is?"

Chapter 30

P aige felt a shiver of apprehension. What was she doing, helping break into someone's house, Reilly's, at that? She darted a nervous glance over her shoulder when she heard the lock click open in the back door. The black paint on the door was peeling, the small porch full of debris. Rotting fruit and vegetable peelings, dirty TV dinner trays, and empty beer and whiskey bottles lined the porch.

She noticed Jamal took a big breath before he actually opened the door to enter. Apparently, breaking and entering made him a little nervous too.

They stepped into the kitchen. Scarred linoleum, holes worn through in places, covered the floor which canted a bit, like a ship's deck on a roll. The room was filthy. The smell was overpowering—a mixture of grease and sweat and who knew what else. Paige sniffed in disgust, but she wasn't really surprised.

Stacks of clothing lined the walls of the room. A cursory examination showed that there were both men's and women's clothing of wildly varying sizes. "How weird!" Paige whispered.

Jamal nodded. He pawed briefly through the clothes, then shrugged. "Who can figure?"

He proceeded into the next room of the small house, and again, they were confronted by piles and piles of clothes. The overpowering odor followed them throughout the house. Next to the front door was a narrow bed, a dirty mass of blankets and unwashed, black-stained sheets. The coppery smell of blood mingled with those of feces and urine. Paige covered her mouth and nose with one hand.

Jamal twitched a blanket aside with one hand. "Blood is my guess, but old blood."

"But there's so much of it," she said, almost gagging at the sight.

Jamal's lips were set in a hard, straight line.

"This reminds me . . . reminds me of my dog." She stopped, nearly unable to speak, eyes wide with horror. "Do you remember my basset hound Beau?"

Jamal turned to look at her. He examined her face for signs of overwhelming stress, but she appeared calm. "Why does this remind you of Beau?"

"One of my recurring dreams . . . it was Charlie's hands putting poor dead Beau in my bed and his blood all over. The sheets were dark blue, and it was hard to see the blood," she faltered, then regained her composure. "But it was there." She bowed her head, tears flowing. "He had said he'd kill my mother or Carter if I didn't let him . . . if I didn't . . ."

Jamal reached out to wrap one arm around her shoulders. "I'm sorry. Paige, I'm so sorry. Do you want to go back outside?"

She shook her head no, forcefully. "Why would someone kill a defenseless pet, how could someone be as inhuman as Charlie?"

Jamal had no answer to that. After a long silence he said, "I don't think this is going to turn out to be animal blood, though, Paige. I'm going to have to call in the cops now."

She grabbed his sleeve. "No! Oh, we can't tell anyone what Charlie did!"

"I don't have a choice. I can't conceal evidence. And this is what Reilly has done, not Charlie." He put a guiding hand on her arm. "Let's get out of here. I'll call Wopat—he'll love the favor."

"Not Wopat! That man hates me! He acted as if he thought *I'd* killed Jerry and Stacy, so cold and suspicious." She was shaking and her teeth were chattering.

"Just hold on, Paige. Wopat doesn't need to know you've been here, so chill," he said sternly.

As they retraced their steps through the distasteful debris around them, a car door slammed in front of the house. They froze. She looked up wildly at Jamal. "What can we do? Reilly's back!"

He put a finger to his lips and drew her back into the shadows by the large, old refrigerator humming in the silent house. Then he strode quickly to the front door and peered out the door. "Just the neighbors, I think. Let's go."

✢ ✢ ✢

Later, they sat in the car in a Sonic Drive-In lot, drinking lots of hot coffee. Jamal had called Wopat and then Paul. He'd told Paul where to find them; they had left the Elpyco house before the cops arrived. While they waited for Paul, Jamal had eaten a pork tenderloin and fries. Paige refused any food, saying she couldn't keep anything down. But he'd forced the coffee on her. "You just drink up before I pour it down your throat."

She smiled through her tears. "Yes, sir."

When Paul arrived, he opened the door on her side of the car and slid in next to her, scooting her over into the center of the seat. She flung her arms around his neck and began sobbing. "I'm so glad to see you."

He pulled away to look into her face. Worry was etched into the fine lines around his eyes. He kissed her tenderly and she returned his kiss.

"Harumph!" Jamal interrupted. "Remember me, guys?"

Paul laughed. "I'll remember you in my will and name my firstborn after you, for saving her today!"

"A white baby named Jamal? Hoo boy!" Jamal countered, laughing. He fanned one hand up and down by his cheek. "It be gettin' too warm in here for me."

✦ ✦ ✦

When they drove back by the house on Elpyco, several police cruisers were in front, their lights played around the yard. Jamal didn't park. "I don't think Wopat would welcome me at this point."

He drove off after a few moments and returned to Paul's car in the Sonic lot. "I need to get busy, so I have to dump you guys. Not to be rude or anything, but get out." He smiled.

Paul punched him lightly in his well-muscled upper arm. "Thanks, Jamal. I'll take Paige home now."

Jamal flipped a mock salute with his right hand, and she leaned over and gave him a kiss on the cheek.

She looked at him with great tenderness and gratitude. "Thanks, friend."

✢ ✢ ✢

Paul took Paige back to the Skycrest so she could shower and change. On the way in, they checked with Chester to see if Holder had returned. Chester said he didn't think so, but he'd ring Mr. Danton's apartment for them. Paige grabbed Paul's hand in fright. "No," she said, trying to remain calm, "that's all right. We'll try later. And Chester," she said hesitantly, "don't tell him we were asking, okay?"

Chester looked befuddled, but he promised.

Paul was irate when he learned Paige hadn't seen a doctor about her injuries. Hearing the anger in his voice, Marmalade hid under a chair in the living room. Paul subdued his temper, though, when he saw how upset Paige was about the idea of getting medical attention.

Rubbing her forehead with one hand, she said, "There wasn't anything a doctor could do, and it seemed more important to find Reilly or Charlie."

She glanced around her apartment. "This place looks so strange to me. I don't think I've been home except to sleep a little in the last few days." She paused, then went on. "Looks kind of cold and sterile, doesn't it?"

Paul didn't answer. He merely got up from the couch where he'd waited while she cleaned up and took her in his arms. She settled comfortably in them, and the two of them rocked together, standing there in the middle of the ivory and peach room. It was a quiet, tender dance. She pulled back to look up at him and began to chuckle. "And Armand—I haven't given him a thought!"

At the mention of the man's name, Paul grimaced.

"When I picked him up at the airport, I noticed how silly he was acting, so rude and selfish," she said. "I kept seeing you and Jamal making a comedy routine out of him."

Paul smiled and dashed pretend sweat from his brow with one hand. "Whew, that's a relief."

The phone rang. Paige sighed. "For pete's sake—I ought to tear that thing out of the wall. It drives me nuts!"

He followed her, standing behind her as she spoke into the phone, his arms wrapped around her, his face buried in her gleaming hair.

"Carter!" she exclaimed. "How are you?"

Paul heard the voice quaking on the other end of the line, but he couldn't hear anything that was said.

Carter told her that Reilly had called in a panic. He'd gone home to find the place swarming with cops, so he'd left the scene before anyone could recognize him and stop him. They were even digging up the yard. Reilly knew his property couldn't bear close scrutiny. If the police stopped him now, he couldn't get the job done on Charlie. Paige blanched, grabbing Paul's hand for comfort.

"I'm feeling fine," Carter went on, "and I've got to get out of here. Come get me out! The stupid doctors won't listen to me."

"Stay where you are," Paige warned her brother, willing herself to sound firm. "You can't be that much better so soon." She thought of the sight of Carter wrapped in tubes and wires only hours earlier. "It's ludicrous!" She placed her free hand on her bruised neck and thought about telling him about Charlie's attack on her. She decided against it. Knowing might increase Carter's resolve to leave the hospital. "I think it's safer for you to stay there, Carter," she added softly. "Please don't try to leave."

He hung up on her at that point, and she stood looking at the dead receiver in her hand, then turned to Paul, a panicked expression on her face. "He's planning on leaving the hospital tonight. Reilly called him and told him about the police raiding his house. Now Reilly's on the run."

"The first thing we're doing is getting you out of here," Paul insisted. When Paige pulled away in protest, he held his ground. "No, now listen to me. We're sticking together through the end of this thing—I can't run the risk of losing you now." He hugged her tight and said huskily, "Especially not to vermin like Charlie." He let her go. "Get packed. I'll put you up in my guest room, such as it is." He smiled his warmest smile, and she smiled back. Even in the darkest moments, Paul somehow was able to lighten the atmosphere for her.

"Oh!" she said, realization hitting her. "We have to call the hospital though. They should be alerted to Carter's attempt to leave there. Can you do that? And I need to call Hal. I just have to explain to him." She started to punch numbers on the handset. "Now that I *know* Holder is Charlie, I'll make him understand. . . ."

She didn't reach Hal. He was at a meeting, his wife said. Paige left a message for Hal to call her at Paul's and hung up the phone. "I don't think telling him all this will be easy."

Paul nodded, then reminded her to go pack. "I'll

check with the hospital and then call the desk to see if Holder has come in." Marmalade twisted, meowing, around Paul's left leg. Paul reached down to pet him. "Then I'll feed this cat of yours."

Paige was halfway down the hall to her bedroom, but she called to Paul over her shoulder. "Won't Chester get suspicious if we keep asking about Holder?"

"I imagine," Paul said with heavy irony, "that by tomorrow, everyone will know more than they ever wanted to know about Holder Danton, and Chester will know why we were asking."

✛ ✛ ✛

The nurse Paul reached at Wesley to tell about Carter's planned departure wasn't the least impressed. She said they'd look into it. Paul shrugged after hanging up the phone. Why was it some people just had the knack for making you feel dumb when you were alarmed about something?

Chester hadn't seen Mr. Danton, he told Paul. Paul could hear anxiety rising in the old man's voice. He knew Chester wanted to please. "It's okay," he said comfortingly. "We'll catch up with him eventually."

"You don't want to leave a message?"

"No, we definitely do not want to leave a message. Don't worry about it, Chester. It'll keep."

When Paige was packed, she hesitated at the door before turning out the lights. "This place looks like a stage set, something that belongs to another phase of my life. How strange." She carefully locked the door. "Of course," she said laughing a little, "I never have spent much time in it. When you work and don't have family, the office seems more like home than home does."

"Ha!" Paul said. "You need a dog."

"Well, I *do* have a cat."

"Yes, but cats are so independent. A dog needs more attention. Moses never lets me forget where home is. When you have to feed a big ox like her and keep her brushed and cleaned up after, you know where home is."

He went on, correcting himself. "Actually, you need a husband and a *particular* dog—Moses, that is. We'd never let you forget where your home was. And how about a little boy? What would you think of taking on a ten-month-old human garbage disposal?"

Her eyes widened. "Garbage disposal! What a thing to say about such a cute little kid."

"He eats so much! It's fun to feed him, though. You ought to try it. It would be good for you."

She squeezed his arm and smiled. "Uh huh, yeah, sure. You wouldn't have any ulterior motives, would you?"

He sang off-key, "'I'm only thinking of you, I'm only thinking of you!'"

"*Man of LaMancha,* right?"

"You got it, kid."

Chapter 31

The light interlude ended when Paige and Paul left the building. When Paige looked to her left, down the driveway leading from the porte cochere, she saw Charlie standing under a streetlight, next to his car, door open. "There he is!" she shouted. "It's Charlie!"

They started running toward him. Spotting them, he turned swiftly and clambered into his car. The door slammed, the motor revved, and he sped off down Oakland toward Hillside.

"He's gone!" Paige wailed.

"Let's go!" Paul grabbed her hand, and they ran to his car.

Inside, they stopped to catch their breath and regroup. "I haven't the slightest idea what to do with him if we catch him," Paul confessed. "We'd better get Jamal in on this. He'll know what to do."

After calling Jamal from a pay phone, Paul drove to his house. Out in front of the house, they sat for a few moments in the car and talked.

"Paul," Paige began hesitantly, "I feel I need to explain why I treated you so badly all these years."

He started to interrupt, to argue. "You haven't treated me badly. . . ."

She placed one finger on his lips. "I did. And I'm sorry. But at the time it was all I could do. He made me feel damaged, and I couldn't face you anymore."

"Oh, Paige," he groaned.

"He was trying to get me to do all kinds of disgusting stuff for his videos, and I refused," she went on, hurrying to tell him before she backed out. "So he raped me. Later that night I bathed over and over, trying to get rid of the feeling of dirt all over me." She sat twisting her hands in her lap. "I felt so isolated. Mother wouldn't even listen to me. All that registered with her was that there was an inconvenient fetus to get rid of." She turned tortured eyes to Paul.

He tightened his arm around her shoulders, letting his silence speak the words he could not utter. He felt torn inside. He wanted to destroy something, destroy Charlie, to tear apart the world where such things could happen, but he was afraid to move, to react. Any movement on his part might frighten her into muteness again.

"And where was God in all this, Paul? How could God allow such things to happen? I didn't deserve that . . . I wasn't a bad person." She started to sob, wrenching, gulping sobs, torn from a tormented mind and heart.

Paul took her chin firmly in one hand and turned her face toward him. "He was there, he's here now, Paige. He didn't cause this to happen to you, and it wasn't punishment for anything you might have done. The Evil One has power in the world, and he uses rats like Charlie Keegan to do his rotten work. But God reigns, Paige. He loves you, he loved you then." He kissed her mouth gently. "I can't explain why wicked things happen to innocent children. I just know they do. Life is hard—you said so yourself once—but God gives grace to live it out."

She continued to cry softly. A strange mixture of the old illness and a new healing filled her. She was sick from the injuries of the past, but the cleansing tears falling from her eyes and the love Paul had for her were healing her mind and soul. And maybe, just maybe, there was a loving God who cared about her, unconditionally, like Paul. If Paul could be so loving and forgiving, he must be made in the image of a pretty wonderful God.

Long minutes passed. They sat together in a welcome, enveloping cocoon of silence.

"I think," Paul began, "that you ought to look into that group Jenny told you about. I believe your healing will be spiritual, and that a group of other victims, like yourself, will help you open up and grow."

She recoiled slightly. Her first thought was that he didn't want to be involved with someone as fouled up as she was, so he was trying to get rid of her. Then she realized that wasn't, couldn't be true, and she relaxed again.

"I can hurt for you, but I can't really understand what it was like," Paul went on. "Other victims would know. But I'll still be here, right beside you. Always, Paige."

He kissed her again, and she felt a passion promising years of delight rising in her. "Oh, yes, Paul," she whispered. "Together." She smiled ruefully through her tears. "I hope, somewhere down the road, that you don't decide you're getting a bad deal."

"Never!"

"I love you, Paul, and I always have. Thanks . . . for everything."

✛ ✛ ✛

It was ten o'clock when they went inside. It felt much later. Paige was exhausted. Her face looked gray and pinched, and she was shivering. Her temperature had dropped from shock and fatigue, and Paul was worried about her. "You get into whatever you sleep in and hop into bed. I'll fix you some hot chocolate."

She was too tired to argue, although she rebelled at the thought of turning him into a nursemaid.

By the time he got back with the chocolate, she was fighting sleep. She was wearing an old-fashioned ivory nightdress with a high neck and long sleeves, antique lace foaming around her face and hands. She was breathtakingly lovely. Paul wanted to kneel in front of her and gaze at her forever.

"If my hands and feet weren't so cold, you would have no patient to wait on," she said teasingly. "I could sleep around the clock, I think." She warmed her hands on the hot mug and sighed. "I feel like a well-loved, cosseted child in some Victorian children's story. I loved to read Frances Hodgson Burnett when I was little and imagine what it would be like to live in a wealthy British home with fussy old nannies around to take care of me. We lived in a wealthy American home with business-like, rather stupid hired help to take care of us. I guess it wasn't that much different, except it seemed more romantic in the books."

She took a sip and ran her tongue around her lips to get all the chocolate. "It all boiled down to not having two parents around to see that you were loved and hugged and spoiled and made to mind, in a kind way instead of crossly. That's one reason I never wanted to have children—I'd die before I'd be the kind of mother *our* mother was."

Paul didn't answer. He just listened and nodded, gazing deep into her clear blue eyes. He was enthralled to watch the play of emotions on her beautiful face, like shadow and sunlight chasing each other across the Flint Hills.

She handed him her half-emptied cup. "Somehow I don't think I have to worry about that anymore. You know what? I'm sleepy."

He nodded again and leaned over to kiss her on her forehead. She was asleep already. He stood and watched her for a short time, sorry she was hurt, but thankful to be able to take care of her for a while. He looked at the bruises on her neck and the scratches on her face. He knew she'd heal fast and then she wouldn't let him take care of her. That was okay, too, as long as she was in his life to stay.

Chapter 32

At the hospital, security guards were combing the halls, bathrooms, and utility areas for Carter Brookings. The nurse who took Paul's call had been trying to fill doctors' orders for sleeping pills and had to start over on her counting. She was a large, stolid woman who moved slowly but with purpose. She knew that nurses who rushed around on their shifts and got themselves all worked up didn't last, so she didn't hurry any. Besides, her feet hurt.

By the time she had finished the job of preparing the sleeping pills and managed to go to Carter's room to check on him, he was gone. Tubes were trailing from the life support systems around his bed, and the thin thermal blanket he'd been covered with was gone. She didn't bother to get alarmed. "Humph!" she snorted to herself. "He won't get far. He was nearly at death's door, and the dadblamed fool doesn't even have any clothes."

She moved slowly back to the nurses' station and lifted the phone to call security and activate a search for her missing patient.

Carter was in a utility room on the second floor.

There he'd found a discarded scrub suit. It was slightly stained, with God only knew what, but he couldn't be picky, now could he? He searched in every bin for a pair of shoes or slippers, but he couldn't find anything for his feet. His head was pounding from the exertion, and he was having a hard time getting a deep breath. His lungs wouldn't fill, and he felt as though they were plugged with glue.

He stuck his head out the door and scanned the hall. Everything was quiet, so he ventured out. The first patient room he passed was dark, but the TV was on. He saw, out of the corner of his eye, the occupant of the room sidle painfully alongside the bed and into the bathroom.

Carter retraced his steps and darted into the room. There, under the now-empty bed, was a pair of sneakers. He grabbed them and walked quickly back to the utility room where he put the shoes on. They were at least two sizes too small, but they'd have to do. He didn't bother tying them.

The exertion of dressing and stealing the shoes was almost too much. He wanted to lie down in a corner of the small room and fall asleep, but he knew he couldn't. Reilly was waiting in the emergency entrance parking lot for him, and it had already taken him too long just to get this far.

Carter dragged himself out of the room and forced himself to stand straight and look alert. He made it to the elevator and down to the first floor.

The corridor between the elevators and the emergency room was crowded. People being transported from one part of the hospital to another, in wheelchairs and on gurneys, their worried loved ones following three steps behind, moved around him. He hugged the wall out of a growing fear that one of them would knock him down. *I just have to get to Reilly's truck, then I can collapse,* he promised himself.

Only a large-eyed child on a gurney, leg in a splint and hugging a large brown bear, seemed to notice him. She stuck her thumb in her mouth and watched him go by. Through a fog he heard her say, "Mommy, what's the matter with that man?"

He redoubled his efforts to get through the hall. A large sign ahead of him—black letters on a white Plexiglass background—rewarded him at last: EMERGENCY ROOM. He steeled himself to make just fifty or so more feet, and he'd be out.

I'll probably freeze, he thought to himself. *This outfit is a trifle cool for December.* He made it through the ER door and past the room where the injured, ill, and laboring waited to be seen.

Just when his foot hit the black rubber mat that activated the electric doors, a big cop grabbed him by the arm. "Hey, buddy, where do you think you're going?" Through the double doors, Carter could see Reilly's truck. He could see two heads in the darkened cab— Reilly at the wheel and Charlie next to him. When Reilly spotted the cop grabbing Carter, he hit the accelerator and squealed out of the parking lot.

Carter raised one arm. "Wait!" he tried to yell. He fainted, instead.

✝ ✝ ✝

Reilly sped north on Hillside, slowing at 9th for the light, then speeding up again and careening on two wheels into the cemetery. Once onto the tree-lined service road, he cut his lights, slowed and stopped.

"What do you think you're doing?" Charlie asked crossly.

"Waiting here to see if we're being followed." His tone clearly implied that he thought it was a stupid question.

"I don't know why I let you talk me into this," Charlie fumed. "You could have just brought the stuff to my office and I'd have paid you there. This cloak and dagger stuff is too amateurish."

Reilly smirked and thought to himself, *Just you wait, Charlie old boy.*

They waited in the dark for five minutes. An ambulance, sirens blaring, went south toward the hospital, but there were no police cars in sight.

"I think the coast is clear," Reilly announced, pleased with himself.

"So let's get out of here," Charlie snarled.

Reilly reached under his seat, picking up a long knife. A streetlight glinted off the blade, and Charlie's eyes widened in fear and a belated understanding. "No!" he whispered.

"Oh, yes," Reilly said, plunging the knife repeatedly into Charlie's fat bull neck, then his chest, losing count of the slashing blows.

The still-warm body of the dead man slumped over toward Reilly. He shoved it back against the far door. He replaced the knife under the seat and then tried to wipe some of the blood off his hands onto Charlie's expensive alpaca coat. Reilly made no noise, but his mouth widened in a horrid grimace of fear and sorrow.

He didn't really like killing, once he did it. He liked the planning part better.

He started the truck and drove slowly out of the cemetery. He was sorry Carter hadn't made it out of the hospital. He would have liked for Carter to see what a good job he could do.

Now to dump the body. He headed north on Hillside, planning to drop Charlie's body over the bridge south of 37th, into Chisholm Creek.

He didn't know where he'd go after that. The cops were swarming all over his house. Pretty soon, though, they'd give up and he'd be able to go home.

He drove in a daze. His peripheral vision had shrunk and he could see only a narrow tunnel ahead of him. He couldn't think very well. Where to go? It was too cold to sleep in the truck. Maybe he'd go to Carter's. He could get cleaned up and sleep for a few hours. No one would think to look for him there.

Once he crossed 21st Street, he sped up. He heard sirens in the distance, and he could tell they were traveling north on Hillside, behind him. He floored the accelerator. His heart was racing, and he was sweating in his light jacket. The odor of his fear mingled with the odor of burned oil and drying blood.

Seven blocks later, he saw the warning lights at the train crossing, but he couldn't stop. Panicking, he tried to turn right, to avoid the train, but his truck skidded, hit a pile of railroad ties and flipped. The cab of the truck collided with the side of the train, and Reilly Hoskins died in a commingled pool of his own and Charlie Keegan's blood.

The truck caught fire and exploded, showering

sparks and fragments of metal hundreds of feet into the air. By the time the train stopped, the engine was past Greenwich. The engineer had no idea what he had hit in the blackness of the winter night.

Chapter 33

Paul called the hospital at eleven. When he reached the night nurse, she was curt with him. She began by interrogating him about how he knew Carter was missing, and he explained courteously to her about the call Paige had received earlier in the evening.

"Well, he's still missing!" she snapped. "God only knows where he is."

"You're right, ma'am," he answered quietly. He wasn't too fond of people throwing God's name around lightly, but she was right—God *did* know where Carter was.

He went back to reading *The Brothers Karamazov* and kept one eye on the TV, which was turned on low in one corner of the living room. Some old movie—*East of Eden,* he thought—was playing. He didn't know why he was watching TV, but he felt as though some bulletin would interrupt the late show with news about Carter or Charlie or Reilly. He felt an overwhelming feeling of dread. Whatever happened, Paige would be hurt by it. He closed his eyes briefly to pray for her. If she could survive this, the rest of her life ought to be a piece of cake—please, God.

He dozed off in the middle of his prayer. He'd been doing that a lot lately. Sometime later the phone rang. He sprang out of his chair to get it before it could wake Paige.

"Paul, this is Jamal." His friend's voice was low, heavy with fatigue.

"Yes, Jamal," he said, eager for news.

"Thought you'd want to know. The cops just found Reilly's truck wrecked on north Hillside. The truck burned."

"Reilly's dead," Paul said for him.

"Yeah, and Charlie too."

"Charlie?"

"Yeah. The interesting thing about Charlie is that he was already dead before the crash, it looks like. Stabbed probably, the coroner says, from his preliminary exam."

"Reilly killed him?"

"It looks like it. The truck is a mess, from the crash and the fire, but amazingly the interior was somewhat intact. The firemen can't figure out how. But it's rather instructive—full of blood and a knife convenient to hand under Reilly's seat."

"Whew." Paul ran one hand through his hair. "What about Carter?"

"What about him?" Jamal asked. *What more could happen?* he thought, bewildered.

"He called Paige at about nine or so, said Reilly had called him in a panic. He said he was going to leave the hospital and wanted Paige to sign him out. She refused."

"And?"

"I called Wesley at about eleven, and the nurse I talked to said he hadn't been found yet." He paused, thinking how tired Jamal sounded. "But don't you try to do anything about it. Have you been home yet?"

"No, not yet. I've been at Reilly's with Wopat since I left you. Paul," he said, hesitating, "it won't be easy, but you'll have to tell Paige—they found the remains of seven bodies in Reilly's yard. Wopat thinks maybe they're some teenaged boys who have been missing for the last few years."

Paul gasped. "Reilly killed them?"

"Looks like it."

Paul wanted to vomit. It all just got worse and worse. Charlie Keegan's legacy of blood and death.

"At least I was able to give Wopat some evidence that Charlie had killed Jerry and Stacy. He wasn't happy to see me, but once I told him about Charlie's old nervous habit with the matchsticks, he started smiling, real big."

"The matchsticks!" Paul said, recalling Charlie rolling paper matches into little spirals. "I remember! Why was that significant?"

"The doofuses found five of those little spiraled matchsticks in Jerry Keegan's bathroom where he and Stacy were killed, but didn't connect it up. Fortunately, Eric Johnson is a good record-keeper and made a note. Wopat said big deal, until I showed him an old picture of that Labor Day years ago when Charlie tried to put the move on me. We were all sitting around a picnic table at his house, and there, clear as day in the picture, were those little cardboard spirals in front of Charlie. He was making another in his hand—you can see it with a good, strong lens." Jamal chuckled, his voice hoarse with fatigue. "You sure were a funny-looking kid in high school."

"Very humorous," Paul said. "Say, why don't you go home? You sound beat, man."

"Yeah, I need to. I called Sherry two hours ago and told her I'd be late. She was ticked. The kids had waited up for me. You'd think she'd get used to it by now." He sighed.

"So go home. It's late. Just don't let it go any later. You can't do much at this point about Carter."

Jamal didn't answer at first. Then he said, "At least Carter wasn't in that wreck. You wouldn't believe how bad those bodies were."

"You saw them?"

"Yeah, I identified them unofficially at the scene. It was gruesome, man. . . ."

"I imagine. Jamal, go home to your wife and kids, would you? Tomorrow is another day."

"Scarlet O'Hara in *Gone With the Wind?*"

"Oh, go home," Paul said gruffly. "And see you tomorrow," he ended softly.

Paul replaced the receiver gently and stood staring out the front window. Snow had started to fall, big, fat flakes swirling in the glow of the streetlights. He opened the door and smelled the night air. He could smell the snow, fresh and cold. There was no wind, and the flakes fell gently, nesting between blades of grass and coating the surface of the street. There was no noise except for the swish of the snowflakes. The world always sounded so still when snow was falling. There was no moon. It looked like the snow would stick, and the city would be a different place in the morning.

He was thankful that Paige was safely asleep upstairs, thankful that Charlie could no longer hurt her. *The worst is over, Paige,* he thought. *Now you can get on with the business of healing, get on with your life.*

He went slowly back into the house. It would be great to take a walk in the morning, if Paige was up to it. They could look back at the tracks they made in the fresh snow, their own two pairs of tracks, just as they had as children.

✣ ✣ ✣

Paige woke late the next morning. Her body ached all over. As she rolled over gingerly in bed and tried to ease herself into a standing position, she chided herself. *What did you expect, you goose? Of course you hurt. What do you expect when someone who outweighs you by a hundred pounds throws you on the ground and tries to choke the life out of you?*

She moaned. Sitting on the edge of the bed, she felt her neck and various other body parts. The muscles in her neck and back seemed to hurt the most, probably from the stress of the day before. Her windpipe and larynx felt damaged, but she knew she'd heal.

Moses stuck her nose in the door that stood ajar a couple of inches and pushed it open. She wagged her tail at Paige, then came over to stand next to the bed until Paige leaned over and scratched her behind one ear. Then the old dog sighed and thumped down on the floor, to resume her watch over the visitor.

Paige smiled. "Nice old dog," she said softly. Walking very stiffly, she crossed the room to get her robe off the rocking chair in the corner and then went into the bathroom to wash up.

When she came out, Paul was there with a breakfast

tray. Paige could see signs of a lost night's sleep in his face, around his eyes. When he looked at her expression, though, his face lifted and he laughed. "You just saw yourself in the mirror, right? You look deliciously woebegone."

"Oh, hush," she snapped. She put a hand up to touch the bruise discoloring the side of her face. "And whatever does 'deliciously woebegone' mean? If it's a quote from some movie, I don't recognize it." She was scowling at him, but he continued to stand there laughing at her.

"Nah, it's no quote. I think I'm just slaphappy, glad you're all right, here safe with me. It was too close a call," he said, becoming very serious at the thought of her narrow escape.

"Here," he said, pointing to the tray on the table at the side of the bed. "Come eat some breakfast. It snowed in the night, and if you're up to it, we ought to go out and walk to the park. The snow hasn't been disturbed, so we need to make tracks."

He directed her back into bed and put the tray in front of her. She scanned the amount of food on the tray and started to protest. "I can't eat this much!"

"I fixed enough for two. I didn't know what you'd be hungry for, so I made a variety to choose from. Take what you want and I'll eat the rest."

Paige helped herself to a piece of toast and two strips of crisp bacon. She also let him pour her a cup of tea. Moses sat up laboriously to gaze longingly at the bacon on the tray. "Don't feed that dog, whatever you do," Paul warned. "She's a terrible beggar."

Paige nodded, then noticed that not two minutes later, Paul slipped the dog a buttered corner of toast and then part of a slice of bacon. She giggled, and Paul looked sheepish. "Well, that's how I know she's a beggar," he said defensively.

They ate quietly for a few minutes. When Paige finished her toast, she pushed her plate away and wrapped both hands around the teacup, taking sips as she watched Paul eat.

"Thank you, Paul," she said at last. "I had a great night's sleep." She stretched and grimaced from the pain. "It's incredible, though, how sore a body can feel after a little accident."

Paul looked at her. He cleared his throat. "Paige, speaking of accidents . . . I guess I need to fill you in on what happened last night." The words sounded hesitant, as though they were being dragged out of him against his will.

"What? Is it Carter? Is he all right?" she asked, scared now. Guilt assailed her. She'd slept all night, safe here with Paul, with no thought of Carter's safety.

"No, no, it's not Carter. He's back in his room, under twenty-four-hour guard. It took them a while, but the hospital did finally locate him, just as he was on his way out the door to join Reilly and Charlie."

Paige stiffened. She sat waiting, still as a doe detecting danger in the woods, waiting for what he was going to say. Her eyes, wide with fear, were locked on his face. "What happened?" she whispered.

Paul didn't want to tell her what had happened, but he didn't want her to hear about it from anyone else, either. "Charlie was in the truck with Reilly last night. They waited in the emergency room parking lot for Carter to make it out of the hospital. When a security guard nabbed Carter at the door, they raced out of the lot and up Hillside. Reilly seems to have run into a train at about 37th Street. They're both dead." As if in slow motion, one hand came up to cover her mouth. "Dead? They're dead?" Tears spilled out of her eyes and coursed silently down her cheeks. "And Carter didn't kill him," she said, relief in her tone.

"No, but I should tell you, Paige," he said haltingly, "it looks like Reilly killed Charlie, before the accident."

Childlike, she wiped the tears with the back of her hand. Eyes wide, she looked out the window, perhaps seeing on the frosted glass the images of Reilly killing Charlie, the crash, and Reilly's death. Color rose in her cheeks. "He's dead, he's dead!" She smiled broadly. "Isn't that awful—he's dead and I'm glad." She leaned over the tray and placed a hand on Paul's arm. "He can't hurt any more children now, Paul. Am I a terrible person because I'm glad?"

He shook his head and stood to remove the tray. Then he sat down on the bed next to her. He smiled, gazing deep into her eyes, before he kissed her forehead, then her mouth, a long, lingering kiss.

Joy leapt up in her heart. *Maybe now I will heal,* she thought as she returned his kiss.

Chapter 34

April 24 was a beautiful spring day. The sun was hot on Paige's back as she sat on the balcony of her apartment for the last time. Marmalade was uncharacteristically affectionate at the moment, and he lay across her lap, permitting her to run her hand down his fur. Today she and Paul would marry, and she would move.

She smiled at the orange cat. "I wonder how you and Moses will adapt to each other. I want you to behave yourself, cat," she said with mock sternness. "No hissing or scratching that poor old dog's nose!"

Marmalade turned to look at her and then blinked his eyes once, condescendingly. She was sure he was thinking, *You can want it, but that doesn't mean you're going to get it.*

Paige thought back over the last four and a half months, of the hours spent in the support group for survivors of sexual abuse, of the tears shed, the hearts broken and healed and broken again, only to be stronger in the broken places. *That was Hemingway,* she said to Paul in her head. She smiled as she thought of Paul—

sweet, strong Paul—as he helped her through the dark hours of depression and pain when she relived the memories of Charlie's abuse.

Renee was also getting treatment, but in her case, the healing would take longer. She had been diagnosed with multiple personality disorder, with at least seven alter egos. Her psychiatrist had estimated perhaps two more years of therapy.

Paige knew how blessed she herself was. She thought, too, of Ecclesiastes: three strands in one cord. She and Paul and God. She thought of Paul's prayers for her, of the spiritual depth of the others in the group, and of her own willingness to open herself to God and healing. God did care. She could trust him and love him. She had a long way to go, but at least she knew she was on the right path.

She visualized herself walking down the long, long aisle on Abe's arm. Dear Abe. He was still ill, still fighting the cancer, but his prognosis was good at the moment. "All I have to do is make it through the next five years, Paige," he'd said, "and I'll have it beat!"

She was glad Abe was giving her away. He came as close to being her father as anyone on earth. She appreciated his willingness to give her away in a very Christian ceremony in a very Christian place when he didn't share her religious views. She prayed God would heal him throughout the months ahead.

She thought of Carter. He was still hanging on, as sick as he was. Just yesterday she'd visited him in the hospital. He'd had another crisis two weeks before that had landed him back in Wesley. When she arrived, he was sitting up in bed playing Solitaire. She couldn't help laughing. "Solitaire! Aren't you the one who always made fun of people who wasted time playing cards?"

"Yeah, especially Solitaire," he said wryly. "But it does help pass the time."

She saw a large leather book, crackling new, on his bedside table. "Carter, a Bible!"

"Yeah, Paul and Jamal brought it by." He blushed a little. "Now don't start preaching, Paige. I told them I *might* read it. I didn't make any promises."

She nodded, her eyes sparkling, a smile playing around her lips. She leaned over and planted a kiss on his thin cheek. He raised a hand—to wipe it off—but then stopped the gesture in mid-air. He smiled in embarrassment. He liked the new warm Paige, always hugging and kissing and showing her affection for him, but he still wasn't completely comfortable with the changes.

"Big day tomorrow, huh?" he asked shyly.

She nodded. "I'll miss you, Carter."

"Now don't start that again!" he said gruffly. "You know I want to see you finally married to that big brute Paul, and you just don't know what this stinkin' body of mine is going to do next. I almost lasted long enough this time to make it to church tomorrow."

Again she nodded, tears welling in her eyes.

"None of that, Paige," he said sternly.

"Okay," she said, trying to will herself to be stoic for him. "Even now," she said softly, "I suffer from mixed feelings. I'm so happy that Paul and I are getting married, but I'm sad about you." She turned away and started running one hand down the heavy beige drapes at the window. "Whenever you go . . ."

"Whenever I die, you mean," he said crossly. "Go ahead and use the word, Paige. I know I'm dying."

"Whenever you die, Carter, I'll miss you. I hope you know that."

"Yeah, yeah," he said, waving one hand airily. "Let's play Crazy Eights."

"You feel up to it?"

"Yeah, so shut up and deal," he said with a slight grin.

"That's from *The Apartment,* right?"

She stood up and went inside. The cool darkness of the interior of the apartment was soothing after the light and heat outside. She couldn't believe how calm she was on her wedding day. She felt a deep wellspring of peace inside her.

Back in her bedroom, Paige gently touched her wedding dress. The gown with the fitted bodice and long full skirt lay across her bed. The fine Italian silk was embellished with beading and a touch of Alencon lace. It was beautiful. The ivory tones looked good against her skin.

The doorbell rang. She knew it was Jenny and Sherry, Jamal's wife, here to help her carry her things to the church, where she'd marry her lifelong love and take on Moses and Michael too. She wondered how Marmalade would adjust.

"God," she prayed aloud, "I beseech you—help me be as good a mother as that little boy deserves!" A deep joy filled her as she raised her face toward the sky, hands clasped above her head in a victory salute. "I feel totally whole! Thank you, God."

About the Author

Laurel B. Schunk is a fulltime Christian writer with special interests in child abuse prevention and race issues. She loves books, cats, dogs, and children. She teaches writing and likes to encourage other writers. She lives in Wichita, Kansas, with her husband and children.